W9-CFK-199

"I'm always in control."

Cheryl's voice was growing hoarse with building tension. She knew the slow-burning heat low in her body had melted all the control she was boasting about.

All Pete had to do was touch her. That's all she needed to make it okay to give in to the uncontrollable desires that raged through her.

"Cheryl?" His smoky gaze captured hers. "You know how to let go of the control," he said. "I remember."

Still, she couldn't move. He took the brandy snifter from her hand and set it, with his, on the table. She waited for his touch, never releasing him with her eyes. The touch didn't come. He raised his hand, but only to loosen his tie.

"Don't."

Her soft command surprised her as much as it did him. With trembling fingers she reached over to cover his hand at his throat.

"Let me...."

ABOUT THE AUTHOR

Peg Sutherland earned her publishing stripes as a reporter and editor for local papers in Florida, Nebraska and North Carolina, where she now lives. But she abandoned the hectic world of newspaper publishing for public relations, hoping the change would leave her with more time and energy to pursue her real passion—writing novels. In *Along for the Ride*, Peg's second Harlequin Superromance, she has combined her talent for romance with her love of mysteries, and the result is a gripping tale of passion and suspense.

Books by Peg Sutherland

HARLEQUIN SUPERROMANCE
398– BEHIND EVERY CLOUD

Don't miss any of our special offers. Write to us at the following address for information on our newest releases.

Harlequin Reader Service
901 Fuhrmann Blvd., P.O. Box 1397, Buffalo, NY 14240
Canadian address: P.O. Box 603,
Fort Erie, Ont. L2A 5X3

Along for the Ride

PEG SUTHERLAND

Harlequin Books

TORONTO • NEW YORK • LONDON
AMSTERDAM • PARIS • SYDNEY • HAMBURG
STOCKHOLM • ATHENS • TOKYO • MILAN

Published November 1990

ISBN 0-373-70428-3

Copyright © 1990 by Peg Sutherland. All rights reserved.
Except for use in any review, the reproduction or utilization
of this work in whole or in part in any form by any electronic,
mechanical or other means, now known or hereafter invented,
including xerography, photocopying and recording,
or in any information storage or retrieval system, is forbidden without
the permission of the publisher, Harlequin Enterprises Limited,
225 Duncan Mill Road, Don Mills, Ontario, Canada M3B 3K9.

All the characters in this book have no existence outside the
imagination of the author and have no relation whatsoever to
anyone bearing the same name or names. They are not even
distantly inspired by any individual known or unknown to the
author, and all incidents are pure invention.

® are Trademarks registered in the United States Patent and
Trademark Office and in other countries.

Printed in U.S.A.

Special thanks to Barbara Hardee,
president of Crown Cabs in Charlotte, N.C.,
and to the New Orleans Historic Voodoo Museum
for their help with this project.

PROLOGUE

THE GLINT OF STEEL didn't show up in the pale eyes staring out of the black-and-white photo.

But Kurt Fletcher knew it was there.

He'd seen it often. Over a game of marbles on a dusty street corner more than two decades ago. In a sideways glance to make sure the coast was clear for palming a pack of cigarettes from old man Rouquette's market. And years after that, when Kurt was too eager to test his newly discovered powers of seduction on Pete's blossoming baby sister.

Pete Fontenot had steel in his eyes.

Kurt knew it was there, even if the camera hadn't captured it. He didn't relish the notion of going up against the iron will behind that glare.

But cold metal pressed against the temple had a way of overcoming reservations. Kurt had learned that the night before.

Pete Fontenot had what Kurt needed to keep Monteleone's wise guys off his back. Although Kurt counted on his old buddy's loyalty—and maybe an ounce or two of guilt—to get him out of this bind, he didn't intend to take any chances. Any smart poker player had a hold card. And Kurt planned to play it smart this time. If anybody came up with the short end of this stick, he was determined it wouldn't be Kurt Fletcher.

"That's your man." Ignoring the knot in his gut, Kurt tossed the picture across the desk toward the horse-faced man in the too-tight plaid suit. "I want his soft spot."

CHAPTER ONE

THE MIRROR-BRIGHT LIMOUSINE glided into the last parking space at the end of the row, its engine producing a mellow growl.

Pete Fontenot didn't feel mellow. But he did feel like growling as he grabbed his jacket from the burgundy leather seat. He hated meetings. Ninety minutes of polite babble and jockeying for position. All for a handful of decisions that could be made in ten minutes.

Shrugging into his camel hair jacket as he locked the car door, Pete remembered the sunglasses he'd pushed back on his head when he'd entered the cool dimness of the parking deck. He almost opened the car to toss them back in, then changed his mind.

He liked the reaction he got in business meetings when he left his sunglasses straddling his head. Or didn't wear a tie. Or forgot to take his morning shave. His more conventional business acquaintances would look as if they were experiencing a sudden attack of heartburn—and not just from their bowl of lunch hour gumbo, either.

He liked unsettling them. It was better than feeling unsettled himself.

Pete saluted his image in the smoked glass of the company limo, tightened the knot in his paisley silk necktie so that it almost—but not quite—touched the open collar of his shirt, then headed out of the deck.

That's when he felt it again.

A prickling at the back of his neck. As if someone had just whispered against his hairline. As if he weren't alone but was supposed to think otherwise.

Pete recognized the feeling. And knew better than to turn around.

He kept walking, the rhythmic echo of his Italian leather loafers meeting the concrete, muted and unhurried. His ears strained toward a sound that never came.

CHERYL STOPPED in the middle of the wide hallway and waited for Dave Arnaud to turn back toward her. The stubby executive grinned tolerantly, as if he knew what was coming.

"Are you sure I can't talk you out of this?" Cheryl Steadman's crisp voice reverberated through the marble corridor leading to the Royal Orleans Hotel's most plush conference room.

"Yeah. Positive."

In her eight months as assistant to New Orleans's executive director of marketing and public relations, Cheryl had mastered the art of winning negotiations with her middle-aged boss. But the dark-haired, ruddy-faced, ex-Navy lieutenant had refused to budge when it came to Project Friendly Faces. Nevertheless, Cheryl's aggravation didn't surface to ruffle the expression on her ivory-smooth face.

"Dave, this is a carnival act. It's—"

Walking back to place his arm under Cheryl's elbow and propel her toward the meeting room, Dave looked up into her crystal-blue eyes and chuckled. "It's the best damned idea I've had since we invited that talk-show guy down to film on location with the striptease dancers and the head mother from the Order of the Holy Redemption. Remember how many calls we got after that show?"

Cheryl slipped her elbow out of reach. "I remember, Dave. You made *me* talk to the bishop."

They laughed together this time, Dave's raucous boom drowning out the sedate, controlled laugh that matched Cheryl's sedate, controlled image. The sleek chignon, the svelte but unalluring gray suit, the plain black leather pumps that added three inches to her already long, slender legs gave Cheryl exactly the no-nonsense look she felt she needed to maintain a competitive edge. And the oversize, hexagonal eyeglasses added a hint of maturity that the twenty-six-year-old felt she needed to command attention and respect.

"Okay, Dave. You're the boss," she said as she beat him to the gilded door handle.

Cheryl dropped her briefcase into a chair near the head of the polished oak conference table and scanned the room. About half of the people expected at the meeting had already gathered. They milled around, glad-handing and pouring coffee from the silver service set up on the Queen Anne table below the nineteenth-century tapestry gracing the back wall. Dave had cornered one of his most loyal supporters on the city council, so Cheryl moved toward the coffee to mingle with some of the influentials gathered to pass judgment on Project Friendly Faces.

As the daughter of Cleveland's most prominent attorney and his old-family society wife, Cheryl Steadman had grown up holding her own in rooms full of stuffy businessmen who were on the downside of middle age. So she adapted to the part of her job that called for hobnobbing with New Orleans's power brokers with the same ease with which she slipped into the silk lingerie and cashmere sweaters she loved but could ill afford on her salary.

She also liked working with the news media and taking the lead in producing promotional literature for the

Chamber of Commerce, both skills she had brought with her from her position in Lima, Ohio.

The only part of her job she didn't like was Dave Arnaud's idea of special events. Somehow, Cheryl couldn't reconcile Dave's outlandish notions with the serious demeanor she had tried so hard to cultivate since completing her degree in marketing—a career choice that Huntley and Amanda Steadman had opposed in their usual understated, distant manner.

Lining up bespangled showgirls to ride elephants down Canal Street when the circus hit town. Arranging charity football games between the New Orleans Saints and an entourage of aging politicians who wanted to rekindle some macho flame, even at the risk of getting knocked on their spreading fannies. Juggling the national media when the cast of a popular prime-time soap opera buzzed into town to tape a series of improbable chase scenes and some equally improbable love scenes against a backdrop of French Quarter jazz and oak trees hung with Spanish moss.

It was Dave's flamboyance as a U.S. Navy publicity man that had endeared him to officials in the port city of New Orleans. So when their native son retired at the end of his twenty-year stint with the Navy, his Chamber acquaintances had been glad to put him to work for the Crescent City implementing the wild ideas that hadn't always been popular with the military.

Cheryl sympathized with the starch-collared naval officers who had had to contend with Dave Arnaud. A lovable old softie when he wanted to be, he was also as stubborn as a mule when it suited him. Cheryl had fought Dave on Project Friendly Faces, mostly because his plan was to make her the focal point of the event. And she didn't see herself as the centerpiece in Dave's hare-brained scheme to promote the coming Carnival season.

Dave, however, was now giving the orders, not taking them.

And Cheryl was smart enough to know that you give it your best shot, then go with the flow. Especially if your plans, as hers did, called for moving up the organizational ladder as fast as possible.

Cheryl maneuvered her way into the middle of a knot of businessmen in front of the coffee urn, smiling and exchanging greetings. So far, she was the only woman in the room, although she knew one of the elected officials expected for the meeting was a woman. Being in the minority didn't fluster Cheryl.

"Miss Steadman, what's Arnaud cooking up this time?" The Cajun cadence—an unusual melding of dialects that Cheryl had instantly decided gave the impression of someone from the Bronx affecting a southern drawl—of the city's transportation manager captured Cheryl's attention in the middle of her reach for a cup of coffee.

Turning toward him, Cheryl shifted into the role of Chamber of Commerce cheerleader. "It's his best idea yet," she said, her rose-colored lips turning up to reveal the faintest of dimples at the left corner of her mouth.

"They always are," someone else interjected, drawing a laugh from the group and halting Cheryl again as she reached for a coffee cup.

"Does he sign your checks, too?" she joked back, her easy acceptance of the friendly ribbing setting the men at ease. One of Cheryl's greatest talents was making people forget her carved-in-marble beauty. Too much beauty, she had learned, was as intimidating to those with middle-aged paunches and sallow skin as too much brain was to those who were unsure of their mental savvy. "Seriously, Dave's new plan could reinforce New Orleans's position as a leader in catering to the tourist trade. And with Carnival season just around the corner, a little good ink and a few minutes on the networks can't hurt."

As she turned once again toward the coffee, one of the gold-rimmed china cups was extended toward her, filled with the savory, chicory-laced coffee that was a Louisiana tradition.

"Cream or sugar?" The low words accompanying the camel-clad arm held none of the false heartiness of the other voices swirling around the room. A quiet intimacy laced the voice, leaving the others out of an exchange that had suddenly become private.

Cheryl expected to look up into eyes ripe with seduction. She was wrong.

His pale gray eyes were challenging, almost hard, beneath a high forehead showing the first lines that come with maturity—or worry. His narrow jaw, tapering sharply to a square chin, held a corresponding hint of unyielding hardness. The tie hanging loose under an open collar and the dark sunglasses shoved back onto his head branded him a misfit in this room full of carefully dressed businesspeople, all playing to win.

This man looked as if he didn't even play the game. That made Cheryl uncomfortable.

She reached for the china cup he offered, her smile veiled and circumspect. "Neither, thanks. I was beginning to think I was destined to sit through this meeting without any caffeine."

"Wouldn't try it. The snores give you away."

Cheryl had a hunch that he wasn't just making glib small talk as the others had been. He not only didn't fit in here, in spite of the first-class clothes that hung easily on his lean frame. He didn't even want to fit in.

The class, she suspected, was a veneer. Underneath was a different texture, a roughness, a grit that upset her equilibrium.

"Maybe the meeting won't run that long," she countered. As the sip of strong, hot coffee hit her stomach, a dull burning signaled another bout with what her doctor had diagnosed as an ulcer waiting to be born. Darn Dave, she thought, and his crazy ideas.

"They all run that long."

He was right, but Cheryl wouldn't admit it. Sometimes the bureaucracy drove her crazy, but she was determined to make it work for her. Determined to prove her parents and her brothers wrong. Determined to carve out a niche for herself that was just as lucrative and just as powerful as the ones her brothers had inherited along with the family name and the family connections.

"I'm Cheryl Steadman, with the Chamber," she said, wondering how she could politely break away from the strange conversation with this strange man.

He was silent. Cheryl wondered if he would purposely ignore protocol and fail to introduce himself. It wouldn't have surprised her.

"Pete Fontenot. Bayou Taxi."

He said it as if he didn't expect it to impress her. Bayou Limousine and Taxi Service was the largest independent transportation company in town. Cheryl had heard more than once about the self-made man with a knack for setting himself apart from other business leaders in the city. Pierre "Pete" Fontenot. His youth, his reputation for spending money as fast as he made it and his refusal to hobnob with the right crowd provided plenty of gossip for the business community.

The most talked-about outrage was Fontenot's refusal to join a Carnival Krewe, one of the exclusive, secret organizations responsible for planning the annual festivities surrounding Mardi Gras. Although the story was only told in whispers, even Cheryl had learned that he had miffed more than a few of the city's influential people by turning down invitations to become part of the "in" crowd.

Cheryl also knew, thanks to her habit of doing her homework thoroughly, that Pete Fontenot's reaction could make or break Dave's new project. This thirty-four-year-old who barely topped her by two inches might not act like one of the city's power brokers, but he had more influence than anyone else in this room full of people with considerable power.

In spite of her running battle with Dave over the project, Cheryl knew she wouldn't mind locking horns with this Mr. Fontenot if he didn't take a shine to Project Friendly Faces. His shell looked so tough it would be fun trying to crack him.

"Then you should find Dave's plan exciting," she said, softening the high-pressure words with a low-pressure delivery. "It's a terrific opportunity for you and your men. I believe you'll be as excited as we are once you've heard what Dave has to say."

His raised brows deepened the faint lines in his tanned forehead. "Do you have operators standing by?"

Cheryl refused to rise to his bait. With the pleasant smile she had mastered so many years ago in her parents' drawing room, she said, "And a free gift if you call before midnight."

Over Fontenot's shoulder, Cheryl spotted Dave's signal that he wanted to get started. She gestured toward the conference table with her cup. "Shall we?"

"I can hardly wait."

Within a few minutes, the rumble of voices and the muffled dragging of chairs over the plush carpet stilled, and Dave stood to introduce Project Friendly Faces and outline his plan.

Cheryl found it difficult to keep her gaze from straying to Pete Fontenot, who had eased into the chair beside her. His presence and the anticipation of opposition charged her with a surge of energy that she usually experienced only when a slick publication was falling into place, vivid and imaginative, on the designer's drawing board. Or when she could tell she was managing to infuse an unsuspecting reporter with her own enthusiasm for a story idea.

People seldom fired Cheryl with that kind of excitement. Not even men. Men didn't fit in Cheryl's plan, and she deliberately stayed away from the ones who might make it easy to stray from the goals she had set for herself.

But Pete Fontenot's calculated indolence had caught her unawares. The high energy contained in his lithe body was reaching out to strike sparks against the hard surface of disinterest she cultivated as carefully as he did his own.

As Dave gave a point-by-point rundown on his idea to turn the city's cab and limo drivers into goodwill ambassadors for New Orleans, Cheryl strained to pick up vibes from Pete. He lounged, one arm slung casually over the back of his chair. He sat far enough back from the table to allow himself the room to prop an ankle on his knee. No bored fidgeting or hyperactive impatience spoiled what Cheryl recognized instantly as his public image. Ultracool. In control. With a jolt, she recognized herself in Pete. It was the startled feeling she got upon unexpectedly catching sight of herself in a department store window. Except this time it was Pete Fontenot staring back, wearing the same careful facade she had cultivated for so many years. The revelation quickened her breathing.

Dave droned on, outlining his plan to stage a charm school for drivers and introduce them to the customer service skills that would make them the city's most visible and most valuable ambassadors to the millions of tourists and business people who visited New Orleans annually.

When he finished, no one spoke. Knowing the kind of pecking order that usually prevailed in such situations, Cheryl wondered if she had been correct in speculating whose opinion the others were waiting for before forming their own opinions.

She wasn't surprised when Pete Fontenot's voice broke the silence.

"What makes you think our people aren't friendly now?"

As he always did, Dave looked to Cheryl for the smooth tact needed to defuse an antagonistic reception. He had learned shortly after Cheryl joined his operation that she could turn almost any situation to her advantage.

Preoccupied with the rigid play of Pete's jaw muscle, Cheryl almost missed Dave's signal that the floor was hers.

"No one thinks that at all, Pete," she said smoothly, calling up her ready smile. "In fact, we developed this idea because we realize just how valuable a contribution your people already make. The key here is to remember that we're creating a project to generate publicity as much as anything else."

She didn't flinch while he sized her up. He didn't look her up and down, lingering over the curves or the glimpses of flesh at throat or wrist, as some men did when they sought to intimidate her. He simply stared her down, daring her to blink, as he would another man.

Cheryl was so accustomed to handling the other kind of intimidation that his forthright stare unnerved her. But she didn't shrink from it. He rewarded her with the faintest of smiles.

"So it's all just a publicity stunt?"

Cheryl ignored the remark but responded to the minuscule thawing she saw in his face by allowing a hint of her smile to travel to her blue eyes. "I believe everyone here, Pete, will agree that any group of people who work with the public can benefit from a refresher course in customer service. Handling angry customers. Information giving. Ways to become a one-man welcoming committee, if you will."

The words sounded as weak to Cheryl as they had the first time Dave spouted them at her. But her sole job right now was to sell the idea to a customer who wasn't in the market for her product.

"Who's going to handle this refresher course?"

She could tell from his eyes that he knew the answer. She could also tell that he was simply testing her, that he had no real intention of making her life more difficult by bucking the plan here in front of the C.E.O.'s of the city's transportation companies.

Dave jumped in. "Miss Steadman will."

"Good choice."

Pete's pronouncement signaled the acceptance that made it possible for the others around the table to express their willingness to be part of the project. Although some of the questions were surprisingly tough—especially the ones from Pete—the group had agreed within an hour on a tentative plan for implementing the project.

As the discussion intensified, Cheryl's excitement grew. She never questioned that the heat in her face and the accelerated pumping of her heart had to do with anything except the discussion of Project Friendly Faces.

"If the main idea behind this project is publicity, how do we accomplish that?" Pete asked as the planning stage of the meeting drew to a close.

"Miss Steadman handles that, also," Dave said. "We'll kick this off at a press conference within the week, if you're all in agreement. In fact, it would add weight to the announcement if some of you could be there."

Dave looked pointedly at Pete, once again reinforcing Cheryl's conclusion that Pete Fontenot carried plenty of clout in New Orleans.

When silence met Dave's suggestion, Cheryl looked around. A couple of the businessmen were making note of the press conference on pocket calendars. Pete's attention was once again focused on her.

"I'll be there," he said.

"GOOD JOB, STEADMAN!" Dave beamed as he thrust forward a pudgy hand for a congratulatory shake. "I don't think Fontenot loved our idea, but what could he do? You made it sound like an idea no clear-thinking businessman could refuse. How the hell do you do that? I was ready to snap his head off."

"I'll never tell. You wouldn't need me then." She was only half joking as she shook his hand unenthusiastically. Now that she had done her job of lending public support to her boss's idea, she remembered how foolish she expected to feel taking the lead in a project that seemed doomed from the start: teaching brusque-talking, rough-looking drivers how to become models of welcoming friendliness for the city.

"You'll get busy on the press conference right away?" The last ones to leave the conference room, they headed back down the ornate hallway of the Royal Orleans.

"First thing tomorrow."

Dave paused at the stairway leading out the front. "Preston and I are going to talk about some bond issue strategies over a martini. Join us?"

Always reluctant to mix after-hour socializing with business talk, Cheryl begged off. "I've got reading for class tomorrow night, Dave. Maybe you can fill me in."

"Really cuts into your leisure time, doesn't it, Steadman?" He reached up to loosen his tie in preparation for the casual meeting.

"I enjoy the class," Cheryl said evasively. Like a nosy father, Dave always wanted to know more than she was willing to tell about her social life. "And I'm getting to know my instructor. I think she'll be a big help in getting me through this."

Dave nodded, his mind obviously already on the Cajun martini waiting for him in the lounge. "Yeah. An M.B.A. never hurts. Give you a real boost over regular Joes like me. See you tomorrow, Steadman."

The uniformed doorman nodded respectfully as he held the massive door for Cheryl. Horse-drawn carriages lined the street in front of the hotel, luring tourists eager for a picturesque ride through the Vieux Carré—the Old Square, as the city's French Quarter was called.

Cheryl was eager only to get away from the narrow streets and the grimy character of the Quarter, which was painfully apparent to her in the harsh light of the waning afternoon. A couple of winos were parked on the low brick wall across from the luxury hotel, paper bags abandoned in the grass giving an unmistakable signal that they were prime for panhandling. Two college kids, giggling and walking unsteadily down the middle of narrow Saint Louis Street, were clearly high on more than the taste of their freedom from classes.

But a look toward the curb revealed no cabs to help Cheryl make her escape from the Quarter back to her apartment in the city's sedate Garden District. Everyone had warned her that a car was more trouble than it was worth in New Orleans, where a parking space was as rare as a street that wasn't congested with traffic. But every morning and every afternoon when Cheryl jumped onto a bus or streetcar to head to and from work, she missed the roomy sedan she'd sold before making the move from Ohio.

Her good pumps, Cheryl knew, would be coated with grime by the time she trekked six blocks through the Quarter to pick up her bus on Canal Street. She'd left her sneaks under her desk at the office, unable to fit them and her Friendly Face file into her briefcase. At least, she thought, she could follow Royal Street, which housed mostly high-rent antique and specialty shops instead of the jazz clubs and strip joints along Bourbon Street.

As she set off down the sidewalk, a sleek black limousine pulled up beside her and the door on the passenger side popped open in front of her.

Sandy hair and a pair of familiar sunglasses leaned across the expansive front seat. "Taxi, lady?"

The turndown that rose to her lips was automatic. But the memory of that moment of discovery—when she'd sensed that Pete Fontenot's public polish might cover the same insecurities that hers covered—almost changed her mind.

"It's the express line," Pete added when he noticed her hesitation. "Goes right to your front door."

Cheryl was tempted. She was tempted to save her shoes. She was tempted to save herself the possible aggravation and embarrassment of being accosted by the tipsy teens who were just ahead of her on the sidewalk. She was tempted to save herself bus fare.

But most of all she was tempted to slide in beside Pete Fontenot and study his finely chiseled profile as thoroughly as he had studied her during the meeting.

It was that temptation that made her decision.

She forced her professional smile and fought the impulse to draw her briefcase against her chest. His self-confidence wasn't the only thing Pete cultivated carefully, she suspected. Something about Pete Fontenot belied the smooth sophistication of his pricey clothes and his cool-as-ice demeanor. Something that told Cheryl he could be as uncompromisingly indecorous as his city.

She wasn't sure her country club upbringing had prepared her to handle a robust town like New Orleans. And she was sure it hadn't prepared her to handle a man like Pete Fontenot.

"No, thanks," she said, her grip tightening involuntarily on her briefcase. "I like to walk."

CHAPTER TWO

VISIONS OF PIZZA, piled high with pepperoni and delivered steaming hot to her front door, obscured the page of notes Cheryl had taken during the past three hours.

Trying to ignore her hunger and the imaginary pizza she could almost smell, Cheryl closed her notebook and dropped it into her briefcase as Professor Fay Thurston reviewed the reading assignment for next week's accounting class.

As usual, dashing from her uptown office to her six o'clock class on the Tulane campus had left no time for food and Cheryl was famished. Also as usual, her late dinner would probably be a bowl of cold cereal instead of the spicy pizza she craved. One part oregano plus two parts garlic added up to trouble for the nervous stomach New Orleans seemed to have given her.

The problem, she knew, wasn't surfacing because of her penchant for spicy foods. It had much more to do with daily deadlines. And projects such as Friendly Faces, with its promise of regular contact with people who made her acutely aware of the sheltered, plastic life she'd led—people like Pete Fontenot.

Reaching under her oversize glasses to rub her weary eyes, Cheryl let out a sigh of relief as Fay dismissed the class. Food and a soft pillow were less than an hour away.

"Rough day?" Fay glanced up in the middle of packing away her teaching materials when Cheryl paused to wait for her.

"It was a great day. The printer delivered our newcomers brochures today—printed blue where we wanted silver and silver where we wanted blue." Cheryl winced at the memory of the eight offending cartons stacked in her office. "That was 8:30 a.m. Things went downhill from there."

Fay chuckled as they started out the door together. The thirty-five-year-old professor's theatrical classroom delivery of her dry subject and the flamboyant fashions that made her petite figure hard to miss in a crowd had appealed to Cheryl's quiet traditionalism. Despite their busy schedules, they met for lunch or went for dinner after class as often as possible.

"I know just what you need to relax tomorrow." Fay snapped her fingers, adorned with no less than six handmade silver rings. "Let's take a long lunch to check out costumes for Mardi Gras. I've got a free stretch between classes, and we could roam the Quarter."

"Thanks, but tomorrow's going to be hectic." Cheryl thought with dread of the press conference to announce the Friendly Faces project, scheduled for late morning. "Besides, I think I'll pass on the Carnival revelry this year."

"Pass!" Fay's purple cape flapped its protest in the January breeze. "How can you pass on Mardi Gras? It's the most exciting, most bizarre, most unforgettable thing since...since...well, I can't even think of anything to compare to it. It's even wilder than a Mississippi tent revival. It's your first Carnival season, Cheryl. You can't take a rain check on Mardi Gras!"

Cheryl smiled at the horrified consternation in her friend's voice. "You don't have to give me a hard sell on Mardi Gras. That's my job, remember? And I've written enough hype on it in the past few months to know that I don't have what it takes to survive that kind of street brawl. A party animal I'm not, Fay."

Fay shook her head in disbelief. "Then you've got a long month ahead of you. This town lives and breathes Carnival until Ash Wednesday. And if you're not in the spirit, it'll drive you crazy long before then."

"I don't doubt it. My boss is already driving me crazy with this asinine project of his." Fay had already been subjected to more than one after-class gripe session on the subject of Dave's newest scheme.

"Have you started your new career as a teacher yet?"

"No, but the press conference is tomorrow." A nagging unease gnawed at her. Cheryl typically enjoyed the challenge of getting a handful of cynical reporters to share her excitement. Being center stage, fielding questions, coming up with an off-the-cuff quote clever enough to make the evening news—the experience was typically exhilarating.

But she wasn't looking forward to unveiling Project Friendly Faces for the media.

She wasn't looking forward to confronting Pete Fontenot again, either. What if he'd had second thoughts? He hadn't been wholeheartedly behind the project to start with. He'd made it abundantly clear that, to him, it was little more than a publicity stunt, not to be taken too seriously. What if he treated the issue lightly in front of the reporters who assembled tomorrow in the Chamber's meeting room?

What if she couldn't shake the feeling that she was treading dangerous territory every time she thought of him?

"So I can catch you on the tube tomorrow night?" Fay stopped at the fork in the sidewalk leading to faculty parking.

"Take in all the details," Cheryl warned. "It could be the most you'll see of me for a few weeks. I might miss a few of your classes before it's over."

"I understand. Just give me a call and I'll fill you in so you can keep up with the reading." She shifted the multicolored woven shoulder bag that held her books and papers. "Want a lift?"

"No, thanks." Cheryl waved and headed toward the streetcar stop on Saint Charles Avenue.

"Listen, change your mind about Mardi Gras," Fay called out. "Be crazy or go crazy. It's your choice."

Cheryl smiled to herself in the illumination from the streetlight. Fay had moved to New Orleans from Mississippi right after college and, like so many others, had fallen in love with the City that Care Forgot.

She wondered if the city would ever be able to weave such magic around her. Cheryl couldn't imagine abandoning herself to the carefree, fun-loving spirit for which the city was so famous.

As the old wooden streetcar rumbled to a stop in front of her, Cheryl took consolation in the fact that plenty of jaws would drop if her family could see her sharing public transportation with a bleary-eyed rummy, a punker whose head was shaved on one side and tinted orange on the other and a couple of domestic workers returning from a long day's work.

Although her feet ached in her sneaks and her fingers were chilled, she thought with no envy of the sleek limo

Pete Fontenot had pulled up to the curb the day before. She had walked away from that kind of life with no regrets whatsoever.

After moving from Cleveland to Lima, Ohio, she had learned that her new job had been arranged by her parents. And so had Geoffrey McMillian. The button-down nephew of family friends, he had been encouraged to make her feel at home in her new town.

It had been the final straw. As she'd searched for another job, Cheryl had considered only those positions more than five hundred miles from Cleveland and her parents.

Amanda Steadman had wept, in her genteelly formal way. Huntley Steadman had raged, in his intimidatingly formal way. And her older brothers, Allen and Kevin, had cajoled, in their condescendingly formal way.

But Cheryl had stood her ground. At twenty-six, she was tired of being smothered and manipulated. New Orleans, surely, was far enough away to escape the reach of her father's influential helping hand.

Right now, the drafty, noisy streetcar that said she was making it on her own seemed much more comfortable than Pete Fontenot's luxury limo.

In fact, Pete Fontenot seemed more daunting company than the forlorn wino who had just drained the last drop from his bottle. She couldn't say why, but the businessman seemed like a legitimately dangerous character.

And whatever else she did, Cheryl didn't want to run the risk of having anyone in her family say "I told you so."

PETE GAVE THE DIAL on the safe a spin, then tugged sharply on the handle to assure himself it was tightly locked. Closing the wood-grain door on the built-in credenza behind his desk, he patted the hefty bundle of checks tucked away in the inside pocket of his charcoal gray jacket.

Payday.

Handing out paychecks always reminded Pete that he'd made it. No one else had believed he could. No one but Pete. And payday was his vindication.

On payday, he handed out more money than his old man had ever seen in a good year.

Pete liked the feeling.

He glanced at the face of the slim gold watch on his wrist, figuring he had just enough time before the press conference heralding the Snow Princess's little tea party. If this Friendly Faces racket had been just another one of Dave Arnaud's crazy schemes, Pete had been prepared to give it thumbs-down. Those jokers with the Chamber might have time to waste playing footsy with the news media, but Pete had a company to run. And especially with Carnival coming up and its inevitable onslaught of tourists, he had no time to horse around.

Then he had laid eyes on the Snow Princess.

The chill she had sent through him reminded him of the chill you get when you're half-gone with fever.

Miss Steadman. A prim and proper name to go with her prim and proper veneer. Wearing that stuffy little suit and the prissy little bow at the neck of her blouse, with her white-blond hair sleeked back in a knot.

He hated women like that. Always ready to look down their perfectly straight noses at people who didn't grow up eating goose liver pâté and Oysters Rockefeller. As if they'd eyeballed him hard enough to spot the grease he always imagined lingering under his fingernails, even after all this time. As if they could somehow read in his face that he'd learned more from bookies and wise guys than books and professors.

Sure, she was just a twenty-five-grand-a-year flunky at the Chamber, but Pete knew breeding when he saw it. The Steadman broad was a blue blood. He would bet on it.

So when Pete found himself reacting to those long, slim legs, the perfect Miss Steadman had raised his hackles like all the other society babes did at first.

At first.

Then he'd noticed the freckles. Just a few over the bridge of her nose and, faintly, on her high cheekbones. Freckles. Girl-next-door, riding-bicycles-in-the-sun freckles. Under the fluorescent light in the Royal Orleans's glitziest meeting room, even the most artfully applied makeup couldn't hide the single flaw that stole her veneer of diamond-bright sophistication.

Freckles. And Pete was a sucker for freckles.

Since the first time he'd kissed nine-year-old Shea Darensbourg the day they dived for the same string of plastic beads tossed from a Mardi Gras float, Pete had been a sucker for freckles. Shea's face had been rosy with freckles, and Pete had never seen a woman with freckles since who he didn't want to kiss.

So after he'd spotted the freckles, finding things to like about Cheryl Steadman had been easy. He'd recognized the quick-witted intelligence in the luminous blue eyes she tried to hide behind those deadly serious glasses. He'd seen the touch of apprehension countered by the edge of self-confidence when he'd started giving her a rough time over this silly project of hers. He'd admired the way she refused to cash in on her femininity with clothes that were too snug or too short.

Miss Steadman had started to look human.

That was when he'd decided to play along with the Chamber's latest publicity charade. At least give it lip service long enough to see just how human the Snow Princess might be. If none of his drivers actually ended up in that hokey class of hers, who'd know the difference?

Hoping for one more swallow of coffee before he headed out with the paychecks, Pete discovered three foam cups with healthy penicillin cultures before he found the current model. The vending machine brew tasted bland and flat without the chicory he was accustomed to in most New Orleans coffee. But he smiled anyway, imagining Cheryl Steadman in action as star of the press conference later that morning.

With a final regretful look at the scattered piles of paperwork hiding the top of his desk, Pete sailed out of his office and into the hurly-burly that was the transportation empire he had built from a single taxi and a penny-squeezing nature so relentless he put Ebeneezer Scrooge to shame. Pete knew he'd earned a reputation as a spendthrift in the years since he'd made it, but no one knew about the frugality that had finally earned him the money he enjoyed spending so freely.

The outer office was plush and quiet, shielded from the din in the garage and dispatch areas by thick carpet, good soundproofing and piped-in music. Pete draped himself over the desk while Elaine Burton shooed him off her paperwork with one hand and handled a telephone call with the other.

"You maniac!" When she finished the call, the plump secretary swatted him on the head with a rolled-up section of the morning paper. "I'll never figure out what's what now. Besides, there's a *beignet* under there somewhere."

"A *beignet*!" Pete jumped up and started looking through the papers for the square, sugar-coated dough-nut. "And you didn't bring me any? You must not want this paycheck very badly."

She dimpled cheerfully, finding the last of the pastry and popping it into her mouth. "You don't pay me enough to mother you, Pete."

"Then I'll have to give you a raise." He tucked the en-velope into the keyboard of her word processor. "Here's lookin' at you, kid."

"You're awfully chipper this morning." She glanced at her watch. "How about if you hustle with those checks so you don't miss the press conference?"

Before he could get out the back door leading to the rest of the building, Elaine stopped him with a gentle accusa-tion. "By the way, the hospital sent the final statement from Mom's surgery yesterday. It was marked 'paid in full.'"

Pete winked. "See, I told you not to worry."

"Pete..." Elaine opened her mouth in grateful pro-test, but Pete blew her a kiss and hurried out the door.

Doors slamming, the sharp bleat of car horns and the din of voices raised to overcome the cacophony in the cavernous gray garage greeted Pete on the other side of the heavy metal door. The smell of exhaust fumes and just-pumped gasoline blended with the pungent aroma of burning tobacco to say "home" to Pete more surely than the fragrance of fresh-baked cookies.

A small horde of men in the gray-and-blue uniforms that were the trademark of Bayou Taxi slowly gathered around Pete. Laughter and good-natured ribbing were swapped with every paycheck that exchanged hands, and some lingered for more than a friendly joke or two.

"Ah, there's a cold beer with my name on it when this shift is over!" A dark, towering driver kissed the envelope before slipping it into his shirt pocket.

"Now, Fats, don't drink this up before you get home to Louise," Pete said with a grin. Lafayette "Fats" Peychaud's booming laugh drowned out the hoots of his co-workers. Everybody knew that Fats allowed himself only one beer on payday before he headed straight home.

"How's that new baby?" Pete asked another driver, a fair-haired young man who'd moved his family into bayou country from the flatlands of Texas.

"Doin' fine, sir." The young man blushed.

"She'll be asking for red beans and rice any day now," Pete warned. "Bet on it, Freddie."

Pete made his way through the garage, collecting the latest news about wives and children and new girlfriends and aging parents from the drivers who were his friends as much as they were his employees. When he'd left the checks for the drivers who were out or working another shift with the dispatcher and was heading back to his office, he spotted another young driver who had just returned from a run with one of the fleet limos.

Sammy Reilly, a wiry redhead, had captured Pete's attention—and respect—his first week on the job by suggesting that many of the cabbies would like to double as limo drivers. The change had saved money and enabled the company to cut its response time to a call for a limo. A dress blazer slipped on over the crisp uniforms Pete insisted on for his drivers, and a cabbie was metamorphosed into a chauffeur.

Pete walked over as Sammy glided the stretch into its berth.

"You shoulda seen this place, Pete," Sammy exclaimed as he bounded out of the car. "No foolin', you could set this whole garage down in the ballroom, I'll betcha anything. I'm gonna buy me an old plantation house just like it someday.''

The youthful dreams shining in Sammy's eyes struck a familiar chord. A chord that carried Pete back almost thirty years. He remembered the first time he and his buddies—Kurt and Tony—had wandered a few blocks from the rough and run-down Irish Channel neighborhood and discovered New Orleans's elegant Garden District.

The ornate mansions, shielded from the tree-lined streets by carefully tended gardens, were like a fairyland to the boys, who had grown up in peeling, narrow row houses shoved so tightly together on the busy, dusty streets that everyone could hear what the next-door neighbors argued about over supper.

Although he pretended to share his street-tough pals' scorn for the opulence, Pete had ached to peek inside the sparkling leaded-glass windows to find out how the royalty inside lived.

Years later, Pete heard the story of the Garden District—a section of town first inhabited in the mid-nineteenth century by wealthy American businessmen who had been shunned as upstarts by Creole society. He had been intrigued by how the success of Yankee commercialism, with its promise of renewed wealth and much-needed industry, eventually won over the aristocratic French and Spanish descendants who inhabited the declining French Quarter.

Pete had been about twelve when old man Rouquette, who ran the corner market, told the colorful tale, embellished with details of crystal chandeliers and marble entry halls at the base of wide, winding staircases, where raven-haired Creole maidens of marriageable age became the key to an amicable blending of the old and new.

The gangly, sandy-haired adolescent understood immediately what had made the Yanks acceptable to Creole society—money. He'd asked Rouquette for a job sacking and delivering groceries, promising to work for tips. It hadn't been long before Rouquette realized that Pete's hustling was resulting in more business for his quiet market.

Pete had decided, as Sammy Reilly had, that he would have a taste of the good life behind those leaded-glass windows. And if money was the key, then money he would have.

Knowing that those who made good their escape were rare, Pete wondered whether it was fair to encourage Sammy to believe in such unrealistic optimism. He also wondered, suddenly, if all the money in the world could ever make him the equal of people like the sleek Miss Steadman. Something about her cool perfection still made him feel like the grimy kid yearning to press his nose against the windowpane.

To hell with Cheryl Steadman, he told himself. He'd made it, and people like her could be damned if they still didn't think he was good enough.

Pete clapped the youth on his slender shoulders and smiled. "You can make it happen if you believe you can, Sammy."

Suddenly the bright light in Sammy's eyes dimmed. "Yeah. But first I've gotta find the time to go back to college. I finished my first two years already. At the community college. You gotta have an education to get anywhere these days. Right, Pete?"

Once again, Sammy's words echoed a passage from Pete's past. He remembered only too well the years he had struggled to keep up with reading assignments and to study for tests while working the graveyard shift for one of the city's independent cab companies. He had been twenty-six before he held a diploma in his hand. Eight long years of going to college part-time.

Eight long years he'd worked for a piece of paper that would serve as the key to the world he so desperately wanted to own.

"You going to go to college, kid?"

Sammy shrugged. "Want to. But it's hard to find the bucks. And..."

"And what?"

"Well, my girl and I were gonna get married this summer."

"You and Marie?" Pete remembered the exotic face and the lilting laughter of Marie Broussard, the young woman who often brought Sammy an oyster po' boy sandwich or a container full of steaming red beans and rice for dinner when he worked the second shift. She worked in one of the French Quarter's voodoo shops, dressing like a Gypsy princess and pushing gris-gris— voodoo amulets and dolls.

Sammy's face turned soft but didn't lose the forlorn expression in his eyes. "Yeah. Marie's got a little girl, you know. She thinks I'm gonna make a great stepdaddy. But I don't see how, if I never amount to anything. Only Marie doesn't want to get married until after I finish college. But I don't want to wait that long. I want to take care of her now."

"That's rough." He couldn't help thinking, though, that Marie might have a clearer head than the young man in front of him.

"She doesn't think I can swing school and work and marriage and raisin' a kid all at once."

Pete shook his head, admitting to himself that Sammy's obstacles were stacked up about as high as his own had been when he'd started out more than a decade earlier. "Sounds like a lot to take on, all right."

"I can do it, though. You'll see."

Slapping Sammy on the back, Pete gave his driver an encouraging smile. "I've got faith in you, Sammy."

"You do?"

"Sure. With that kind of determination, you're already ahead of the pack."

"Thanks, Pete."

TWENTY MINUTES LATER, after Sammy had picked up his check from the dispatcher, Pete's words still rang in his head.

I've got faith in you, Sammy.

Coming from a man like Pete, those words were a real shot in the arm. Not like when his mom or Marie said them.

Sammy didn't have the courage to tell Pete that one of the reasons he'd come to Bayou Taxi to work was the story of Pete's rise. Every cabbie in town knew that Pete Fontenot had been one of them, with no better start in life than they'd had. But he'd managed to make good. Sammy's plan was to find out what had made his young boss a success and turn himself into a carbon copy of Pete Fontenot.

He'd already seen one of the reasons for Pete's success—Pete was a regular guy. He never treated his drivers like another piece of equipment, but like an important part of the business. He made them feel as if they mattered. And they paid him back by working hard and taking care of the business entrusted to them.

Plus, Bayou Taxi was one of the few cab companies in town where you didn't have to own your own cab—and keep it running and filled with gas. Pete didn't work it that way, which meant guys like Sammy had a chance to get started even if they didn't have the bucks to lay out to buy their own cab. Some of the guys said, though, that Pete would give you a hand if you wanted to buy your own cab one day.

All the guys liked Pete. And Sammy wanted to be just like him. Maybe someday he'd tell Pete that, too.

As the young driver turned away from dispatch, he spotted a man leaning against the garage door opening, silhouetted against the brilliant January sunshine. He'd seen the man earlier, a sloppy-looking mug with a toothpick behind his ear, nosing around asking questions.

Maybe, he thought, he shouldn't wait for someday to tell Pete about that.

PETE WAS PULLING OUT in one of the company's rental cars, a vintage roadster he reserved for special clients, when Sammy flagged him down.

"Hey, Pete, I hope you don't think I'm out of line," Sammy started uncertainly, "but I thought you oughta know. Some guy's been nosing around."

The hairs stood up on the back of Pete's neck the same way they had the night before, when he'd walked home with a bag of fresh croissants from the French bakery on Jackson Square to his town house on Dauphine Street. The streets had been busy, already clogged with the first burgeoning crowds that would continue to grow in size and intensity during the six-week Carnival season leading up to Mardi Gras. Despite the crowds, Pete had felt in his gut there was something on those streets to be wary of. He had tried to shake off the uneasy, instinctual feeling that he was being watched. Followed.

"What do you mean, nosing around?" Pete wanted to convince himself that Sammy's imagination was working overtime, as he had tried to convince himself the night before.

"You know. Askin' questions. Tryin' to buddy up to some of us. But he looks like a real loser to me."

"What kind of questions?"

Sammy squirmed. "You know. What kind of boss are you? Who're your friends? Stuff like that."

A chill flashed through Pete in spite of the suit coat and the pleasant hum of the heater in the roadster. Looking up into the concerned blue eyes in front of him, Pete cleared his expression and smiled. "Probably just the licensing guys, Sammy. They like to play Sam Spade when you're up for renewal."

Sammy nodded uncertainly.

"If he keeps it up, we'll have Marie cook up a potion for us," Pete joked, hoping to allay the young man's worries.

"Sure, boss." Sammy grinned, but Pete wasn't sure if he'd convinced the driver not to worry or if Sammy had simply decided to copy his boss's deliberate lack of concern. "I'll have her make up an amulet."

As the roar of the roadster's engine hummed through Pete's body, he couldn't help but wonder if the old days on the streets were finally moving in to catch up with the fairy-tale existence he'd managed to make his own.

People who were born to wealth and refinement didn't have people following them on the street.

Only people who were half a step away from being thugs themselves fell victim to other thugs.

CHAPTER THREE

SHE WAS BORN to be center stage.

Pete marveled at Cheryl Steadman's finesse in front of the cameras as he sneaked into the back of the brightly lighted auditorium.

Oblivious to the tangle of microphones at her chin, she smiled a dazzling smile without missing a beat in answering the reporters' questions. Every question sounded to Pete like a land mine set up to trap an unsuspecting bureaucrat. But by the time Cheryl had worked her magic, her answers made it seem as if she had scripted the press conference ahead of time.

Cheryl's skin was translucent alabaster against the royal blue of her trim suit. Her hair gleamed in the lights and her eyes, free of the hexagonal eyeglasses, were fiery with excitement.

She loved it; that was clear. And he loved watching her. He loved listening to her carefully modulated voice, deliberately laced with just enough folksy friendliness to counterbalance the no-nonsense professionalism of her appearance.

Savvy *and* freckles. Who said there was no such thing as the perfect woman? Pete thought, a self-deprecating smile playing across his lean face.

"Miss Steadman, what's this project going to cost the taxpayers?" Pete recognized the voice of Tony Alonzo, one of his boyhood gang from the Channel. Pete strained forward, looking for the tweed cap that Tony was never without when he left the newsroom of the *Times-Picayune.*

"That's the question I've been waiting for." Cheryl's confident quip drew a chuckle from the reporters, a certain clue, Pete knew, that they liked this spokesperson from the Chamber of Commerce. "Project Friendly Faces won't cost the taxpayers a penny. This is strictly no-budget."

Pete felt his excitement rise as Cheryl prepared the crowd for the punch line with a carefully measured pause, while making eye contact with a half dozen reporters around the room.

"But the payoff, in terms of visitors who go away from the city with smiles on their faces, is more good word-of-mouth advertising than we could buy with two-hundred million dollars during the Super Bowl."

"But how do the cabbies feel about it?" interjected another reporter. "This seems to suggest they don't have friendly faces right now."

Cheryl didn't flinch at the question, although Pete knew this was the point at which she had expected him at her side, a reinforcing presence. As she opened her mouth to speak, he stepped out from the crowd at the back of the room.

"I think I can answer that, if it's okay with you, Miss Steadman."

Her eyes widened almost imperceptibly as she traced the sound of his voice. He saw the welcome in her eyes, as well as the instant of wariness she didn't hide quickly enough.

"Welcome to the party, Mr. Fontenot. I think we can find a microphone for you, if you'd like to join me."

Once again the reporters laughed as she gestured to the overload of microphones on the lectern in front of her, each one with a different radio or TV station logo emblazoned on it, each one hooked up to recording equipment that would bring her voice to everyone who tuned in for their daily news.

"If you're sure you have a little limelight to spare, I'm game." He captured her eyes with his and dared her to reveal something besides the varnished perfection of her public image.

The image never cracked. The smile she directed at him, the welcome in her eyes, were as impersonal as the friendliness she fabricated for the members of the press.

He joined her on the elevated stage, noticing immediately that her high heels brought her eyes level with his. The eyes didn't waver. It was a shame, Pete thought, that her freckles wouldn't show up on TV.

He pressed closer to join her behind the microphones, and their shoulders brushed. She stiffened as he started to speak but didn't move away, bowing to the watchful eyes of the TV cameras looking for a hint that they weren't really allies.

Although Cheryl's expression never changed, Pete noticed that her hand trembled as she adjusted a microphone.

CHERYL DREW a deep, unsteady breath as she slipped three leftover press kits into her briefcase. As grateful as she had been for Pete Fontenot's timely arrival and his show of support for Project Friendly Faces, she had to admit she had been steadier on stage before he showed up.

Nervous, no doubt, that someone unaccustomed to working with the media might say or do the wrong thing, she decided as she retrieved her eyeglasses from the bottom of her briefcase. But the businessman had handled himself well. Smoothly. Almost at ease, in a way that people seldom were when the cameras were rolling.

Much better, she told herself, slipping the eyeglasses on and looking around as the long meeting room, still busy with reporters knocking down TV equipment, came into clearer focus.

She rarely set the glasses aside for vanity's sake, but the lenses glared under the bright lights of the TV crews. So she left them off for the cameras but relied on them to lend her added maturity and needed authority the rest of the time—both functions that her seldom-used contact lenses wouldn't serve.

Glancing down once again to make sure her project notebook was in her briefcase, Cheryl was startled when a hand brushed her arm.

"Sorry I was late."

She looked around into the contrite gray eyes of Pete Fontenot, standing almost as close as he had on the stage. The urge to back up was strong, but the folding table at her hip left nowhere to retreat. Her palms, already warm from the lingering stimulation of the animated question-and-answer period with reporters, dampened as she tightened the grip on her briefcase.

"It's no problem. I'm glad you arrived when you did." She smiled and leaned away as much as possible, hoping he would take the hint and back off. "Your timing was perfect."

"Thanks. Seemed like a good send-off for your idea."

"We'll know by dinnertime." Had the man never heard of the concept of personal space? she wondered, gritting her teeth in irritation at his nearness. "And it's not my idea. This is Dave Arnaud's baby."

She was grateful when he finally moved, until she realized he intended to slip a hand under her elbow and walk toward the exit with her.

"No kidding? If I'd known that, I wouldn't have been so agreeable." His easy smile softened the words.

"Then I'm glad you didn't know. We need your help," she admitted, switching her briefcase to the arm he cradled and slipping out of his loose hold. Pete's barely perceptible touch was even more disturbing than Dave's possessive naval-officer grip.

"Anything. You name it."

"Just get your drivers there when the classes start. And remember to wax enthusiastic when the cameras are rolling."

"Are you guaranteeing a bang-up class?"

She smiled. She'd been asking herself the same thing in the past week. "Actually, I've been burning the midnight oil trying to figure out what I can tell these people that they don't already know. This is Dave's idea, remember?"

She could see the wheels turning as he nodded. "How much do you know about cabbing?"

"Even less than I know about New Orleans," she admitted. "And what I know about the city I learned from rewriting old promotional brochures for tourists. I've been here less than a year."

"That's it, then." He propped one of his glove-soft loafers on a chair in the front row. "I'll give you a crash course."

"What do you mean? A crash course in what?" Cheryl longed for the hard-bitten looks he'd given her the first day they met. She had been more comfortable with that than she was with the devilish dare in his eyes that seemed to say, "See, I knew I could get under your skin." She could think of no way to blot the moisture from her palms without being obvious.

"A crash course in New Orleans." He tapped his sunglasses, which he'd pulled from his inside breast pocket, slowly against his knuckles. "In being a cabbie in New Orleans, which has got to be the best place in the world to roam the streets for a living."

"Oh, really?"

"Absolutely. Trust me."

Not on your life, she thought as his slow smile deepened.

"Here's how we work it. I'll drive one night and you can ride shotgun—collect the fares, handle the radio. See what it's like firsthand." He nodded slowly, as if the plan were slowly taking form in his mind. "Then I can show you around for a day, including some of the sights you wouldn't catch your first few hundred trips to the city. How about it?"

This press conference was as close as she wanted to come to a relationship with Pete Fontenot, Cheryl reminded herself. And having him volunteer to become her personal tour guide was not part of the game plan.

"That's very generous of you, Pete, but I don't think it will be necessary." She could see in his eyes that he suspected exactly how phony her gratitude was.

"It's a good idea. An insider's view. My guys could be pretty hostile to some babe coming in telling them how to do their job." He glanced over a shoulder at the last two reporters remaining in the room. Cheryl realized for the first time how close the reporters were and hoped they hadn't overheard. "Especially if they get a hint she doesn't know her rear end from a pirogue in the bayou."

Cheryl felt a flush of irritation heat her face. "A what?"

"See what I mean?" Pete shrugged and shoved his sunglasses on, his disarmingly easygoing smile once again taking the sting out of his words. "Could get rough out there, Cheryl. Well, let me know if you change your mind. See you around."

Dumbfounded, Cheryl watched him take two sauntering steps toward the reporters before she turned on her heel and left by the back door.

His casual warning did just enough damage to convince her that Project Friendly Faces could be the kiss of death to her plans for a meteoric rise through the ranks at the New Orleans Chamber of Commerce. A group of streetwise cabbies would be able to see through a phony facade as quickly as she could spot a takeoff on a designer dress.

A LONG, LOW WHISTLE escaped Tony's lips as his eyes swept from one end of the sporty roadster to the other. "That, old pal, is better lookin' than the new chick takin' obits in the newsroom."

Pete chuckled, tossing the keys to the fleet car up and down in his hand. "Give me a call when you've got something special going on. She'll be yours for the night."

"You're on, pal." Tony peered inside. "But for now, how about a lift back to the *Picayune*?"

"Hop in."

When they were gliding through the sluggish lunchtime traffic along Canal Street, Tony's fascination with the high-priced toy diminished the closer they came to the building that housed the city's morning newspaper.

"Give me something inside on this Project Friendly Faces, Pete." Tony pulled his cap down over his eyes and lounged back against the crushed velvet headrest. "This story's just another dog from the chamber unless I can get a little something special.''

Pete thought once again about the long-legged Snow Princess. But the heat Cheryl Steadman cooked up in him wasn't the kind of inside scoop Tony was looking for to spice up his news story.

"Sorry, Tony. Nothing to tell."

"But you'll keep an eye out. Right?" Tony grabbed his canvas attaché from the floor as the vehicle eased to a stop in front of the *Times-Picayune* building.

"You've got it. And don't forget about the car. Anytime."

"Hey, that's one promise you'll deliver on."

CHERYL STOPPED long enough to peel off her royal-blue jacket and seek out a dust-free spot in the storeroom to put the garment out of harm's way.

"Dave, why on earth are we doing this?" She leaned over to lug another box of brochures onto the hand truck Dave had brought in from the mail room. "Don't we pay other people to do this? People who aren't wearing silk blouses and five-dollar stockings?"

A cigar pointed heavenward from his clenched teeth, Dave grunted. "It's good for morale, Steadman. Convinces the underlings that us suits in the fancy offices aren't above doing a little real work." He took the last box from her, plopped it on top of the others, brushed his dusty hands together and grinned. "Wanna push?"

She honored him with a withering frown and grabbed her jacket, following him out the door toward the loading dock, where his Jeep waited.

"Besides, the mail room kid who usually does it is out with the flu," he explained.

"At last, a good reason." Her heels clicked on the linoleum, a sound she never heard on the carpeted floors of the administrative offices. "The things I do for you. Like this Friendly Faces business. You wouldn't believe what Pete Fontenot suggested today."

He cut her a quick sideways glance. "Oh, wouldn't I? You stay away from him, Steadman. He's too sly for a nice girl like you."

Cheryl refrained from reminding him once again that she wasn't a girl. Old habits died hard, she reminded herself, and Dave Arnaud had been a chauvinist too long to do much about it. In spite of it, he always listened to her ideas and gave her opportunities to take the lead in plenty of high-visibility projects.

Like Project Friendly Faces.

"He wants me to spend an evening with him playing cab driver," she continued as they took the ramp down to the Jeep. "Show me the sights as cab drivers see them. Learn what it's really like out there. Can you see me playing cabbie?"

"Steadman, that's a great idea!" He tossed his spent cigar in the gravel. "That's gonna give this project just the kind of headlines we need."

"You have got to be kidding," she said, looking down into his beady brown eyes, a warning tone in her voice. "Me? In a cab? Collecting fares all night from drunken conventioneers and party-time tourists?"

A familiar, elfish smile brightened Dave's face as he contemplated the publicity potential. "That's great, Steadman. Remind me to get you a raise."

"I'll do no such thing. I'm not riding in a filthy cab with some..." She could see by his eyes that there was little point in arguing. Dave Arnaud had learned in the navy all there was to know about pulling rank. And he was definitely in a rank-pulling mood these days. "Dave, you just finished telling me to stay away from him."

Dave waved a dismissive hand as he pulled another cigar from his inside coat pocket. "You can take care of yourself, Steadman. Set it up right away. And don't forget to call the press. I can see the headlines now."

CHERYL'S GOLD METAL BALLPOINT beat a rapid-fire rat-a-tat against the side of the phone on her desk.

Nothing she said had changed Dave's mind. Not the reminder that he didn't own her after hours. Not her suggestion that the new assistant copywriter was aching for such a chance and might do a better job with Friendly Faces than Cheryl could. Not even her rigid silence during their ride to the hotel to deliver the brochures.

He hadn't budged.

Suddenly irritated at the clatter she was creating, Cheryl placed the pen with forced calmness in the marble vase she used as a pencil holder.

How could she call that man and tell him she'd changed her mind? Worse even than giving in, how could she get through a night of—as he put it—riding shotgun in one of his grungy cabs?

Not to mention putting up with the cold appraisal of those steely gray eyes of his. A prospect that was worse, even, than spending hours in a smelly, drafty cab.

Cheryl stood up abruptly and marched to the bookcase across from her desk. Tearing into a pouch of gunpowder-green tea, she dropped a tea bag into one of the china cups, dowsed it with hot water from a steaming electric pot and marched back to her desk.

Fuming at her helplessness, she wondered if her family was right. She wasn't cut out for business. She wasn't made of the stuff that would enable her to do whatever was required, no matter what. How long would it be before she did just what they had predicted and went crawling back to the safety of their two-story Tudor?

The very thought squeezed a knot in her stomach.

By the time she remembered the tea bag steeping in her cup, the brew was too bitter to drink.

Grabbing the telephone, she punched out the number staring her in the face from her leather-bound notepad. She bit out his name to the pleasantly efficient voice that answered and waited, the rate of her pulse accelerating with each note of the insipid music spewing into her ear.

"Pete Fontenot."

She almost dropped the phone, the sound of his voice close to her ear was so alarming. She opened her mouth and found no words. When he spoke into the silence moments later, she could hear the aggravation threatening his quiet voice...and envision the quick suspicion in his gray eyes.

Quietly, as if to avoid detection, Cheryl replaced the receiver in its cradle.

Her hands were trembling again. Her hands never shook. And today, it had happened to her twice. She made a mental note to see if trembling hands were another symptom of ulcers. Maybe her nervous stomach was, as her doctor predicted, becoming something worse. And shaking hands were the first warning signal.

She doubted it.

I'm just not gutsy enough for New Orleans, she told herself bitterly. *I can't handle people like Pete Fontenot. Dave is right. He's too sly for me.*

"WHAT DID YOU DO to this one, boss man?" Elaine's dimples came right through the intercom. "It's the same lady who hung up before. And she sounds ready to spit nails. Didn't I tell you to let 'em down easy?''

"Oh, go file some letters." Pete looked at the blinking line and wondered who had an ax to grind now. Probably some huffy society doll who didn't make it on time to a meeting to plan the carnival ball. He grabbed the phone and leaned back in his swivel chair, propping his feet on the chaos he called his desk. He focused on the framed watercolor of a lush bayou swamp on the opposite wall and prepared to tune out an angry customer.

"Pete Fontenot."

The line was silent. Pete wondered if she planned to retaliate for whatever beef she had by hanging up on him all afternoon. Or would she finally work up the nerve to spill her guts about whatever she wanted.

"This is Cheryl Steadman, Pete." He heard the forced lightness in her voice and instantly lost sight of the bayou. "I've changed my mind about your offer. I think a preview of life as a cab driver would go a long way toward making this project a success."

He recognized the same practiced party line she had used on the reporters earlier in the day. Sounded as if Dave Arnaud was once again pushing her into something she wasn't nuts about getting pushed into.

Whatever the case, he didn't mind at all that she was getting pushed right into his arms.

He caught himself short and reminded himself that a couple of nights sight-seeing with the Snow Princess didn't mean that she'd get anywhere close to his arms. Her ploy of moving her briefcase from one hand to the other earlier in the day hadn't been so subtle that he didn't get the message. Cheryl Steadman was as untouchable as she looked.

"Terrific." He smiled anyway, imagining a whole night with her—eight straight hours—during which he could see what it took to rattle her chain. "Want to start tonight?"

He could almost see her scrambling for an excuse, looking around her pristine office for some way to weasel out of it, to put it off as long as possible.

"That sounds fine, Pete."

His brows arched in surprise. As he scribbled down her address and they agreed on a time, Pete wondered if it was too late to put his hands on the rattiest cab in the fleet.

"Oh, and, Cheryl . . . dress casually."

NUMBER 26 TEMPTED PETE as he passed through the garage a few hours later. The old cab had been shelved two weeks ago for repairs—ratty interior, a cracked windshield and shocks that would rattle your teeth.

He was sorely tempted to live down to every one of the expectations he was certain Cheryl Steadman had of him. But the potential for bad publicity wasn't worth it, even to put the Snow Princess through a few hours of discomfort.

Curbing his devilish inclination, Pete grabbed the keys to a more acceptable taxi. When he turned away from dispatch, a short, wiry figure silhouetted against the lights in the front of the garage stepped forward. The suit was almost as shiny as the patent leather shoes. And the hair, long and slicked back, had a sheen of its own. The face, in shadows, was sharp and pointed, stretched into a smile that dared you not to smile back.

Pete recognized Kurt Fletcher right away and felt a moment of unreasoning panic at seeing him, once again, in the garage of Bayou Taxi. He had paid dearly to get Fletcher out of his life—and his garage—once before. His heart galloped erratically at the prospect of Fletcher worming his way once again into his life.

"How's the old partner?" The oily voice matched everything else about Pete's boyhood friend. "Doin' pretty well for yourself, huh, chum?"

The greedy bitterness in his ratlike face as Fletcher took in the garage heightened Pete's apprehension.

"Doin' okay. How about you?" Pete didn't care how Kurt was doing. He'd heard enough to know that, by whatever standards you wanted to use, Fletcher hadn't done well at all since Pete bought out his half of the business four years earlier. He knew that being sought out by his old chum was nothing but bad news.

"Great! Doin' great!" Fletcher's eyes still darted around the garage, which bustled with activity as dusk settled over the city. "Listen, how's about a drink? Catch up on old times?"

What had he heard, and promptly tried to forget, on one of his Sunday visits with the folks? Nothing that should surprise him after the problems that had prompted him to buy out Fletcher's part of the company they had started on a shoestring and a dream. A little drug hustling. Running numbers. In the pocket of the wise guys who were responsible for most of the city's illegal activities.

A drink with Kurt Fletcher was an invitation to trouble. The kind of trouble Pete had tried to steer clear of for years.

"Thanks. But I've got to be somewhere." He couldn't bring himself to be any more polite. Pete was surprised to find that it still hurt to be so distant, so cold to Fletcher. For a fleeting moment, he could see Fletcher's youthful face—as narrow and pointed as it was today but aglow with the excitement of youth—as he had accepted Pete's dare to swing from a frayed old rope on the dock over the muddy Mississippi River that flowed past rows of battered old warehouses. Pete and Tony had roared with laughter at their friend's bloodcurdling whoop when the frayed rope broke and landed him in the icy river.

"Just a short one, pal." Fletcher's smile stiffened. "Got a little business to discuss."

"What kind of business?" Pete's eyes narrowed. The vision of twelve-year-old Kurt Fletcher faded. In his place stood a low-rent hood whose mere presence spelled trouble.

"I need a little help." The smile disappeared completely now. The shadows under Fletcher's heavy brow deepened with his frown. "You know how it is. You get in a little bind now and then. And I figured I could count on my old partner for a little help getting straightened out."

Pete steeled himself against the appeals to their old friendship. Fletcher had sold out that friendship years ago, when he had jeopardized their fledgling company with shady shenanigans that had added up to a clear-cut case of embezzlement.

"You want money. Is that it?"

The ugly sneer that passed as a smile reappeared. "Naw. Not money. Money I got. Just need a little helpin' hand from an old pal. Won't take ten minutes, Pete. Just a short Sazerac and you're back here in a quarter hour."

The mention of a Sazerac twisted Pete's heart the few degrees necessary to win his reluctant agreement. Sazeracs. The first time he, Tony and Fletcher had tasted the forbidden temptation of hard liquor had been over a jug of Sazerac cocktails Tony had mixed at his old man's bar. They had pedaled furiously to the solitude of a nearby walled cemetery and proceeded to desecrate the eternal rest of the city's ancestors with the drunken giggles of thirteen-year-old boys on their first real rampage.

Well, maybe just a short Sazerac.

WITHIN MINUTES they were seated across from each other in a dark dive around the corner from the garage. Fletcher tossed back his concoction of rye whiskey and bitters. Pete watched, his Sazerac untouched, irritated with his soft-hearted capitulation.

"Get to the point, Fletcher. You've got five minutes."

"Busy man, aren't you, pal?" Fletcher waved his glass at a passing barmaid. "Now that business is doin' so well, it's hard to find time for your old friends, ain't it?"

Pete maintained a stony silence. Fletcher hadn't given in willingly when Pete had bought out his share of Bayou Taxi. It was no surprise that he was still bitter.

"What I need's pretty simple, Pete. Friends of mine deal in a high-profit product. And they need transportation. A way to deliver their product from one side of town to the other." He paused while the waitress set another drink in front of him. "Low risk for you, but a nice cut of the profits. Your guys are on the road all the time anyway, so it's sheer profit. No risk for you, pal. None at all. But plenty of green stuff to make it worth your while."

So Fletcher was looking for a way to run drugs. Pete downed his own drink quickly, tossed a bill onto the table to cover the tab and stood up.

"Not interested, Fletcher. Thanks for the offer."

A powerful hand caught his forearm.

"Don't decide yet, pal. Let's go over the details. It's a sweet deal. You'll see." Fletcher's eyes were cold with desperation and angered at having to plead. "I owe some money, Pete. This'll wipe the slate clean. I figured I could count on you, bein' from the old neighborhood and all."

Pete looked down at the hand gripping his arm and pointedly looked up into Fletcher's dark eyes. Fletcher dropped his hand.

"I don't care about the details, Fletcher. You ought to know that. Bayou Taxi is clean and it's going to stay that way."

Fletcher took a careless swig from his Sazerac and wiped his mouth on the back of his hand. "You owe me, Pete. You know you do."

"You used up your tab with me years ago, Fletcher."

Fletcher's eyes froze into an icy glare.

"Lotta people depend on you, Pete. I wouldn't want you to make the wrong decision. Wouldn't want to see people get hurt."

Pete's fist closed; the muscles in his forearms flexed automatically. He remembered without trying how easy it would be to grab this lowlife by his shiny green tie and yank until Fletcher was gasping for air. With great effort, he forced himself to relax his taut fist.

"Think it over, Pete. I'd hate for you to make a decision you'd regret."

The B-movie dialogue was surprisingly chilling delivered face-to-face. Pete turned and walked out of the bar and into the dark street. He took long, deep breaths of the pungent river air to get the stale smell of the bar out of his nostrils. He brushed his sleeve where Fletcher had grabbed him but couldn't brush away the prickling discomfort Fletcher's veiled threats had left behind.

CHAPTER FOUR

EACH TICK of the captain's clock on her mantel was an irritant, a grain of sand grinding against Cheryl's nerves.

She hadn't been able to concentrate on anything since she walked in the door from work.

Who are you kidding? she thought, pushing another piece of puffed oat cereal below the surface of the milk and watching it pop up again. *You haven't been able to concentrate on anything since you called Pete Fontenot.*

After accepting Pete's offer to squire her around town in one of his taxicabs, she had lost her ability to focus her thoughts. Editing a simple press release for Risa, the new copywriter in the office, had taken an hour. An hour! It was a page and a half, double-spaced, on the number of dollars conventions had brought into the city during 1989. Not *War and Peace*, for goodness' sake!

Wrinkling her nose at the cereal that was rapidly turning to mush, she emptied the bowl into the disposal, rinsed it and placed it in the compact dishwasher next to an identical bowl from breakfast. And another from dinner the night before.

"No wonder you can't get interested in eating," she chided herself, wondering if all people who lived alone talked out loud simply to break the silence with the sound of a human voice.

But she wasn't fooling herself. The monotony of her diet had nothing to do with tonight's lack of appetite.

That could be traced back to the phone conversation with Pete Fontenot. To be more specific, it had to do with the fact that he would be here in less than twenty minutes.

Nineteen, in fact, according to the clock. Every minute of the past half hour had ticked off ominously, distracting her as she searched her closet for something to wear. Ecru fisherman's knit sweater. Or the striped cotton crewneck, in complimentary colors that went with every pair of casual pants she owned. Or the cranberry angora.

She had spent an unconscionable eleven minutes deciding on the fisherman's knit.

She had fed the fish in the twenty-gallon aquarium, not pausing as she usually did to enjoy the graceful swish of the mollies and angelfish. She had plumped the tapestry pillows on the silver-gray couch, pausing to contemplate where she had seen that exact color recently. She had straightened the edge of books hemmed between two chunks of smoothly carved marble at the back of her desk and changed the angle of the gooseneck lamp on the desk's polished edge.

Now, as the clock continued to tick, the little bit of cereal she had managed to swallow was rolling around in her stomach in a way that was becoming increasingly and unpleasantly familiar.

Seventeen minutes until Pete Fontenot. She plopped down on the couch and pointed the remote control at the TV. The evening news would distract her. Sixteen minutes. There she was, with Pete Fontenot at her side, touting Project Friendly Faces. Grimacing, she pointed the remote control again and the screen grew dark. Fifteen.

Her foot tapped soundlessly on the winter-white carpet. She stilled it. *This man,* she argued with herself, *should not rattle you.*

She reached for the accounting textbook on the marble-topped coffee table and opened it to the place marked by a strip of ribbon.

Fourteen minutes. Thirteen. The tassel on her leather loafer swished as her foot once again picked up the clock's persistent tick. Twelve.

She closed the book with deliberate calm, without reading a single word. *He'll be here in less than ten minutes,* she told herself. *Surely you can sit here without fidgeting for ten minutes.*

The telephone trilled from the kitchen. Cheryl's heart lurched—what was wrong with her nerves!—but she sat still, waiting for the answering machine to take over at the end of two rings. Whoever it was would have to wait; she was in no mood to talk to anyone right now.

"Sorry we missed you, sweetheart." Amanda Steadman's response to her daughter's taped message was clipped and precise. With distaste, Cheryl realized she probably sounded just like her mother. "We just wanted to say hi."

The voice faded, as if she were talking to someone in the background. Cheryl felt a twinge of guilt. *It's your mother,* she told herself. *Go talk to her.*

"And your dad wanted to see if the two of you could get together." Cheryl hated the hint of imperial command in her mother's voice. "Dad knows you're busy, but he'll be in town on business a few weeks from now and thought the two of you might have dinner. Let us know if that suits you."

Cheryl sat, unwilling to take the steps necessary to interrupt the tape and talk to her mother. As the recorder clicked and rewound, her forehead puckered almost imperceptibly at the thought of her father coming to town. Huntley Steadman would march imperiously into her world and somehow make it seem smaller, less important than it seemed now.

The Garden District apartment of which she was so proud would become, through his eyes, no more than a three-room garage apartment behind one of the city's old-money homes in one of the city's old-money neighborhoods. He would be disdainful that his daughter rented someone's garage, without ever noticing the few tasteful antiques she had picked up or the elegant architectural touches—French doors, crown molding, mirror-bright hardwood floors—that made it special.

To him, it would be just a garage apartment. And not nearly good enough for the daughter of one of Cleveland's best families.

And the job. Looking down the angle of his patrician nose, Huntley Steadman would label Dave Arnaud a no-class little hustler. He wouldn't see that the job brought his daughter into contact with the city's power brokers. He wouldn't notice that she had at least unofficial authority over two copywriters and a graphic artist. He wouldn't make the distinction that she wielded, in an exciting, glamorous city that relied upon its public image, not a little bit of power.

She considered trying to think of a way to put him off. Maybe the business trip would be canceled.

Her heart lurched again at a knock on the front door. Not so much a knock as a controlled pound. She hadn't heard the car on the cobblestone driveway. She had let Pete Fontenot sneak up on her. She felt unprepared, somehow unarmed.

And that, she told herself, was ridiculous. She could hold her own with anybody. Especially a man who didn't even know to leave his sunglasses in the car.

Cheryl forced herself to walk calmly to the drop-leaf dining room table to pick up her leather shoulder bag on the way to the door. She opened the door in midpound, searching for something coolly dismissive to say about his overzealous knocking. But she didn't voice her irritation.

"Is this casual enough?" she asked, holding out her arms to display the sweater and pulling a smile out of that part of her that always responded with social appropriateness. "I hope I won't give the company a bad name."

"Maybe not." He grinned easily, unexpectedly, and the corners of his eyes crinkled. "I usually insist on a necktie, but I decided we'd make an exception tonight."

Pete's crisp slacks and windowpane-checked shirt weren't part of the uniform his drivers wore, Cheryl knew. But he had pulled on one of the navy blazers sporting the Bayou Taxi logo on the breast pocket. On Pete, it looked like the yacht-club jacket of the upper crust.

The man definitely wore his clothes as well as he wore his finesse in a business meeting. She had to give him that. No one would notice that his blazer wasn't tailor-made any more than they would notice that his confident composure was manufactured.

Only another expert manufacturer would know, Cheryl thought as they walked down the wooden steps to the cobblestone driveway.

"Guess this is quite a switch for you," Pete said, holding the door of the cab with studied gallantry while she slid into the front seat, "riding in front with the hired help."

Cheryl could have sworn his face twitched with the hint of a grin as she reached to pull the car door closed herself. So he was going to make this difficult, was he? After he crossed to the driver's side and settled into the front seat, she turned to him with one of her canned public-relations smiles. "Not at all. I love a good adventure."

He stared at her in the glare of the floodlight bright-ening the lush gardens between the main house and the garage. Damn the man, she thought again, wondering what those hard gray eyes were looking for.

A crack.

The thought came to her as she held his look without flinching. The same thing she was waiting for. A crack in the veneer.

It would be snowing in August before he found one, she promised herself, confident that her placid expression would never fail her.

"What's it like when you really smile?" His voice was so impersonal he might have been asking how long she had worked for Dave Arnaud, but the question was un-expected. Designed, she knew, to throw her off balance.

She smiled again. It was harder to pull off this time, but she found one and pasted it on. "Like this."

His chuckle was much more sincere than her smile. "Great. This should be a lot of fun."

He started the engine with a rumbling rev but turned back to her before pulling down the long driveway to-ward Saint Charles Avenue. "Here's the game plan, Slick. I'll drive, you take care of the radio."

Every minute of her social training, the training that decreed that one never show one's irritation, was put to the test. Slick? Who in blue blazes did he think he was?

She squelched the protest that bubbled to the surface as Pete pointed to the radio microphone hanging on the car's dash beside the meter that kept track of the fare. She wasn't a cab driver and her name wasn't Slick. But she would be damned, she vowed, if she wouldn't be the best sport Pete Fontenot had ever tried to snooker.

"Fine. What do I do?"

Cheryl listened closely as he told her how to work the radio and how to respond to calls. She ignored the brusqueness of his voice. She also ignored the fact that he seemed as determined as she that they not touch—not the brush of a finger, not the nudge of a knee. Cheryl was to be guardian of all equipment on her side of the front seat; Pete would oversee everything on the driver's side. And never the twain shall meet. Which was more than fine with her, Cheryl told herself.

With businesslike dignity, Cheryl contacted dispatch for their first address, then listened silently as Pete gave her a blow-by-blow on the way. A brief history of the Garden District. Dates and architectural styles and family business connections.

She wondered, as she listened, how he could possibly know so much. He wasn't old money himself. She knew that much from doing her homework. She had a hunch that, if she asked, he could tell her which families had daughters who slept around and sons with a weakness for nose candy.

But exploring the life-styles of the rich and famous wasn't the game for the evening, Cheryl discovered when their first fare staggered down the sidewalk toward the cab.

The tall, barely dressed woman with the whiskey bottle peeking out of her beaded bag lurched toward them with precarious dignity, the embodiment of every bad impression Cheryl had of New Orleans. Cheryl wondered, as she carefully averted her eyes, if Pete was smiling again. And what kind of instructions he had left with the dispatcher. Surely, she thought, this had to be a setup.

"Should you help her?" Cheryl asked, holding tightly to her imperturbability. *Just pretend you stop at the curb to pick up tipsy women in scandalous clothes every day of the week,* she told herself.

"Lucy never falls."

A shiny black dress clung snugly to the woman's tall, thin frame. Her breasts, disproportionately large for her sparse build, were thrust upward to make the most of the gown's plunging neckline. Her hair was a tangled mass of shoulder-length black curls. Her heavily outlined eyes drooped. And the shoulder bag, weighed down by the whiskey bottle, kept slipping off her shoulder.

"How's it going tonight, Lucy?" Pete greeted their unsteady passenger cheerfully as she slumped into the back seat.

"It's a son of a . . . Hey, what's the special occasion?" In spite of the slur, her voice held a husky melody. "What are you doin', Font'not, slummin'?"

"Been missin' my old friends, Luce."

Lucy grunted, clearly not convinced. Without asking, Pete pulled out into the traffic and headed toward town. Remembering his instructions, Cheryl radioed dispatch to let them know they had picked up the fare on Magazine Street.

"Hey, Pete." The deep voice called from the back seat. "How 'bout a quick stop?"

"Bottle running low?"

Lucy's laughter rolled, raucous and raspy, into the front seat. "Yeah. You know me pretty good, babe. Always did."

"No need to stop, Luce. Jasper'll take good care of you when we get to the club."

"Aw, Pete. You know he waters down the juice. Thinks I can't sing if I get too tanked up."

The rest of the ten-minute drive Pete spent gently distracting Lucy from her interest in making a stop for liquor. His steady run of quiet conversation kept Lucy from realizing they had reached their destination without making a stop along the way.

Was she imagining it, Cheryl wondered, or was Pete actually being human? He seemed to actually care that Lucy didn't go into her job with a full bottle of whiskey for reinforcement.

Even more interesting, the guard was down. The guard he had put up at the meeting earlier in the week, the guard he had used to keep her and the rest at a distance. With this woman, there was no guard. Curious.

Cheryl cringed as they pulled up at the back entrance of one of Bourbon Street's more notorious night spots. The alley was heavy with the odors of stale beer and rotting food and others best not identified. Out front, she knew, men enticed customers by offering a teasing glimpse of the ample flesh that pranced and paraded onstage inside.

Tomorrow, Cheryl told herself, she would cheerfully kill Dave Arnaud for getting her into this.

"Font'not, you sorry so-and-so, you tricked me again." The singer's smile was bleary as she looked down on the cab from the back door. "Mama always told me you'd come to no good. Too bad I listened to her."

Cheryl was glad Pete couldn't see her smile as he joined Lucy in a laugh. She didn't see any need for him to think she was thawing. He waved at Lucy as she took a final swallow from her bottle before letting it fall to the ground.

The cab eased down the alley, which fed into one of the side streets in the French Quarter. Cheryl wished she had locked her door when she first buckled herself in. Now, she refused to reveal her uneasiness.

"Your old friends are certainly interesting."

Pete's answer, as usual, was slow in coming. She wondered if he always weighed everything he said so carefully. Or if that was only a signal that his guard was up once more.

"Yeah. Which way, Slick?"

Another check-in with dispatch and they were heading to a high-rise hotel off Canal Street, less than a mile away. In spite of the short distance, the crawling traffic slowed them down.

"What kind of people become cab drivers?" she asked, then decided her question had the condescending tone that had come from years of practicing to be the daughter of Huntley and Amanda Steadman. She tried to salvage the question. "If I'm to make these classes something they'll enjoy and learn from, I need to know who New Orleans cab drivers are."

Pete's left arm hung casually out the window; his right arm was draped lightly over the top of the steering wheel. He could have been asleep, his don't-give-a-damn attitude was so perfectly in place.

"They're everybody," he said finally, checking his rearview mirror as they crept through traffic. "Dumb. Smart. Black, white and everything in between. Honest. Sometimes. Whatever else they've got going against them, they want to make their own way and be a little bit better off tomorrow than they are today."

"Can they do that driving a cab? Better themselves?"

In the darkness, Cheryl almost missed the twitch of his lips that served as a smile. Or served to hide one. She couldn't be sure which. "If they're smart."

Cheryl recognized no answer when she heard one. What, she wondered, did he mean by smart? Street smart? Smart enough to know when to turn an easy profit? Smart enough to take advantage of the system? Pete Fontenot needn't think her naive just because she hadn't spent her life on the street. "Were you smart?"

His expression never changed. "Sometimes."

His game playing irritated her, but she was determined to cover it. "Tell me how you got started."

"Why?"

The pulse quickened in her throat. He was as leery, as defensive, as she. "Why not?"

"Because I'm not one of your students."

Cheryl pursed her lips. This man was definitely a hard case. "Fine. Is it a second job for most people? Is it something they do until they can get into something better? Or do they see it as their life's work?"

"Yes."

The ambiguous answer ended the conversation as Pete pulled in front of the hotel and jumped out to put some luggage in the trunk for two well-dressed men. The next half hour was a whirl of headlights and city lights seen mostly from the freeway on the way to the airport. But scenery—the ornate headstones of a centuries-old cemetery amid block after block of down-at-the-heels commercial buildings and miles of nondescript industry that could have been anywhere in the country took a back seat to the conversation going on behind them.

Cheryl listened intently, intrigued as the businessmen ironed out the details of a million-dollar construction deal. Although it was clear from their conversation that leaking news of the deal too soon could up the price of the riverfront land they hoped to purchase for the project, the two seemed oblivious to the four ears absorbing all the facts from the front seat.

"My gosh!" Cheryl exclaimed after Pete deposited the two men and their luggage at a bag check outside the terminal. "We could snatch that deal right out from under them if we had the right money or knew the right people. Are they crazy, talking like that in front of us?"

Pete looked at her quizzically before buckling himself in. "You call dispatch yet?"

Cheryl responded with prim efficiency. "Yes, boss. We're heading for the Cornstalk Hotel in the Quarter. If we're lucky, we'll get our next insiders' business tip of the week."

In spite of her exasperation with him, Cheryl felt a surge of satisfaction as laugh lines suddenly appeared at the corners of his eyes. Maybe she was more sly than Dave Arnaud thought. Sly enough to hold her own with Pete Fontenot, anyway. The thought accelerated her pulse and made her feel a little bolder than Cheryl Steadman of Cleveland was accustomed to feeling.

"And yes, they *are* crazy for talking like that in front of us," Pete replied at last as they zipped into the freeway traffic. "To them, we're just part of the equipment. If they were sitting in K-Paul's having dinner, they'd check over their shoulders to see who's at the next table before they blabbed so much. But, hell, we're just cabbies. Never occurred to them we might be able to use the information."

"It's a wonder cab drivers don't get to be millionaires," she said, almost missing his chuckle in her apprehension over the rear end of the vehicle in front of them, which they were approaching far too quickly for comfort.

She held her breath until Pete let up on the gas, then glanced at him for a response to her last statement. He scanned the freeway traffic intently.

"Yeah. Isn't it?" He whipped the rattling old vehicle around a tour bus.

If she hadn't been brought up oh, so properly, Cheryl couldn't have stopped herself from asking if Pete had made his money by keeping his ears open. It was no secret he had started out as a cab driver. But it was certainly a mystery how he'd managed to turn that into a respectable financial empire.

"This isn't a confessional." Pete eased back in the seat and punched the gas as a stretch of freeway opened up in front of them. "How I made my money isn't any of your business, either."

His blunt words stung, but she forced her voice to remain cool. "I didn't ask."

She sensed him turning his head in her direction, but she feigned interest in the skyline of the city.

The young couple they picked up at the Cornstalk, a historic inn adorned with a distinctive wrought iron fence molded to look like a row of cornstalks, had another kind of business on their minds. Muffled signs and the occasional rustling of clothes were hard to ignore as the cab crept along Saint Charles Avenue parallel to the streetcar line.

When the giggling, flushed couple were finally deposited—in what state of disarray she didn't dare look to discover—Cheryl found she couldn't bring herself to look at Pete, either.

The next fare was a blessing. An older woman from a genteel but decaying apartment house on Louisiana Avenue, one block beyond the Garden District, was meeting her nephew from out of town at his hotel in the French Quarter. In the soft cadence peculiar to the upper-class Old South, she talked all the way about her nephew's success in women's accessories and his frequent trips to the city where he had grown up.

"He's a darlin' boy," she said in her softly wavering voice. "And he's simply in love with this notorious old city."

"She's easy to love," Pete admitted, smiling into the rearview mirror. "Like a beautiful woman growing even more beautiful with the years."

Cheryl forced herself to keep looking straight ahead but couldn't ignore the affection in his tone.

"But such a naughty lady, wouldn't you say?" A hint of flirtatiousness entered the elderly woman's voice.

"That's one of the best things about her," Pete said, sharing a laugh with his fare.

By the time they saw the woman safely into the hands of the doorman at her nephew's hotel, Cheryl had grown entranced with their exchange. New Orleans—in spite of its sometimes unsavory reputation—clearly captured the hearts of its natives.

"I'm hungry," Pete said abruptly. She wondered suddenly why his voice and actions seemed to hold a kindness, a gentleness for everyone but her. It surprised her to realize she would have appreciated just a fraction of that gentleness coming her way. "Let's eat."

Food was the last thing on her mind after they drove to the Bayou Taxi garage and started out on foot into the Quarter. The crowd was sparse at first, but as they neared Jackson Square the numbers of tourists ambling the streets increased. Most of the artists who displayed their wares on the fence surrounding Jackson Square had packed up for the day, but a few remained, doing caricatures and charcoal sketches of tourists.

A street juggler, a worn felt hat upturned for donations at the foot of his unicycle, captured their attention. When they stopped to laugh at his calculated clumsiness and mile-a-minute banter, the large number of people craning to view the juggler's antics pushed them closer and closer together. Suddenly, the separation they had carefully enforced in the cab was violated. Her shoulder

crushed into his chest. His arm shifted uncertainly against
her back. She stiffened and made her back so straight she
could easily have marched across the square balancing
china plates on her head. Except that her knees felt shaky.
His thigh was solid and warm against the swell of her hip.

Cheryl's mouth went dry. The juggler was no longer
funny. She was near the front, but she couldn't hear a
word he said. She didn't see him. She didn't even feel the
rest of the people crowding in around her, a situation that
would normally have irritated her and sent her heading for
escape.

All she felt was Pete.

She was grateful when his hand at her elbow propelled
her out of the crowd. Not nearly soon enough, they were
walking in the open again. The snappy breeze from the
river cooled her skin.

Except where they had touched. Except along her
shoulder and her back and her hip where his chest and
arm and thigh had been pressed to hers. There, the heat
remained. She walked quickly, as if to outrun the warmth.

Pirate's Alley was dark, darker than the bustling
brightness of Jackson Square. No one else was braving the
isolation of the narrow alleyway that night, and Cheryl
suddenly wished for the return of the crowds. What if
Pete . . . did something?

She clenched her fists at her side. *Get a grip on yourself, Steadman. What if he did what? Kissed you?
Grabbed you and ravished you? This is the real world, not
some inane movie. Besides, if he did grab you, a well-
placed knee would soon rid him of any amorous notions.*

With a controlled shiver, Cheryl recaptured her equilibrium as they stopped in a small, dark courtyard. Giving only a brief knock at one of the doors leading off the
courtyard, Pete ducked his head inside and called out.

"Henri, what's for dinner?"

A short, rotund man with a stained apron showed up at the screen door.

"Pete! You old reprobate! What you been eatin'? I ain't seen you in a rabbit's age. You ain't eatin' nobody else's gumbo, now, are you?"

Pete feigned hurt and surprise. "Henri, I don't even eat my mother's gumbo anymore. You know that."

Laughter rumbled up from the chef's broad, deep belly. "You come in. I fix a bowl for you and the lady."

Cheryl followed as they squeezed through the hectic restaurant kitchen, where huge pots of seafood gumbo and jambalaya bubbled. The rhythmic click of knives chopping efficiently through vegetables punctuated the hubbub of waiters calling out for shrimp creole and cooks protesting that creole sauce can't be hurried and busboys and dishwashers clanging plates and glasses and dishes. And everyone, it seemed, called out a cheery greeting to Pete or paused midchop or between sizzles to slap him on the back.

Through the door into the dining room, Cheryl saw the soft lighting and heard the quiet mood music that was a world away from the chaos of the kitchen.

They stopped in a small room off the kitchen, where a desk piled high with cookbooks and ledgers and accordion files barely left room for three folding chairs. Henri followed close behind with two steaming bowls of seafood gumbo on a tray and two red cloth napkins draped over his meaty forearm.

"Two best seats in the house," he declared, shoving a stack of papers onto the floor with a thud to make room for the bowls. While Pete breathed deeply of the pungent steam and made appropriately pleased sounds, Henri unfurled the napkins and slipped them expertly onto their laps. With a deferential bow and a twinkle in his eye, he turned to Pete. "Wine, *monsieur?*"

"Certainly, Henri," he answered, playing the smiling chef's game. "A cabernet, perhaps?"

Pete didn't hesitate before diving into the stewlike soup of shrimp, crawfish and okra served over a mound of rice. Giving one quick, pitying thought to her delicate stomach, Cheryl took a brave spoonful of the tangy gumbo. The flavors exploded against her tongue and the back of her throat. Her eyes watered at the combination of pungent spice and dark, musky seafood.

"The best in town, isn't it?" Pete asked, watching carefully for her reaction.

Cheryl nodded, wondering if her taste buds had ever been more alive. She would never admit it to Pete, but her first—and until now, only—experience with gumbo during a business lunch with Dave Arnaud had turned into a howling case of heartburn.

"More old friends?" she asked, relieved as Henri slipped in quietly with two glasses of heartily dark wine, then slipped out again.

"Yeah. More old friends." The crinkles around his eyes signaled a smile. "You like them better than the last old friend you met?"

A sip of her wine cooled the spicy burn of the gumbo. "Why, no. I'm just sorry we didn't get to hear Lucy sing."

She was instantly sorry. It was one of those innocuous, socially "right" comments that would come back to haunt her, of that she was certain. But before Pete had time to react—perhaps, if she was lucky, before he had time to register the remark—their dinner was interrupted by a visitor.

A dark-haired young woman who could only be Henri's daughter dropped into the cramped office with a loaf of warm, crusty French bread in a basket. She and Pete talked about her final year of high school and the scholarship to Loyola that was still up in the air.

Then the dishwasher stuck his head in the door, pausing to dry his hands on the dingy white bibbed apron tied around his waist. Pete introduced him as another Pete—Pedro Alessandri—who had been in a high school class taught by Pete's sister, Angie. Pedro's teeth gleamed brightly against his nut-brown skin as he talked about the new baby in the family.

"Not too many years and your sister, she'll be teaching the second generation of Alessandris," Pedro boasted.

"I'll remember to razz Angie about that the next time I see her," Pete promised.

Although they both tried valiantly to turn down a serving of Henri's famous bread pudding, topped with rum sauce and shavings of white chocolate, their protests were no match for Henri's determination. As they nibbled at the sinfully delicious dessert, Henri leaned against the door frame and talked about the old neighborhood.

"Your folks, Pete, they're doin' better than any of us," Henri said, his thick arms crossed over his belly. "Millionaire sons, so lucky we should all be. Millionaire sons who ain't stingy, right?"

Directing a wink at Cheryl, Henri talked right over the objection Pete was opening his mouth to make. Cheryl didn't look directly at Pete, but she had the distinct impression he was uncomfortable. Henri didn't slow down, just kept up a ten-minute dissertation on how well Pete's parents were doing in the business he had set them up in, who in the old neighborhood was in failing health, who had died and married and had babies.

The steady stream of gossip didn't end until the screen door to the kitchen closed behind them. After the steamy kitchen, Cheryl welcomed the cool evening air. She raised her face to the hint of a breeze.

"What now?" he asked.

The gumbo was a cozy warmth in her tummy and the wine was a lightness spreading through her limbs. But his voice—ah, his voice. His voice negated all the mellowing influence of good food and drink. His voice crackled against her nerve endings, snapping and stinging wherever it touched. His voice reminded her of the heat of his body pressed against hers.

The night was not as gentle as it seemed, she reminded herself.

"Back to work, I suppose," she said purposefully.

"You've seen enough of that, haven't you?" His hand on her wrist stopped her. She turned to face him, slipping her wrist out of his reach. "I thought you wanted to hear Lucy sing."

His silvery eyes, which looked almost directly into hers, were teasing. She hardly heard his words, but her all-business instincts went on automatic.

"I don't think that's part of what I need to see in order to relate to cab drivers, Pete."

Turning, she started to head back toward Jackson Square and Bayou Taxi.

"Hey, Slick."

Her long stride slowed at the command in his voice. Looking back in his direction, she watched him watch her. He didn't say a word, then slowly walked toward her. When he was so close she could almost count the stitches in the collar of his shirt, he stopped.

"Hey, Slick, when are we going to stop playing games?"

The longing in his eyes was curbed but naked. He wanted her and his words issued a challenge. *Deny that you want me, too.*

"I don't know what you're talking about, Pete."

Even in the darkness of the alleyway, Cheryl could see the shutters close on his emotions. His gray eyes grew cold, glitteringly icy. Cheryl shivered.

"Come on, Slick, let's get you safely home before you figure it out."

CHAPTER FIVE

GETTING CLOSE to Cheryl Steadman might not be such a hot idea after all, Pete thought as he strode the last half block to his Dauphine Street town house.

On his territory, she had been the Snow Princess times two. Cold and rigid and absolutely unbending.

He hadn't helped matters, either. No matter how hard he tried, he hadn't been able to shake the uneasy feelings he had carried out of the meeting with Kurt Fletcher. Uneasy and teed off. What a slime. Imagine thinking, for even a minute, that Pete would be party to one of his two-bit drug deals.

The way their partnership had ended should have given Fletcher all the answer he needed.

Pete felt as if he'd spent half the evening looking over his shoulder. And the other half feeling the prickle at the back of his neck.

But, no, that wasn't true. At least half the evening he'd been trying hard not to imagine how Cheryl Steadman would look with that corn silk hair of hers spread out around her face. Trying hard not to imagine whether she had freckles on her shoulders, too. And other places, as well.

No, he hadn't worried about Kurt Fletcher the entire evening. Just enough to make him as uptight as Cheryl Steadman obviously spent her entire life.

Just enough to make him jump when a kitten stood up and yowled from the oversize flowerpot outside his wrought iron gate. Still fishing in his pocket for his key, Pete stared down at the tiny animal. So scrawny and dirty it could only be a stray, the black-and-white kitten looked up at him and spoke in indignant tones.

Pete knew that tone of voice. It held him personally responsible for hunger and damp alleys and unfriendly dogs. Somehow, Pete knew, the network of stray cats was efficiently and unerringly spreading the word. Pete Fontenot. Dauphine Street town house. Pushover.

"Yeah. Right. Keep your shirt on, Spot. I gotta find the key first."

Without waiting for Pete, the kitten bounded friskily through the gate, urging him on with impatient demand. The stray, at least, knew he wouldn't bite.

Pete almost smiled in spite of the frown furrowing his forehead. Then again, he told himself as he followed the kitten up the unlighted stairway, maybe Cheryl knew things the new animal on the block didn't know. He wouldn't mind, now that he thought of it, giving the lady a nibble or two.

Hanging his Bayou Taxi blazer haphazardly on the back of a molded chrome dining chair, Pete walked over to the TV and set the VCR to play. A boxing match from earlier in the evening popped onto the air. He watched for a few moments as the commentators debated the pros and cons of the two fighters, then turned the sound up so he could hear it in the next room.

"Meow, yourself, Spot. I guess that means you're hungry," he said to the kitten, which had followed him and now stood on his shoes and called out reproachfully for attention. "Yeah, thought so. Come on, let's see what we can round up."

He leaned to pick up the handful of fur. Demanding cries instantly turned to surprised silence, then a hesitant purr. The tentative chug of the kitten's purr grew steadier, more certain, as it turned wide golden eyes on its new protector. Checking the kitten's plastic collar for a tag, Pete discovered that the metal ring had stretched open. The tag identifying the kitten had disappeared in the streets.

Cradling the kitten against his neck, Pete noted there were no messages on the machine as he passed the kitchen wall phone and opened the refrigerator door.

"How about a beer?" Spot's purr said the choice was fine with him, but Pete was skeptical. "Nah. You're not legal yet. How about an artichoke?"

Popping open a bottle of beer for himself, Pete surveyed the refrigerator. Artichoke. Two half bottles of hot sauce. A bottle of champagne, another of soda water, four limes and leftover jambalaya from a restaurant down the street.

A small pink nose nudged the cold bottle. A rough pink tongue followed, sampling the dampness.

"Poor guy. You're thirsty, too, aren't you?" He set the kitten down on the counter beside the beer bottle while he filled a plastic bowl with water. But when he set bowl and cat down together on the black-and-white tile floor, the tiny animal couldn't reach over the side of the bowl. Before Pete could react, Spot tipped over the plastic dish with a dirty white paw. The kitten jumped back in time to avoid wet paws, then ventured forward to lap from the spreading puddle on the floor.

"Resourceful little beggar," Pete said, rummaging through the cabinet for a kitten-size bowl and leaving Spot to enjoy the water. "I like that, Spot. But don't get any bright ideas. This is my place, not yours. You're still the visitor. A *temporary* visitor. Tomorrow, we run ads to find the people who really belong to you. Got it?''

After setting down a fresh bowl of water and mopping up the other with a couple of paper towels, Pete went back to the refrigerator for the jambalaya. Skeptically, he set the take-out tray down next to the kitten and stood back to watch. The kitten circled the tray and edged cautiously close to the food. He looked up helplessly and, at Pete's shrug, touched a tentative nose to the concoction of sausage and rice.

After one reluctant bite, hunger took over.

With one ear on the replay of the boxing match, Pete sipped at his beer and watched as the kitten wolfed down the food.

''. . . very different styles make this battle a tough one to call,'' one of the announcers proclaimed solemnly to the other.

Pete ran the back of his hand over his chin, which was working on a healthy stand of stubble. Different styles. No kidding, he thought, envisioning Cheryl's flawless perfection.

It wasn't just her looks, either. Look how she dressed. Like nobody ever had to tell her to keep her shirt tucked in; she'd been born with her shirt tucked in. And that hair. It was so damned perfect he'd been hard-pressed to fight the urge to run his hands through it until it was thoroughly messed up.

Different styles. What an understatement.

Spot, a round bulge of satisfaction now replacing the hollow over his ribs, sat back on his haunches and looked up expectantly. When Pete turned his empty hands palms up, Spot began an after-dinner cleanup that was long overdue.

"...without a doubt as evenly matched as any two boxers in their weight class," concluded the pompous voice of the second announcer.

Evenly matched? That remained to be seen, Pete thought, picking up the kitten and cuddling it to his chest as he headed back to the living room with his beer. Completely mismatched was more like it. This babe had class up to her eyeballs. Right up to her pretty blue eyeballs. Class. *You can't buy class, Fontenot.*

He'd heard that before. From Eleanore, the day he asked her to leave. With the passion of newborn hatred flickering in her eyes, she had calmly placed the big diamond solitaire in his hand and curled his fingers around it. That was class, too. Her voice, when she spoke, had as many sharp edges as the two-carat rock in his palm.

Just remember, Pete, you can't buy class.

"Hell, yes, you can, Spot." He settled deeply into the familiar softness of the leather recliner positioned in front of the TV. Absently, he scratched behind the ears of the kitten that rested on his belly and tried to concentrate on the prefight hype.

If scrappy Americans could buy class in a Creole society almost a century and a half ago, Pete Fontenot could do it in 1990. His parents were proof of that. That had taken money, hadn't it? Today, their souls didn't belong to other people. Today, they worked for themselves. They ran the best cleaning service in town. A first-class cleaning service. That's what money could do. It could save his mom from taking the bus to the rich folks' homes every day.

This town house was proof, too, wasn't it? He didn't even bother to look around at the expensive furnishings he had copied right out of one of those trendy home magazines two years ago. Parqueted teak and chrome in the dining room. Black-and-white sofa stretching for miles. Torch lamps on the wall. The only change from the magazine photo was his collection of Mardi Gras masks dotting the walls instead of the pen and ink drawings. It was classy. His cars were classy. His clothes were classy.

"But you've still got dirt under your fingernails, Fontenot," he told himself.

He looked down at his neatly trimmed nails. How many years, he wondered, had he been unable to scrub away the grit and grime that came with working under the hoods of cars?

He kept his hands clean now. But he could still picture the dirt under his nails every time he looked. Surely everyone else could, too.

Cheryl Steadman had probably seen right through him, too, the first time she'd leveled that Snow Princess look at him. She had country club upbringing written all over her, just the way Eleanore had. And she no doubt knew when someone didn't belong, just as Eleanore had.

To hell with Cheryl Steadman, he told himself, grinning in spite of himself as he looked down at Spot, now sleeping contentedly in a tight ball on his stomach. But Spot, whose whiskers twitched in some kitten dream, deserved a rest.

He turned his attention back to the fight, where the two middleweights were dancing around each other, each checking the other's stance, each looking for the right opening before throwing the first punch. With one hand on the kitten, Pete watched the two sweat-glistening bodies. By the end of round two, his eyes had drooped shut. Spot hadn't moved, but his purr could be heard even over the voices of the TV commentators.

PETE JUMPED at the sound of the ringing telephone. Spot peeped out a sleepy protest at being disturbed so abruptly.

Clearing the grogginess out of his voice and trying not to stumble over the kitten scampering along at his feet, Pete picked up the kitchen phone on the third ring.

"Hey, partner, I know it's late. Hope I didn't interrupt anything." The oily voice was cheerful, friendly.

"What do you want, Fletcher?"

"Just wanted to see if you'd had a chance to think about my little proposition, partner. I think if you'd listen to some of the details, you'd see that—"

"I'm not your partner anymore, Fletcher." Pete's jaw clenched angrily. "And I'm not going to be. I don't need to hear the details."

"Listen. I'm a fair man. I remember how you operate, Font'not. You don't like to make rash decisions. Why don't you think about this—say until the first of the week. I'll see if I can't come up with a few...incentives...in the meantime, to help you make up your mind."

Pete hung up. He was surprised he hadn't noticed before how cold the town house was. He adjusted the thermostat, turned off the TV, picked up Spot, headed for the bedroom and spent the next two hours staring into the darkness.

"I CAN'T EAT DOUGHNUTS for breakfast," Cheryl protested, looking up from the small plate of sugar-dusted squares into Pete's frowning gaze.

"That's not a doughnut. It's a *beignet*. Ben-yay. It's French for...doughnut, or something. Now eat it."

Cheryl swallowed a chuckle. Pete Fontenot was the only person she'd ever seen who could frown and grin at the same time. Well, he wasn't actually grinning. But that little twitch at the corner of his mouth seemed to be his way of saying that his furrowed brow didn't mean he was ready to bite nails.

Although she had wondered when he picked her up that morning—this time in a fancy roadster bearing the license plate BAYOU-1.

He had certainly looked at ease. With the top down on the shiny silver car, the wind had blown his straight blond hair back from his forehead in reckless disarray. Nothing else about him had given any indication that mussed hair would concern him. Sandy stubble darkened his cheeks and a battered leather jacket covered a gray T-shirt. His jeans were . . . well, the most polite thing to say was that they were most assuredly comfortable.

And although he had settled his rangy frame easily into the low-slung seat, to Cheryl he still looked poised. Ready to strike. Despite his casual carriage, she had sensed right away that he was looking for something. Waiting for something. Maybe it was the way he'd glanced in the rearview mirror or swept his eyes in a 180-degree angle every so often.

Pete had something on his mind. And it was making him quiet. It had also turned his eyes to a flinty coldness that almost made her shiver.

Her reluctance to breakfast on sugar and caffeine had gotten the first rise of the day out of him. She decided to make the most of it.

"Pete, I've heard all about *beignets* and coffee at Café du Monde," she said tartly. The breeze ruffling the blue-and-white awnings whispered over her ears. "I don't see why I have to experience it just so I can talk to cab drivers about customer service."

"Because it's part of the experience, Slick." He licked sugar away from the corner of his mouth, and Cheryl's first bite of *beignet* stuck in her throat. "You can't talk about serving tourists if you don't even know what a *beignet* tastes like.''

"That is nonsense." She choked down the bite and chased it with a swallow of chicory coffee. She felt suddenly short of breath. "That makes no sense at all, Pete."

He snapped his fingers and pointed at her, nodding. "Exactly. The whole town makes no sense. See, you're starting to get the picture already. And only one bite. By the time we've sucked the heads off a few crawfish for dinner, you'll feel this city in your blood, Slick.''

Cheryl wasn't sure which idea sent the chills up and down her spine—eating those creepy-crawly little creatures from the bottom of some bayou creek or spending an entire day with Pete Fontenot. One was just as daunting as the other. She wasn't sure she had the gumption for either.

Pete glanced up from his watch and popped his last *beignet* into his mouth. "Eat up. There's a voodoo queen waitin' for us.''

Closing her eyes in dismay, Cheryl followed his lead and swallowed her final bite of the light pastry. "A what?"

As he pulled her to her feet, Pete stepped closer. While Cheryl stood frozen in panicked expectancy, he stared down at her lips for what seemed like an eternity. Then, with a half grin that almost crinkled the corners of his eyes, he licked the end of one finger and reached over to blot sugar off the edge of her lower lip.

"Where do you society babes learn to be so messy?" he teased, something besides humor burning in his clouded, pale eyes. His tongue flicked out to capture the specks of sugar on the end of his finger.

The tiny spot where Pete's touch had left her lower lip damp electrified every inch of her body.

THE BRISK TWO-BLOCK WALK took care of the insistent stirring in his groin that had threatened to embarrass Pete when he'd touched her face. By the time they reached the garage, where they had parked the roadster before going to the Café du Monde, he had just about—not quite, but just about—pushed out of his mind the soft swell of her lip against his finger. And the sudden paleness that had made her freckles stand out against the creamy whiteness of her skin.

He couldn't forget the haze in her eyes, however. A lack of focus, a shimmering blue confusion that said his touch had knocked her knees out from under her, just as it had him. His body stirred again, threatening to harden, suggesting ever so gently that he should do something more, something a bit more conclusive, to wipe the control out of her eyes.

Oh, hell. What had he done now?

For two blocks she had talked calmly about the cleanup of the riverfront warehouse district that had taken place thanks to the 1984 World's Fair. Her voice was just a tad frostier around the edges than usual, but she wasn't fooling him. Nevertheless, focusing on her words and the long, brisk stride that had easily kept up with his own had made it easier to dowse the heat in him.

Then she started in with her griping again. The stirring he couldn't control settled down the minute he suggested they leave the roadster in the garage and take two of the bicycles he kept stashed in the back.

"A bicycle? Why don't we just drive, Pete?" She, too, seemed to regain her momentum with the words. "This isn't a pleasure tour, you know."

"Oh, yeah?" His head rolled back and he laughed soundlessly. "I noticed. No wonder Arnaud stuck you with this Friendly Faces business. He's probably relieved to have you out of the office for a while.''

She surprised him with her own laugh—the first he'd heard from her. A golden, soprano bell of a laugh, trilling out and washing over him and sweeping away too quickly. Go figure it. First, she got her back up because he suggested a bicycle tour of the Quarter. Then, she laughed right out loud when he all but called her a pain in the ass. He'd never get this one figured out.

But, Lord, she looked delicious when she laughed. Her blue eyes turned cagey, almost flirtatious, and that little dimple at the corner of her mouth appeared. Of course, she was delicious today, anyway. Gray corduroy pants that didn't cling anywhere—just brushed over the rounded edges of her compact little tush. In fact, she was compact everywhere—she wouldn't be giving Miss April much competition for cleavage. But every inch of skin would be as creamy smooth as her face and as soft to the touch as the angora sweater that whispered over her small, high breasts.

He couldn't remember his reactions in a female's presence being this automatic since high school. Latent adolescence rearing its ugly head, he supposed.

''Dave Arnaud had better enjoy the peace and quiet. Lead me to the bikes, Mr. Fontenot,'' Cheryl said, tossing her head with a smile that was meant to be haughty but ended up only looking coltishly daring. Pete wished once again that she had her hair down around her shoulders instead of twisted up and tightly restrained.

Just like the rest of her, he thought. *She probably wears iron underwear.* But actually, he saw cotton. Pristine, little-girl cotton with a bit of cotton lace at the V between her breasts. Or silk. Vanilla ice-cream silk that rose in rustling points over her small, dark nipples.

He shook his head and cursed his imagination while he yanked a bicycle off the rack with fierce strength. He thrust the red bike in her direction. "Here. Ride this."

THEY RODE. Pedaling a little too furiously at first, they wove in and out of traffic and pedestrians already filling the streets of the Vieux Carré at midmorning. Shoppers in the expensive garb of tourists, clutching cameras and packages and oversize shopping bags. Shoppers in the funky casual of natives who lived and worked in the Quarter, heading home from the bakery with breakfast. Street vendors and delivery trucks and noise were their companions.

Noise. The rattle of panel trucks and the crash of crates hitting the sidewalk as they were muscled off the trucks. The chatter of voices with accents foreign and diverse—southern drawls and the quick, nasal clip of midwesterners, the singsong of the Orient. A horn bleated at the prodding of an impatient driver. Music bleeding out of the confines of canopies covering sidewalk cafés. Noise and a parade of colorful aromas kept them company as they pedaled from one wide boulevard to another narrow lane.

Aromas. The fresh-baked heaven of croissants and crusty French loaves. The caramel sweetness of praline candies hanging heavy in the air. The clean perspiration of hard work from one passing body overtaken and extinguished by the overpowering floral perfume of the next. Hot dogs, cotton candy and popcorn fighting for air space with shrimp and oysters frying for po' boy sandwiches. The dank, nose-wrinkling fragrance of the horses that pulled picturesque buggies for tourists.

Cheryl's senses had never been so bombarded. But none of the sensations carried the impact of the man who pedaled at her side. Ever since he'd touched her, the war had raged within her. And she had seen it raging within him, as well. It was, she knew, what had made him so short with her at the Bayou Taxi garage. It was responsible for the freeze in his eyes and the tension around his mouth.

He had been trying once again to find the crack in her veneer, pushing her to the limit with an outrageous bit of game playing. And it had backfired.

Her nipples grew taut once more as she thought of the touch. His damp finger—damp from the brazen touch of his tongue—on her lower lip. The power of her response had been almost savage. She would gladly have traded the bare, fleeting little touch for one of those ravishing, hungry, violent movie kisses.

It had made her downright giddy. Why else would she have laughed out loud that way when he was doing his darnedest to be irritating? She could have dismissed his wisecrack about Dave with a cool rejoinder. Instead, she had laughed out loud. How un-Cheryl-like. She just hadn't been herself.

In fact, the Cheryl Steadman she had known and kept on careful track for so many years was getting off track in too many ways. Displaying a singular lack of planning, she had gone to bed the night before without laying out her clothes for this morning. And without taking any precautions against the heartburn she was certain would wake her once the spicy seafood gumbo did its job on her. It wasn't like her to be so thoughtless.

It had been sheer luck that the gumbo hadn't once interrupted her dreams.

But here she was this morning, acting very unlike herself once again. She was even enjoying the bicycle tour of the Vieux Carré. It was exhilarating and a little bit breathtaking in its magnificent decadence.

She was under control now, however. Despite the sweet tightness in her breasts, which traveled lower and became a flowing lushness that turned her knees to rubber, she was under control. She could listen as Pete told her the history of the ornate buildings around Jackson Square, pointing out where hangings and duels were said to have taken place and the apartments where wildcats reputedly once made their homes—along with more than a smattering of the nation's most famous authors. Now that she was under control again, she could look around as he pointed to the ornate wrought iron balconies and explained that their Spanish influence pegged them as newer than the few squat, stark French buildings that had survived two devastating fires in the late 1700s.

"And there's where this part of the country got its name," he said, pointing to a nondescript corner drugstore.

"What do you mean?" This, too, was a new story to Cheryl.

"From 1854 to 1881, the Citizen's Bank issued ten-dollar bills printed with *dix* on the back—that's French for 'ten,'" Pete said. "Everybody called them dixies. And the rest, as they say..."

"Is history," she finished skeptically. "Are you sure that's a true story?"

He shrugged, amusement in his eyes. "Does it matter?"

They both had to stop and dismount when they encountered a horse-and-carriage traffic jam. He offered a hand to lead her around, but she ignored his chivalry and followed behind, instead. Not that she was afraid of her reaction if they touched again. It wasn't that at all. She was definitely under control.

But a part of her was still registering things she would never have registered the day before. Like the golden down that covered the rangy muscles of the forearm that peeked out when he pushed up the sleeve of his well-worn leather jacket. The perfect bow of his upper lip that would almost, not quite, border on unmasculine, if it wasn't for the square rock of his chin and the stubble that signaled he had slept too late to shave. Or just didn't give a darn if he looked good in her eyes or not.

That, Steadman, is much more likely the case, she told herself as they ordered lunch—oyster po' boys from the propped open screen window of a hole-in-the-wall sandwich shop.

Balancing a paper-wrapped sandwich in one hand and a plastic cup of ice-cold beer in the other, she watched in silence as Pete eased down to sit on the curb next to their bikes. "Isn't that dirty?"

"Mmm-hmm." He nodded, looking up at her with a dare in his eyes as he munched on a mouthful of his sandwich. "But if a horse and buggy come by, we can always lift our feet."

She wanted to shove the toe of her loafer rudely into the backside that sorely strained his threadbare jeans. In fact, she thought about it long and hard before she gave in and sank down beside him on the curb. In the end she'd decided that would be too much of a departure, even for a Cheryl Steadman who was quickly learning to enjoy things she wouldn't have dreamed of two days ago.

Before biting into the sandwich, she peeked between the thick slices of the French loaf. Crispy fried oysters, with lettuce and tomatoes and what looked suspiciously like hot sauce for seasoning. *Hello, ulcer.*

"It won't bite back."

"I didn't think it would."

"For a rich kid, you don't get around much."

His words ruffled her feathers, but she tried not to let it show. So that was what made him so darned disagreeable, was it? He had her pegged as a rich kid and didn't like it. "I'm not rich. And I'm not a kid."

"You were once. Rich. And a kid."

The cold beer, she discovered, was a crisp complement to the tang of the spicy, musky oysters. She reached the tip of her tongue out to lick away the foam remaining on her upper lip and instantly thought of the sugary doughnuts from their breakfast. Without thinking, she looked over at Pete to find he was staring at her. Or more precisely, at the tip of her tongue, which had ground to a halt at her upper lip.

There was no doubt in her mind he was remembering exactly what she was remembering. Her face grew warm as his eyes grew dark. She wished suddenly, more than anything, that she was the kind of person who acted on impulse. The kind of person who could ditch her sandwich in the gutter and reach over and land a long, hard kiss on that too perfect bow.

But Cheryl Steadman was not that kind of person. She looked away and decided to take another long swallow of beer, instead. Did beer, like wine, steady the nerves? she wondered.

Pete wasn't so quick to return to his meal, Cheryl saw from the corner of her eye. But she ignored him and concentrated on her sandwich, knowing that a woman with a mouthful of food would be a major deterrent, even for the kind of person who might act on impulse. Because if Pete Fontenot had the same impulse she had, she didn't want to know about it.

"So," he said at last, "where were you a rich kid? Des Moines or Kansas City or somewhere like that?"

"Cleveland." Her response was clipped. He never let it rest, did he? "What were you? A poor little street urchin here in Sin City?"

"Yeah, basically." He grinned. No, he did more than grin. He tossed his head back and gave a silent laugh. The laugh lines crinkled around his eyes; some of them reached down to his cheeks and tracked through the golden bristle. His teeth were impossibly straight and white. "In the Irish Channel."

"That's near the Garden District," she said. "Where the Crescent City's rich kids live."

"Yeah. Nearby and a million miles away," he said, staring down at the dust on his tennis shoes. "A politician from the Channel once said that if you read about it in the society pages, it always happened in the Garden District. But if the news came from the police blotter, it happened in the Irish Channel."

He was laughing, but Cheryl sensed his amusement didn't go very deep. She was also surprised to realize that, for the first time, he had dropped his protective shield for her, too.

Then, before she could react, he seemed to realize the same thing and the wall went back up. "So, tell me about being a rich kid in Cleveland."

"It wasn't as much fun as being a street urchin in New Orleans." She balled up the sandwich wrapper and napkin.

He grunted his skepticism, took her trash and pitched everything, piece by piece, into a nearby trash can. He made a basket with every shot.

"We didn't shoot baskets, for one thing," she said. "At least, little girl rich kids didn't shoot baskets. We took dance and piano and wore braces and brushed our hair a hundred times every night."

Pete made a wry face. "You know what?"

"What?"

"You could be right. Makes stealing cigarettes and fighting over marbles and walking some old lady's dog for a half-buck for the movies sound like fun."

She nodded, seeing for a moment the little boy face of three decades earlier. With pale, trusting eyes and a skinny little chest and knees forever scabbed over.

"You had Mardi Gras, too," she pointed out.

He grinned again. "Yeah. We made masks out of glitter and milk cartons every year. The glitter wouldn't half stick to the cartons, and we looked awful by the end of the day. But it was better than no mask at all."

He laughed, staring down at his hands as if he could see something more than she could see. "When plastic milk jugs came out, we really hit the jackpot. They were so big, we could make sensational masks. And every year we followed the walking parades all the way into town. Felt like we were in our very own parade.

"Still do. Every year, a couple of us from the old gang still follow along behind the Half-Fast Marching Parade."

She waited for him to go on; he looked lost in thought and she was certain he would tell her more. Instead, he abruptly jumped up, grabbed her hand and pulled her to her feet.

"Your wretched life in Cleveland is over, Slick. You're in fast company now."

"What next?" she asked as they pushed their bicycles down the street. She hoped he wouldn't touch her again.

"A graveyard."

"A graveyard?"

Within five minutes they had biked out of the Quarter to the city's oldest graveyard, on Basin Street. Cheryl had heard of the need to bury the city's dead above ground, as the city was below sea level. The rows of above-ground crypts, dating from the 1700s, were engraved with a half dozen or more names. As the vaults filled, Pete told her, bones were shoved to the back to make room for the next tenants. Even the wall surrounding the cemetery was made up of adjoining burial vaults—a wall of bodies.

The narrow walkways between towering crypts gave an eerie, mazelike aura to the graveyard.

Then, in the middle of the graveyard, near a spreading oak dripping with Spanish moss, was a brightly decorated crypt. Plastic Mardi Gras beads hung from the corners and dime-store trinkets were piled in front of the name marker. Two cookies in bakery wrap and a full, unopened bottle of wine sat at the base, as amazing to Cheryl as the coins and dollar bills littering the ground. The crypt was marked with large red *X*s.

"What in the world?" She looked at Pete, her eyes wide, as they left their bikes under the tree and walked closer to the gaily decked out grave.

"Gris-gris," Pete said, as if the words were self-explanatory. "Voodoo offerings."

"But why?"

"This is allegedly the burial place of Marie Laveau. New Orleans's most notorious voodoo queen."

"But . . . but why do people leave all this stuff?"

"To be protected from evil. To take hexes off. So maybe Marie will ward off somebody else's evil eye for them."

"You're kidding."

"Hey, street urchins don't kid."

"But don't people take the food and the money and the wine?"

"And rile the voodoo queen? Slick, you've been in Cleveland too long."

Cheryl studied the grave for several minutes, considering the folly that some people apparently took all too seriously. Then, the new Cheryl, the Cheryl who had frustrated her by doing too many un-Cheryl-like things since she had started hanging around with Pete Fontenot, turned back to Pete with a playful glint in her eyes.

"Why didn't we bring an offering? Isn't that likely to rile her, too? Just coming to gawk empty-handed?"

Pete shook his head contritely. "How thoughtless of me. There's only one thing we can do to salvage the situation. We'll run down to The Gris-Gris Shoppe and pick up an offering."

"Are you serious?" Her blue eyes really sparkled now. "There's really a place where we can go buy an offering to get Marie Laveau off our backs?"

"Street urchins—"

"Don't kid. I know." She grabbed him by the hand and turned toward their bikes. "In that case, let's get going before old Marie starts shooting us the evil eye."

But he didn't move. Instead, he pulled her back toward him like a yo-yo. His hand was still in hers, but his fingers had tightened. She felt the breath rush out of her at the dark look in his eyes.

"Does this mean we've stopped playing games, Cheryl?"

His voice caressed her name. She wanted to run but couldn't. She wanted to stay right here, inches from his chest, too much to run. "I don't know what you mean."

What had happened to her voice? It was a whisper. A wimpy little whisper, while this man had a fierce grip on her hand. She should wrench it away. Ask him what he had on his mind. Stalk away, nose in the air.

She didn't. She stood and waited. And prayed the kiss, when it came, would be fierce enough to match the passion that was building in her.

"Are you waiting for me, Cheryl?" His voice was still whiskey smooth. His hair unruly. His lips barely teasing with a smile that glimmered only fleetingly in his eyes.

He had no intention of kissing her. He intended to make her come to him. And right now, rivulets of passion she had never known existed were running too deep and long to let the Cheryl who never acted on impulse get in the way.

"No, damn you," she whispered huskily, inching closer, feeling the ache run deeper when his breath reached her lips. "I'm not waiting."

She crushed her lips to his. The need that had exploded in both of them hours earlier had simmered and boiled and left them with a hunger that bordered on the violent. His mouth was hot and waiting, open to the ravenous seeking of her tongue. His day-old whiskers rasped against her face, and she reveled in the angry pain that was the only feeling strong enough to check the passion he had unleashed.

His hands were at her back, pulling her closer even though she was already pressed tightly enough to feel the rivets of his jeans against her hipbones. Even though she was pressed tightly enough to feel the insistent thrust of his arousal prodding at the V of her corduroy pants. Even though her breasts, aching for the touch of his hands, were flattened against the solid flesh of his chest.

She ran her hands along his jaw, felt the movement as he returned her kiss and wondered if Marie Laveau would take offense if they fell in a heap under her oak tree and made loud, aching, furious love.

CHAPTER SIX

THANK GOODNESS for the wino. If the grubby old man hadn't ambled up to the voodoo queen's crypt, Cheryl might never have regained her control. Her face burned as she propped her bike next to Pete's against the nondescript storefront.

Thank goodness for the bicycles, too. They made it much easier to avoid conversation as they completed their original plan of seeking out an offering for Marie Laveau's grave. Surely, she thought, she was smart enough to figure out a good excuse for not returning to place the offering on the tomb.

The isolated Basin Street cemetery was the last place Cheryl needed to be with Pete Fontenot right now.

Not that she hadn't regained control, she told herself as she followed Pete to the door. Her heart no longer thundered wildly. The prickling weakness along her thighs had receded. Mostly. And the tender abrasion of his whiskers around her lips was now mostly irritant, not aphrodisiac. Mostly.

She paused for a breath as Pete held the door open, expecting him to step aside so she could enter without passing close to him. After all, he had been gentleman enough not to mention the kiss— The kiss? Was that all it was? It seemed so much more—while they pedaled the two blocks to the Gris-Gris Shoppe. But he didn't move aside, which left too little room to get by without brushing against him. She was forced to look him in the eye.

The pale eyes were still stormy with desire. But there was more. Amusement. A teasing certainty. He was laughing at her!

"I like a woman who takes charge, Slick." His voice was low, full of the heat of appreciation. And his grin was languid, heavy with desire.

"Good," she said calmly, looking at him boldly as if she dallied with hot-blooded men every day. Then she squeezed past him and, in a last-ditch effort at defiance, took care to linger as her breasts grazed his T-shirt. A wave of desire weakened her temporarily, but she ignored the sensation and returned his lingering appraisal.

Damn the man! If he wanted to play it cool, nobody could do it any better than Cheryl Steadman. At least, she hoped she could play in his league.

The bell over the door jingled as it closed, and Cheryl's gaze swept over the tiny, crowded shop. She set her mind to focusing on the oddities that lined the shelves, determined not to think of The Kiss again.

The musky scents of incense and lighted candles swirled around her, captivating her senses as powerfully as the low, sensual music with its pulsating drumbeat. The shelves were lined with hundreds of jars of different shapes and sizes, some filled with annointing oils and others with healing herbs and roots or seeds with special properties. Candles flickered in front of small altars in one corner of the store. Over the door, the head of an alligator looked down on all who entered. And one large glass case housed a gleaming boa constrictor.

"Don't worry. He won't jump you," Pete said, gesturing toward the reptile, which stared intently at Cheryl.

"Oh, really?" She trembled as she returned the snake's unblinking stare. "How can you be so sure?"

"You're not his type."

When she turned to glare at him, he had turned his attention to the crystals behind another glass case at the counter. Before she could spit out a sharp retort, the shopkeeper came through beaded curtains at the back.

"Mr. Fontenot!" The young girl's dark face, surrounded by a cascade of shiny black waves, broke into a wide smile. "You may not remember me. I'm—"

"I remember you, Marie. It's good to see you again." Pete placed a hand on Cheryl's shoulder and led her to the girl, who had been followed through the beaded curtains by a curly haired toddler sucking her thumb. "Cheryl, this is Marie Broussard. She's the friend of one of my friends at Bayou Taxi, Sammy Reilly. Marie, this is Cheryl Steadman with the Chamber of Commerce. And this must be Shanna."

He squatted to bring himself closer to eye level with the toddler, whose Mardi Gras T-shirt came almost to the knees of her pint-size jeans. Shanna gave a big, dimpled grin when Pete held out his hand, then hid behind her mother's skirt. Cheryl could tell from the brief conversation he had with the toddler that he knew his way around youngsters.

"Sammy told me she's a cutie and he's right," Pete said, standing again. "How is Sammy? I haven't seen him today."

Marie's eyes flashed. "Him. I am angry with him. First, he says he will not go back to school this semester. Next, he cancels our date tonight because of an accident."

Pete tensed. "An accident. What accident?"

"Another driver wrecks his car and leaves them short-handed, so Sammy must work," she said with a shrug, then smiled coquettishly. "I am not truly angry, but Sammy must feel a little contrition before I accept his apology. Then he might appreciate me enough to go back to—"

"Marie, can I use the phone?" Pete's voice, when he interrupted, was on edge.

She nodded and led him through the beaded curtain to the office. Cheryl strained to hear as he spoke to someone at Bayou Taxi but could only hear Shanna jabbering to her mother and the continuous drumbeat of the exotic music throbbing through the store. When Pete came back through the curtain, his jaw was set tightly.

"I'm going to the hospital. I've got a driver in serious condition," he said hurriedly, taking her shoulders in a firm grip. "You wait here and I'll send a cab around for you to take you home."

Cheryl had no desire to brook the vexation in his voice. Judging by his reaction, the accident must have been serious. The last thing he needed, she knew, was for her to argue with him.

Before he released her shoulders, he held her eyes with his for a long, searching look. She knew with certainty that he planned to kiss her before he left.

Then he dropped his hands, turned and walked out the door.

HOSPITALS GAVE PETE the willies. Some people thought they smelled like antiseptic and medicine; to him, they smelled like the first step to the next world. Death and pain and fear hung in the sterile air. Pete felt claustrophobic the minute he walked into the lobby.

He found Elaine Burton already there, in the intensive care waiting room with Fats Peychaud's wife. Depend on Elaine, he thought, watching the concern in her plump face as she took Louise's order for coffee. Elaine thought of everything. Always did. Thank goodness someone had thought to call her at home, even though it was Saturday.

She saw him as she headed toward the elevator to the first-floor vending machines.

"Pete, I'm so glad you're here. We didn't know where to find you."

"How's Fats?" He put an arm around her shoulders and gave her a reassuring hug.

"Not good. He had some internal injuries, and he lost quite a bit of blood." She swallowed hard to steady her voice. "They think he'll be okay. But Louise has just fallen apart."

She gestured to a gray-haired, slender black woman huddled in the corner in a vinyl chair, her face tear streaked and her eyes vacant.

"She's about cried herself out now, but I don't think she's any too stable yet." She shook her head. "Their two kids are on their way from out of town to be with her, but until then..."

"Don't worry about it, kid. I'll see she's taken care of." Pete's stomach did an uneasy tap dance as he anticipated spending endless hours in the hospital waiting room with Louise Peychaud. But he wouldn't have her sitting here alone. "What happened?"

Elaine passed a hand before her eyes and took another steadying breath. "It's so crazy, Pete. Apparently, this big, black Lincoln went flying past Fats on the causeway, sideswiped him and kept on going. Just one of those crazy accidents. Fats was lucky, I guess, that the cab was impaled on the bridge railing instead of flying right through it into the lake."

Elaine went down for coffee while Pete took over the job of comforting the distraught woman who just might have cheated widowhood.

Just one of those crazy accidents, he thought as he introduced himself and took Mrs. Peychaud's trembling hand in his. *A big, black Lincoln. Just one of those crazy accidents.*

The pounding in his head suddenly gave way to Kurt Fletcher's voice on the telephone not twenty-four hours earlier. *I'll see if I can't come up with a few... incentives... in the meantime, to help you make up your mind.*

Pete felt the prickles on the back of his neck. And wondered if Cheryl had made it home safely.

DESPITE THE EXOTICA on sale in the tiny shop where she worked, Marie Broussard was little more than the girl next door, Cheryl decided.

While she waited for the ride Pete had promised, Cheryl visited with the young woman, who looked barely twenty in spite of the three-year-old clamoring around her knees. The aura of mystery created by Marie's flowing black cotton gauze skirt and hand-crocheted black sweater was a total fabrication, Cheryl learned as the young woman chattered away.

"So there I was, with a baby on the way and not even out of high school and scared to death of my mother and the priest and Sister Therese." She laughed brightly, the silver earrings jingling cheerily against her shoulders. "Especially Sister Therese. And nobody had any money. No money for doctors, no money for hospitals. I thought I should just die and save everybody the trouble."

"It looks as if you've managed well, Marie," Cheryl said, glancing out the door and wondering how long her ride would be. She could have ridden the bike back to the garage herself, she knew, but she had promised Pete she'd wait, so wait she would.

"Oh, I managed well, all right," Marie said, hefting the chubby Shanna onto her hip. "Thanks to Pete."

"Pete?"

"Well, nobody can say for sure. But Rosa—that's my older sister—Rosa said that Pete heard about it from his mama and suddenly help was coming out of the woodwork. The doctor in the neighborhood, he said all his fees would be free, if only I would work in his office four hours a day. And Sister Therese—Sister Therese!—said I could study at home and still graduate with my class. I know that had to be the first time a girl out to here—" she mimed a rounded belly in front of her "—received a diploma with Sister Therese's blessing. And the hospital... Nobody knows, but the hospital sent a bill marked 'paid in full.'

"And then, after Shanna was born and I was well enough to go back to work, the woman who owns this shop called and offered me a job. Rosa says everybody knows that Pete's good friends with her, so..."

"So Pete has been a real knight in shining armor?" Cheryl fingered the edges of a stack of parchment that Marie had told her was used for making talismans.

"Well, he's helped a lot," Marie admitted. "But Sammy's my real knight. We want to get married, but I think he should finish college first. He thinks he can work and be Shanna's daddy and go to college, and I say—"

Her stern dissertation on her disagreement with Sammy ended with the tinkle of the bell over the front door. Although she had been expecting someone, Cheryl felt surprisingly apprehensive as she looked toward the door. Pete had seemed so agitated when he left that she had remained on edge in the half hour since. The familiar Bayou Taxi uniform on the rusty-haired young man who entered the shop set her mind at ease.

"Sammy!" Marie's bright face was a dead giveaway that she had forgotten her pique. Sammy smiled back, pausing to pick up Shanna, who had scampered over to him and clutched his legs delightedly.

"Hi, squirt." He deposited a kiss on the giggling youngster's nose, then walked sheepishly toward Marie. "Hi, Marie. Still mad?"

Suddenly remembering that she was supposed to be making Sammy regret canceling their Saturday night date, Marie tried to summon up a pout. But it unconvincingly dissolved into another smile. "I tell you what. I let you off the hook if you promise to sign up for classes next week."

"I tell you what," he countered, handing his company hat over to Shanna's eager hands. "I let you off the hook if you marry me next week."

She gave him a playful shove. "Then I guess I'm still mad at you."

For the first time, Sammy noticed Cheryl, who had feigned an interest in a book on tarot readings while the two carried out their charade of a fight. "Say, you must be Miss Steadman. Pete asked me to come give you a lift home."

"I appreciate the effort, but it's really not necessary," Cheryl said, smiling.

"That's okay." Sammy grinned. "If it makes Pete feel better, well, I don't mind a bit."

The two young people made an almost incongruous couple, Cheryl thought. He was so red haired and ruddy and she was so darkly beautiful. The one thing they clearly had in common, she decided quickly, was a youthful naiveté they each wore like a badge. It glowed in their eyes and their cheeks and their smiles. Even a teenage pregnancy hadn't been able to put out the fire of youthful innocence that burned in Marie's face.

That, and one other thing, she decided as they prepared to go. They were both crazy about Shanna. Sammy tickled the youngster under her chin and kissed her on the head as they were leaving the shop.

"Miss Steadman—Cheryl—you come back to visit sometime," Marie called out from the door while Sammy loaded the bike into the trunk. "I'll make you a talisman. On the house. Money. Fame. Love. Whatever you want."

THE NIGHT STRETCHED OUT endlessly in front of Cheryl. She couldn't believe how disappointed she had been to learn from Sammy that Pete had asked if he could postpone their evening out for one night. The wife of the injured driver would be alone until her children flew in early the next morning, and Pete insisted on sitting up with her at the hospital.

When Pete had first suggested, earlier in the day, that they spend the evening together taking in a jazz club and having dinner, she had been skeptical about its value to her as a teacher.

But Pete, persuasive as ever, had promised to tell her enough about the life of a cab driver that she could write a doctoral dissertation on the subject. So she had agreed. Reluctantly. At least, she told herself her agreement had been reluctant.

Now, staring down at an accounting textbook that grew more tedious with each word, she was disappointed. Although she couldn't for the life of her imagine how she could look Pete in the eye after the spectacle she had made of herself in the cemetery, she was disappointed. She relished the challenge.

She relished the man. That was the bottom line, she admitted. He was slender and not very tall and didn't care whether or not he combed his hair or shaved before they met. He was too cocky for his own good, and his idea of answering a question was to return a smart-guy comment or a question of his own.

But she relished him. Lord, how she relished him. Geoffrey McMillian was a cartoon character of a man compared to Pete Fontenot. Determined to move into the ranks of adulthood when she left her parents' home for Lima, Cheryl had accepted Geoffrey's halfhearted advances with equally apathetic ardor. It was as proper as it was boring, and she certainly hadn't regretted the loss of the lovemaking when she discovered that Geoffrey's primary interest was in cultivating Huntley Steadman. The idea of marrying a woman simply because she was the "right" kind of woman hadn't seemed to appall Geoffrey.

So here she sat, an accounting book for company, confronted with longing for a man for the first time in her life. And shying away from the knowledge that she had no doubt made a fool of herself in letting him know so . . . so vividly just how much she longed for him.

What she longed for now was a phone call. Pete's voice at the other end, telling her he was sorry, telling her he couldn't wait for Sunday night, telling her The Kiss had set him on fire.

Well, that wasn't very likely.

But he could call. Surely he would call to make arrangements for Sunday night. Unless he intended simply to let things slide. Unless he had decided she was so hot to trot that he could string her along and keep her guessing.

Who knows what kind of games men like Pete Fontenot play, she warned herself. *You can't play in his league, Steadman. You're a novice. A rank beginner. A—*

When the knock on the door broke into her thoughts, she jumped up excitedly. Pete! He had changed his mind. He had gone out for dinner and decided he just had to stop by to make sure she wasn't angry about his canceling out. Of course she understood; staying at the hospital was such a decent thing to do.

She dashed quickly into the bathroom to make sure her hair looked okay. She had washed her face and her freckles were shining through a bit more than usual, but—

Another knock. She ran to the door and opened it without bothering to check through the peephole. Fay Thurston's tiny face, framed by a thirties vintage big-brimmed fedora, greeted her.

"I was in the neighborhood," Fay announced.

Cheryl instantly banished the disappointment from her expression. Fay was wonderful, but seeing her face certainly hadn't done for her what seeing Pete's face would have done. "I'm so glad you dropped by."

She pulled Fay into the room, surveying the dramatic cut of the Joan Crawford-style jacket that topped tight jeans in a leopard-spot print. It was not a style Cheryl had seen lately in any fashion magazine. Where, she wondered, did the woman find these clothes?

"Actually, there's this funky little restaurant that's just opened about eight blocks from here," Fay chattered, looking around the traditionally furnished apartment. "So I thought I'd take a chance that a knockout like you would be footloose tonight and join me."

"Actually, I'm studying accounting," Cheryl said, glancing once again toward the silent telephone. "But..."

"If that's all," Fay waved her hand dismissively. "Listen, I've got connections in high places. I'll put in a good word for you with the professor."

They laughed and Cheryl made up her mind. She had never in her life sat by the phone waiting for a call, and Pete Fontenot would not prompt her to any more un-Cheryl-like conduct in one day.

"I'm not dressed, but—"

"If you were dressed, I wouldn't be caught dead with you," Fay vowed. "Bad for the ego of a little shrimp like me. Just grab a jacket and we'll knock 'em dead."

"Well, you may knock 'em dead," Cheryl agreed, getting a tweedy jacket from the hall closet. She avoided another longing glance at the telephone as they walked out the door.

"And let's stop by the little shop where I bought these pants and browse before dinner," Fay suggested. "They've got some things that might make great Mardi Gras costumes. You have changed your mind about Mardi Gras, haven't you?"

"No, Fay, I don't think so." They were too far from her apartment now for her to notice that her telephone had just started ringing.

BEFORE THE THIRD RING, Pete heard the distinctive click of an answering machine kicking in.

Damn it, she wasn't home.

He listened to her carefully modulated voice delivering the carefully chosen words and felt himself stirring again. Stirring on the inside, definitely stirring on the outside.

The Snow Princess had melted this afternoon. Just thinking about the way she had gone after that kiss made him hurt all over.

Could she really want him as much as that kiss seemed to indicate? Or was the unruffled taunting she had displayed when they reached Marie's shop the real Cheryl Steadman?

The beep sounded. Should he leave a message? Where the hell was she, anyway? Glad to have her night to herself again, no doubt. Out with one of her smooth-as-butter pals who knew what it was like to grow up a rich kid in Cleveland. Glad to be free of a street kid from New Orleans whose idea of a good time was dragging her through a two-hundred-year-old cemetery.

To hell with her.

"Cheryl, this is Pete. Sorry about tonight." *But not sorry about today,* he thought. Lord, if only he could bring out another response like the one today. "Let's make it eight o'clock tomorrow night, instead. I'll give you a call tomorrow."

Get a grip on it, he chided himself. *Why get yourself all worked up over a babe like that? You're not in the same league and you know it. And so does she.*

THE BLINKING RED LIGHT on the answering machine was a welcome beacon in the dark kitchen. With a pounding heart, Cheryl stood and looked at it. It had to be Pete. It had to be.

Blackened chicken and Fay's best stories about growing up next door to the Curl Up and Dye Beauty Salon in coastal Pascagoula, Mississippi, hadn't been enough to distract her from worrying all evening about the telephone call that hadn't come. Still, she had laughed so hard she had tears in her eyes when Fay told her about the time Jimmy Lee Atwater held everyone in the Curl Up and Dye hostage with his squirrel gun until Leona, who owned the Curl Up, had covered Jimmy Lee's wife's frosted tips with a Silky Sable rinse. Terrorism, Pascagoula-style, was definitely slapstick material.

Resisting Fay's efforts to talk her into a Mardi Gras costume had been just as much fun but not more distracting. In her search for a disguise in the funky little shop a half block off Saint Charles, Fay had tried on everything from a feather-boaed negligee—"I could go as Mae West," the hundred pounder had suggested—to a satin and sequins bowling shirt—"How about Dolly Parton? And don't you dare say I have delusions of grandeur!"

Cheryl had never, she was certain, laughed so hard.

But the laughs hadn't lingered. They were squeezed off quickly, the breath choked out of them by Cheryl's memories of the day: Pete's fingertip at her mouth; the teasing eyes that turned to brooding so quickly; the working of the lean muscles of his thighs as he pumped the bicycle through the Quarter; the faint flavor of beer when their lips had met with a hunger so demanding they might both have been making up for a lifetime of longing.

And now, listening to Fay's car with the hole in the muffler thunder its way down the cobblestone driveway, the answering machine winked invitingly.

Taking a deep breath, she pushed the message button and waited for it to rewind.

"Cheryl, this is Pete. Sorry about tonight." She frowned. She didn't hear much regret in his cold, abrupt voice. In fact, none at all. "Let's make it eight o'clock tomorrow night, instead. I'll give you a call tomorrow."

Standing in the dark and staring at the wicked box, Cheryl felt her blood begin to simmer. *How tender,* she thought. *How thoughtfully sweet. Sorry about tonight. I'll call tomorrow. So be there and maybe I'll make it up to you.*

"Damn the man," she fumed, walking back through the front room to hang up her coat and turn off the aquarium light. "Here I spend the whole night feeling like some silly high school kid with a crush, and he sounds like the czar handing down orders to the underlings."

To hell with Pete Fontenot, she decided. Let him learn some manners; then they could talk about tomorrow night.

But she knew, even as she laid out a fresh pair of corduroy pants and a crewneck sweater for the next day, that when he called, she would say yes. She didn't have the will to do otherwise, anymore.

The old Cheryl, the Cheryl who held herself aloof and stayed away from complications and had a plan mapped out, was slowly, but surely losing control of this new Cheryl who kept surfacing whenever Pete Fontenot was around.

EVEN THE NEW CHERYL was not ready for the conga line that formed halfway through the ten-minute version of "When the Saints Go Marching In" the next evening at the Juke Joint, Pete's favorite jazz club in the French Quarter.

But she and Pete both laughed as most of the other patrons in the club snaked through the smoky room, holding on to the hips of the strangers in front of them and only barely managing not to step on toes and knock over tiny round tables cluttered with empty bottles.

"Do people get this drunk every night?" Cheryl asked, looking down at her watch. After ten on a Sunday night. Why, she wondered, wasn't she home herself, getting ready for the workweek that would start the next morning?

"No," Pete admitted. "Saturdays and Fat Tuesday are much worse."

The partying patrons collapsed in their chairs and ordered another round when the band segued into a mellow version of "Do You Know What It Means to Miss New Orleans" followed by "Tin Roof Blues." As the number drew to a close and the band excused itself for a break, Pete swallowed the last of his Sazerac.

"Ready for stage two?"

"You mean there's more?"

Dinner at Antoine's had started this evening. It was a meal marked by ever present but never intrusive service. By a quick calculation, Cheryl decided there were as many serving people in their dark, intimate dining room as there were patrons. A regal waiter led them on a tour of the fabled restaurant's extensive wine cellar and insisted on sending around a bottle of the house's best to Bayou Taxi the next day.

"So you'll think of us when you celebrate your next special occasion, Monsieur Fontenot," the waiter intoned.

The bill for the dinner, Cheryl knew, would keep her in silk scarfs for a year.

From Antoine's, they had walked over to Bourbon Street to a small comedy club, where Cheryl had surprised herself by loosening up enough to enjoy the bawdy routines of a comedian whose favorite subject was sex. After that, the Juke Joint.

Now, they walked down Bourbon Street until the neon ran out. The crowds that kept the streets lively in the French Quarter turned back toward the garish lights as soon as they realized they had run out of souvenir shops and girlie shows. So they were soon alone on the dark street. A block away, the clop-clop of a horse kept pace with them.

"Is it safe this far down? So far from the crowds?" Cheryl asked, looking around uneasily.

"Sure. All the pickpockets are back there," Pete said, nodding in the direction from which they'd come. "This is mostly residential. My place is just a few blocks over."

He gestured to the left and Cheryl was grateful when he turned their steps to the right at the end of the block. Pete's place was not where she wanted to end up this evening.

Well, that was not entirely honest, she realized. The new Cheryl had been at war with the old Cheryl all evening over how to handle her blossoming desire. She had wanted to touch Pete. To feel her hands on him, the texture of his skin against hers. She had wanted to run her fingertips over the light dusting of golden hairs on the backs of his hands. To mold her palm to the squareness of his shoulders.

Nevertheless, she was glad he had headed away from his place. She had a great deal of mental preparation to do before her imperturbable finesse could handle that.

Neither of them had mentioned the day before. Or The Kiss. In fact, although he had seemed to be having fun, Pete had also seemed preoccupied and tense. When she'd asked about the injured driver, Pete had said he had improved enough to be moved out of intensive care. But now she wondered. It had been clear when Pete left the Gris-Gris Shoppe the afternoon before that the accident had upset him. And tonight, he hadn't been his usual needling self.

"You're sure the driver is okay?" Something had to be responsible for Pete's brooding.

"Fats? Sure. He's going to be fine. Drivers get hurt sometimes."

But Cheryl could tell from his voice, from his rigid stance, from the hands that suddenly plunged deeper into his pants pockets, that he wasn't as blasé as he wanted to sound.

"But you feel responsible." She hazarded a guess. Reading people had always been her specialty, but reading Pete Fontenot was like trying to translate a handwritten Russian manuscript.

He shrugged. "That's part of it, I guess. They're my men. They trust me. And..."

He shrugged again and pursed his lips tightly.

"It wasn't your fault, Pete. He was sideswiped. You're not responsible for that."

Suddenly, as if banishing all dreary thoughts, Pete whirled around to face her. "It's time for dessert, Slick. Let's go down to Madelaine's."

Cheryl regretted being unable to corral Pete long enough to get into his head a bit. But she understood his shying away from her probing; no one was more reticent about sharing than the Steadman family. It was as much a part of family tradition as goose and wild rice dressing and hot cranberry punch on Christmas Day.

"After all we've had to eat and drink tonight? Dessert?"

"Sure." Turning her from side to side with a teasing appraisal, he reached out as if to touch her and ran his hand along the imaginary line of her subtle curves. "You can stand the calories, Slick."

"You are incorrigible." A quivery warmth started to glow deep in her loins as she imagined his hand actually molding itself to her.

"That's what my momma always said. Actually, that's not what Mom said." Pretending to think, he raised her hand and tapped her fingers against his lips. "What she said, actually, was—now how did she put it?—'You better get yourself some respect, boy, before I take this broom to your backside.'"

"She should have done it," Cheryl said.

"She did. Last time I was home, I think."

Cheryl chuckled, unable to imagine anyone taking a broom to Pete. "That I would like to see."

"I'll take you next time I go. She'd love to put me in my place in front of a fancy lady friend."

Knowing how lightly such things were said, Cheryl attached no significance to the casual comment. Pete Fontenot was no more the kind of man who took a woman home to meet his mother than she was the kind of woman who would take him home to meet her father.

For a moment, the thought pleased her. Pete Fontenot and Huntley Steadman across the parlor from each other, measuring each other's worth over a snifter of brandy. If either of them came up short in the other's eyes, she suspected, it wouldn't be this street-smart kid who had turned himself into a millionaire.

Funny, but during the past two days, a millionaire was the last thing Pete had acted like. And his mother, Cheryl surmised from what he said, was as unimpressed as her son appeared to be by his wealth and power. Which was probably what had kept Pete from falling into the traps some men new to wealth fell into so easily. Although she had heard plenty about Pete's penchant for spending money on the fastest and loosest of the city's old-society daughters, what she had learned about him since made her wonder if that wasn't an image he cultivated merely to cover the truth.

The truth? At least if Marie and Sammy and the other people from his old neighborhood were gaining the right impression, he was a man who looked after his own people. He was a man who would rather eat in the kitchen where his parents' neighbors worked than be served at the candlelit tables in the dining room. He was a man who would rather work behind the scenes to help a pregnant teenager than write out tax deductible donations to the charity of the month.

The cozy French bakery was still teeming with people, even this late at night. Coffee and pastries seemed a popular way to end the evening in the Quarter. Others were buying the morning's baked goods at day-old prices to take home for Monday's breakfast and lunch.

"Pete, you're not out of croissants already?" The woman's pointed face, topped with a traditional fluffy white chef's cap, barely reached the top of the display counter.

"Yeah, already, Madelaine. I've got a guest that's eating me out of house and home."

Cheryl looked at Pete quizzically, and the proprietress looked at Cheryl with equal curiosity in her face. "Hmm. She doesn't look like such a big eater, your friend, here."

Pete's lips twitched, then he leaned over the case and said in a stage whisper, "Wrong friend, Madelaine."

The woman raised her dark eyebrows and shrugged in Cheryl's direction. "You watch yourself with this one, dearie. He's so bad. I promise you. So bad."

"What about a Napoleon?" Pete asked, pointing to the cream-filled pastries.

"What about a fruit tart?" Cheryl countered, pointing to the miniature custard pies topped with kiwi, strawberries and blueberries.

Pete looked skeptical. "Nah. I vote for Napoleons."

"But I want a fruit tart." She turned to face him with hands on hips.

He turned to face her, stepping so close she imagined she could feel his heart pumping. "But Napoleons are messier. And this time, you get to handle the cleanup."

Cheryl's vision blurred momentarily. So he hadn't forgotten yesterday, after all. She remembered, with knee-weakening clarity, the moment at Café du Monde that had been the first step on the way to The Kiss.

She wondered if it would throw him at all if she leaned over and kissed him right now, under Madelaine's frankly curious gaze. She doubted it.

"Suppose I'm not in the mood for cleaning up tonight, Mr. Fontenot?"

"Then I'll take them home to my visitor, Miss Steadman."

She wanted to shove one of the gooey treats right into that smug face, but she knew how much he'd love seeing her lose her cool, so that would never do. Besides, she wasn't really angry, just frustrated that she could never seem to get the better of him. And dying of curiosity about his visitor. Street smarts, she decided, counted for a lot more than parlor game experience when it came to one-upmanship.

"Fine." She turned back to Madelaine. "A fruit tart for me, a Napoleon for Mr. Fontenot and one for his friend at home."

And when the order was bagged up, Cheryl insisted on paying. "With my compliments to your friend while she's licking your face," she announced as they walked along the edge of Jackson Square toward the riverfront walkway.

A lone saxophone player was set up at the corner, sweet and mournful blues spilling from his shiny instrument.

They stopped and watched as they ate their pastries. Pete asked for a Rodgers and Hart ballad and tossed a bill into the sax case at his feet.

Cheryl finished her tart and was about to pull her napkin out of her skirt pocket to wipe her fingers when Pete seized her wrists. She looked up in surprise.

"I give in." He raised her hands to his lips.

"What . . . ?" Before she could finish framing the question, he had taken one finger gently in his mouth and swirled his tongue around it. The core of warmth that started in Cheryl's loins began to simmer and spread as he took each of her fingers in turn and sucked them slowly, never taking his eyes off hers as he did so. When he reached the last finger, he applied gentle pressure with his teeth before he released it.

"Pete . . ." she breathed, wondering if his seductive playfulness had left him as ready for lovemaking as it had left her. The warm dampness of his tongue had seemed to touch her everywhere.

"I want you to want me, Cheryl," he whispered as the saxophone moaned low behind them. "I want you to want me so bad you'll beg for it if you have to."

The words were meaningless to her for the moment. But when he leaned close and captured her lips in a hungry, bruising kiss, she knew exactly how it would feel to be willing to beg for the hard thrust of his body to ease the ache in hers.

CHAPTER SEVEN

CHERYL WISHED FERVENTLY for the day when Dave Arnaud would learn to leave his cigar behind when he entered her office.

The No Smoking sign hadn't worked. A polite but very clear-cut request hadn't worked. Gentle reminders hadn't worked. Dave just grinned and puffed.

"So how's it going, Steadman?" He slouched in the chair across from her and propped his feet on the corner of her desk. "Lookin' forward to the start of your new career as a teacher this week?"

"No, I am not." She reached over and pulled the file on a billboard project out from under his feet, giving him a pointed look as she did so. He drew a long puff on his cigar in response. "Dave, it's going to smell like a sewer in here all day. Can't you leave that thing in your office?"

He chuckled. "Whatsa matter, Steadman? I don't ask you to leave your perfume in your office."

"I don't wear perfume to work, Dave." He was hopeless. What she always failed to remember about the boss was that he loved to aggravate. So why was his impish grin so engaging? This morning, it was hard to remember.

"'Zat right? Maybe you—"

Before he could finish whatever clever rejoinder he had thought up, the telephone rang. The voice on the other end introduced itself as Tony Alonzo, a reporter with the *Times-Picayune*.

"I remember you, Tony. From the press conference last week." Setting aside her irritation, Cheryl infused her voice with a smile for the news media. "What can I do for you?"

"I'd like to do a story about the Friendly Faces campaign, and I've got an angle I'd like your help with," he said. "It's got to do with Pete Fontenot."

Outwardly, Cheryl didn't register the mention of Pete's name. Inside, she sang. And went weak.

"I'm an old friend of Pete's," Tony continued, dragging Cheryl reluctantly from her vivid recollection of their kiss along the riverfront. A kiss that, inexplicably, Pete hadn't repeated when he delivered her to her front door. Almost as if he wanted to leave her guessing; almost as if he wouldn't take another step until she did. "We grew up in the same neighborhood, went to school together, that kind of thing."

Didn't everybody? Cheryl thought. The man seemed to know everyone in town.

"So what I'd like to do is take this idea of Friendly Faces as a jumping-off point for a feature on Pete." As she listened, Cheryl stirred restlessly in her chair, unaware that her uncharacteristic fidgeting had captured Dave's attention. "Pete got his start as a driver, so he's built sort of a reputation for giving his drivers the chance to make something of their lives. We could weave in the story of the class with Pete's own education on the street as he rose from driving a cab for somebody else to buying his own cab and eventually turning that into a major company. What do you think?"

"The self-made man angle?" At least, she thought, she'd find out how he turned himself into a millionaire in less than two decades by driving a cab. It was a cinch Pete wouldn't tell her.

"Well, yeah," Tony said. "So, could I come by to interview you, maybe after class starts this week? In fact, I'd like to sit in on some of the classes, if that's okay."

"Sure, that's fine," she said, absently toying with the telephone cord. "But I'm not sure how the class fits in with a story about Pete. Maybe I don't need to—"

The telephone receiver was snatched from her hand. She looked up into Dave's frown. "Hold on a sec, okay?" he said to Tony, then punched the hold button. "What's the problem? We're looking for publicity, right? This guy wants to tie in our classes with this story about Pete, it plays right into our hands. Don't forget to tell him how Fontenot offered to be your tour guide. Maybe they ought to get some pictures of the two of you together."

Cheryl took a deep breath. She wanted to swat him with a file folder. "I don't think so, Dave."

"Why the hell not? Publicity. That's what this is all about. Remember? I'll expect to see those pictures in the paper, Steadman." He turned and walked toward the door, then stopped to wave his cigar in her direction. "And, hey. As soon as you get this turkey taken care of, give the wire services a call. See what kind of angle you can cook up for them."

She saluted crisply. "Aye, aye, Captain."

Before Dave was out the door, one of the receptionists stuck her head in. "Another call for you. Long distance."

"I'll get it in two seconds, if they can hold." Staring for a split second at the two blinking lines, she punched the first one and quickly made arrangements for Tony to visit the class and interview her afterward. Then she took the other blinking line.

"This is Cheryl Steadman. May I help you?"

"Cheryl, how's the world treating you?" Her father's deep, formal voice reverberated all the way from Cleveland. At least, she hoped he was still in Cleveland.

"Fine. No complaints," she said, knowing he would approve of what an accomplished social liar she had learned to be in the parlor of the carefully appointed Tudor. "How are you and Mom? And Allen and Kevin and all the little second-generation Steadmans?"

"Top-notch. We're all just top-notch." Knowing her father had spent as much time on small talk as he ever allotted during a business day, Cheryl was prepared for him to launch into the reason for his call. "I believe your mother called to say I would be in town in a few weeks. I'd like to take you to dinner while I'm there. I'll be staying at the Hilton, so I could get dinner reservations at the Court of Two Sisters."

Keeping it, as always, ever so formal. Not "Let's get together" or "What would you like to do while I'm in town?" No assumption that he would stay with her. Suddenly, she was driven by a need to try—once again—to prove herself.

"Of course we'll get together, Dad." She kept her voice as even, as unmoved, as his. "I know it's a shame not to dine out in New Orleans, but I'd like to show you my place. Why don't you come there and I'll see that you get one of the best Cajun meals in town."

Now how, she asked herself, *do you plan to do that? You don't know jambalaya from étouffée.*

He agreed and they settled on the date and time. Cheryl marked it in her appointment calendar—as she knew he was doing at the same moment—and they finished the necessary pleasantries as briskly and efficiently as possible.

She stared at the penciled-in appointment. It should be in red, she thought. Never, in all the time she had lived on her own in Lima, Ohio, had her parents visited her. She had never invited; they had never made overtures. Her apartment wouldn't have stacked up, she knew, to the spacious and elegant homes that her two older brothers had already bought and furnished, complete with 2.3 children each and wives who were active in the Junior League.

Cheryl had never stacked up. She had been a girl and no one had expected her to stack up. The fact that she had even tried had been a serious disappointment. Her role in life was to follow Amanda Steadman's lead. Attract a good husband. No, make that the *right* husband. An elegant home. Well-groomed, well-behaved, properly success-oriented children. A place in society, planning charity fund-raisers and hosting cocktail parties for political candidates.

Becoming an ornament in society may have been fine for Amanda Steadman, but it hadn't suited Cheryl. Cheryl had wanted to be like her father. She wanted people to listen when she spoke. She wanted people to ask her advice. She wanted to wield power, calmly and unemotionally. So she had watched her father and learned from him. When to smile. When to nod gravely. When to answer and when to merely listen. By the time she was ten, Cheryl knew more about how to manipulate others than most people learned in a lifetime.

The one person she couldn't manipulate was Huntley Steadman. No matter how hard she tried, she couldn't make the football and basketball teams that led him to cheer for his sons and slap their backs in camaraderie. No matter how hard she tried, she couldn't get him to spend

Saturday afternoon with her Girl Scout troop as he had with the Boy Scout troops.

Even when she tried things his way, by trying to live up to his expectations for little girls, he hadn't responded with the attention she wanted. The lowest moment in Cheryl's young life had been the day she realized Huntley Steadman couldn't be bothered to show up in the audience for her ballet recital.

She had given up ballet the next day.

And had immediately decided she would do what she wanted with her life, no matter how vigorously her parents urged her to do things their way. Because she would never be—could never be—one of the sons that Huntley Steadman clearly cherished.

This visit wouldn't change that fact of life one iota. Cheryl knew that. Fixing dinner, no matter how well it turned out, in her own place, no matter how nice it might be, wouldn't measure up to the country club treatment from his sons. Would it? Even hearing how well her job was going, if he cared enough to ask and she could bring herself to boast, wouldn't hold a candle to the power and prestige her brothers now had at their command.

This visit would be a replay of her entire life. Cheryl tried hard to squelch the hope that just this once she might measure up. Just this once she might make Huntley Steadman proud.

SAMMY'S HEAD WAS SPINNING. Student activity fees and lab fees and placement tests and orientation sessions whirled around in his head and made him wish for something as uncomplicated as Canal Street at rush hour with traffic signals on the fritz. This was nothing like his first two years at the community college; this was big and confusing and made him want to head for home.

What would he have done without Pete?

He stole a quick glance at his boss as they walked out of the bookstore, laden with notebooks and textbooks and workbooks—even a T-shirt that Pete had insisted on buying for him. Class of 1992 it read, in big blue letters across the front.

"Aw, Pete, I'll never finish that soon," he had said sheepishly, running his hand wistfully over the letters.

Pete had shrugged. "Maybe not. But you are a junior in college now. And you need a goal. Something to shoot for. Remember, if you don't know where you're going, how will you know if you get there?"

What Pete didn't know, Sammy thought as they crossed the Tulane campus to the visitors' parking lot, was that he definitely knew where he was going. He was going to be just like Pete. With one big difference. Marie.

"Wait till I tell Marie," Sammy said, flashing an ear-pushing grin. "Maybe she'll be so glad I'm back in school she'll even give in and marry me."

"She still holding out on you?" Pete opened the door to the company car waiting in the lot. Sammy tossed their purchases in the back seat.

"Yeah. She says no Mrs. in front of her name until I've got B.A. after mine." He ran a hand through his wiry red hair. "Are women always so stubborn, Pete?"

Sammy couldn't tell for sure, but he thought Pete's eyes were laughing behind his sunglasses. "Not all of them. Just most."

"Whaddaya do about it?"

Pete kept a close eye on the rearview mirror as they pulled out into Saint Charles Avenue traffic. "Depends. On whether they're worth it anyway."

Sammy settled back in the comfort of the front seat and pulled out the schedule of classes that were starting next week. Marie was definitely worth it; so he'd just have to be as stubborn as her and see who gave in first.

"AM I LATE?" Pete asked as he whizzed past Elaine's desk en route to his office, snatching the fistful of messages she held out for him.

"Is the Pope Catholic?" she called after him dryly. "You guys want coffee?"

He turned around and blew her a kiss. "Why do I put up with you, Elaine?"

She chortled. "Why do I put up with you? That's the question."

Pete turned toward his office, where Tony Alonzo was studying the contents of one of the shelves above the credenza. "Write about this in your newspaper." He gestured toward Elaine. "I'd have *two* million if I could get good help. You want coffee?"

"No, I'd like a beer," Tony said, pushing his cap back on his forehead. "But I'll settle for coffee. Black."

Pete peeked around the corner at Elaine, who had turned back to the ledgers she was balancing on computer. "Sweetheart? We'd love some coffee if you can tear yourself away from debits and credits long enough."

Pete grabbed Tony's hand enthusiastically, pounding him on the upper arm with the other.

"I still don't know why you want to write about a bad customer like me," he said, a grin creasing his unshaved face. "But if that's what it takes to spend some time with you, I'm all for it."

Tony nodded. "You're right. We ought to stop being such strangers. Deadlines come around every day, but good friends . . ."

Both men let the statement trail off, having come as close to sentiment as was comfortable for them. But each knew the other was remembering lazy summer days of roaming the streets looking for entertainment in the form of anything that wouldn't land them in juvenile court, and winter nights when study sessions had been nothing but an excuse to talk about cars and girls and movies and cars and girls and cars. That was before they'd gone their separate ways—Tony having left for college.

"So, have a seat. And let's see what kind of crazy notion you've got here."

Pete motioned Tony onto the couch on the far side of his office, and Pete rolled his desk chair around to face him. Tony explained his idea to Pete, then started ticking off the list of questions he had prepared for the interview.

For almost two hours, with frequent stops to beg coffee refills from Elaine, the two men talked about Pete's start in the cab business. Tony knew bits and pieces of the story from talk around the kitchen table at home. But hearing it from Pete turned the tale into a drama even he hadn't anticipated.

"I drove that damned car hundreds of miles every night," Pete recalled, his eyes focused on something far away from the room, "just praying it would hold together long enough for me to get in another night's work. It took every penny I had earned working for old man Rouquette in the grocery store to buy that run-down heap of junk. But to me, it wasn't a nine-year-old Chevy. It was my ticket out."

And that's exactly what he had turned it into, Tony decided as Pete's story unfolded. He had bought the cab three years out of high school, while taking one or two college classes each semester. For eight years, Pete had driven his cab every night and squeezed in a class whenever he could. The work had been more important to Pete, because he had also been helping out at home and putting money into a college fund for his sister, Angie.

"Angie's the one who really made good," Pete said. "She's teaching high school English now."

"She's not the only one you helped." Tony prodded. "You set your folks up in their business. And helped your brother with his college?"

"Lou was too damned stubborn. Wouldn't take much help." Pete grinned. "But I talked him into finishing two years, and he's the traffic manager at the delivery company where Pop worked for so many years."

"Stubborn must run in the family." Tony returned his old friend's grin. "I remember the time you swore we'd have time to take a case of chocolate bars out of the back of old man Rouquette's store and get two blocks away before he could get to the storeroom to see what the commotion was all about."

"I would have been right, too, if you hadn't decided to stop and straighten up the crate of tomatoes Kurt knocked over on his way out."

The mention of the third member of their youthful musketeers quieted them both. They stared at the tape recorder on the couch. In a moment, Tony reached over and hit the pause button.

"What about Kurt?"

"I don't want to talk about him, Tony," Pete said firmly. "We don't have to bring him into this, do we?"

Tony picked up his cap and ran the brim through his fingers. Stalling for time. Pete recognized the gesture immediately.

"He's part of the story, isn't he?" Tony looked up from the houndstooth cap and straight into the gray eyes that were as familiar to him as the ones that stared at him from the mirror every morning. "He was your partner for three years."

Pete grasped his knees to keep from clenching his fists. "Can't we just say I had a partner and bought him out? Frankly, Tony, I don't want my name linked to his."

Tony sighed. "Can't blame you for that. He's made quite a reputation for himself. I guess you could see that even then."

"Yeah." Pete stopped. He didn't want to talk about Kurt Fletcher. He didn't even want to think about Kurt Fletcher. The last thing he needed right now, with Fletcher breathing down his neck, was a newspaper story linking them. "Can we just drop him out of the story?"

"I'll get around it. Somehow." Tony turned the recorder on again. "So you worked as a cabbie for years, slowly buying up cars as you could afford to. You and Lou worked them over, isn't that right? And after three years in your own business, you were able to buy out your partner and go it on your own."

They were in the middle of a discussion on the work ethic he had learned from his father—who had driven a delivery truck—and his mother—who'd worked as a housekeeper—when Elaine's timid knock interrupted them.

"Pete, I'm sorry, but there's someone on the phone." She made a face. "He's pretty insistent that he talk to you. He won't leave his name, but he said you'd be real sorry if you missed his call."

"Thanks, Elaine."

Giving a little shove with his foot, he rolled the chair back toward his desk and picked up the blinking line. His gut was in a knot; he knew who was on the other end. And the truth of the matter was, he would have been more than happy to miss the call.

"Pete Fontenot." His voice was clipped. He hoped Tony wouldn't notice, although he knew that was hoping for a lot. Tony was, after all, a reporter.

"Hey, partner, how's it goin'?" The voice oozed false friendliness.

"What can I do for you?" He tried, for Tony's sake, to temper his abrupt tone.

"Oh, nothin', Pete. Just wanted to pass on my sympathy."

Pete's pulse suddenly accelerated. He didn't want to hear this. He knew what was coming and he didn't want to hear it. He said nothing, unaware that he had crumpled an empty envelope off the top of one of the many stacks on his desk.

"It was a real shame about that accident on Saturday, pal." The sympathy in Fletcher's voice made Pete want to shove a couple of teeth down his childhood friend's throat. "I know you must hate to see your drivers get hurt like that. And their families...must be a real hardship on their families."

"Listen, you..." Pete bit his tongue, knowing there was nothing he could say with Tony listening from the couch.

"Of course, I know you'll take good care of that fellow's family. You always were a soft touch, pal." Fletcher suddenly switched to all-business. "I know you're a busy man, pal, so I won't keep you. Just wanted to remind you we've got a business deal pending. You ready to get in on the action?"

"No. This is one opportunity I think I'll pass on."

"Why don't you stop by for another visit with Mr. Peychaud and his poor family before you decide, Pete. Catch you later."

The telephone buzzed in his ear. *The bastard.* Pete clamped his jaws tightly shut and struggled for control before he hung up and turned to face Tony again.

"Where were we?" he said at last.

TONY KNEW BETTER than to try to stare Pete Fontenot down. Pete had always been the hard case in the group; the one who rared back against a tree or a board fence and just stared while you tried to convince him it was worth a dollar to ride downtown to see a movie. Then, if you didn't convince him, Pete would likely as not just get up and walk away.

And everybody would follow. With their dollars burning a hole in their pockets and the latest 007 movie just out downtown, he and Kurt would shrug and follow.

Because nobody stared Pete down. Not then. Not now.

But Tony also knew when Pete was trying to con him; he'd watched him operate too many times. And he knew, as he pounded away at the electronic keyboard later that afternoon, that Pete Fontenot had been trying to con him after that phone call.

Pete was in trouble. It had been written all over his face when he hung up the telephone that morning.

Tony scrolled once again through the notes he had transcribed into his computer terminal, looking for the key to Pete's guarded expression. But the only flag he could see was Kurt Fletcher's name, which was conspicuously, blatantly missing.

Wonder what Kurt's up to these days? he thought, flipping his cap toward the corner of his desk and dragging the phone book out of his drawer.

THE NEXT THREE HOURS couldn't go fast enough to suit Cheryl. Once she was standing up in front of the hundred or so cab drivers expected for this first Friendly Faces class, she knew her instincts would deliver her from this funk.

But right now, her mood was as dreary as the chill winter rain drizzling down the windows of Pete's limo.

She couldn't even have said why. Pete's conspicuous absence the first two days of the week might have been the reason, she admitted, although it hadn't cheered her that he'd called today and offered to drive her to the hotel where the class was scheduled. It might have been anticipation of the interview with the *Times-Picayune* reporter, Tony Alonzo. It could even have been her father's call, which had left her regretting her haste in insisting on showing off her apartment and her cooking skills. Definitely a dumb stunt, she thought. It might even have been the overload of work and night classes.

Or it might have been her anxious concern about whether Pete Fontenot ever had any intention of kissing her again the way they had kissed Sunday night.

Cheryl felt like a trembling virgin when she recalled the intensity of their kisses. A quaking innocent who was in way over her head with a man who clearly knew just what buttons to push to turn a woman to jelly in his hands. Jelly she had certainly been.

Worse, she wanted to be again. And again and again. It had been all she could do when he'd walked into her office while she and Dave had been reviewing the art boards for the next issue of the Chamber's newsletter, not to look him up and down as lasciviously as a man ogling an underdressed female.

She wanted Pete. And she couldn't be sure that he wasn't just toying with her. He might want her, all right, the way he dallied with plenty of women. But that wasn't good enough for Cheryl.

She wanted what Pete wanted. She wanted him to want her enough to beg for it.

And that, she told herself, was as unlikely as her ever capitulating and begging for him.

The car slowed, but Cheryl knew it was too soon for them to be at the hotel where the classes were being held. She peered through the rain-streaked window. "What are you doing?"

"I'll be right back." He hopped out, leaving the car running and the windshield wipers slapping back and forth. Cheryl's eyes followed him into the Gris-Gris Shoppe. Impatiently, she looked at her watch, hoping Pete wouldn't make her late for her first class. Nothing threw her off stride more than being late.

Well, almost nothing, she thought as he shot back out the door and dashed through the rain five minutes later.

"Here," he said, pulling something from his pocket and leaning closer to slip a thin ribbon carefully over her head.

Breathing in his closeness, Cheryl closed her eyes until he had retreated to the safety of his side of the car. Then she reached down to lift the tiny red flannel pouch resting against her breasts from the end of the narrow black satin ribbon.

"What is this?"

"A gris-gris. A good luck charm," he said. "I asked Marie what was good for giving you power over people, and she mixed up a bunch of herbs and oils. It's a sure thing."

Cheryl tingled as she fingered the soft pouch, touched that Pete would be thoughtful enough to read her low mood. "Thank you, Pete. I know I'll do a good job now."

"You don't have to wear it, you know. I mean, I realize it doesn't exactly go with what you have on."

"But if I don't wear it, how will it know I'm ready for it to do its thing?" she protested, looking down at her cowl-necked sweater dress.

Pete thought for a moment, then reached over and lifted the gris-gris off her breast. The backs of his fingers were a whisper of fire. She looked up and the sparks flew from his silver eyes to her ice-blue ones. He squeezed the tiny pouch—no bigger than a locket—in his palm for a moment, then pulled the neck of her sweater out just far enough to slip the ribbon down the front of her dress. The flannel was warm between her breasts.

"I think it'll work now," Pete said.

BUTCH WAS GETTING TIRED of schlepping around in the rain. To hell with this Fontenot guy, for today, at least. He was glad, though, to be tailing him for Fletcher. Anybody who had his pick of limos to choose from deserved to get taken down a notch or two. And Fletcher was just the guy for the job.

So to hell with Fontenot and his chick, for today. Maybe the girl in the store could tell him what he needed to know, and he could call it a day. All this voodoo hoo-doo gave him the creeps, but he would reward himself with a side trip to Zodie's after. Rainy days like this were always good for a game of pool over at Zodie's.

The bell over the door jingled when he walked in, which drew the young shop girl out of the back room. She was a looker, just like the chick with Fontenot. He was not only rolling in high-price-tag cars, he was rolling in good-looking chicks, too. The skinny little guy had all the luck, Butch thought bitterly, flexing a beefy arm just to reassure himself. His plaid jacket pulled in the shoulder when he did.

"Can I help you find something, sir?"

Butch picked up one of the potion books in a meaty paw and smiled as pleasantly as his horselike face would allow.

"Yeah. Friend of mine said you could help. My old lad—my wife's mother is in ill health, and Pete Font'not said you could give us something that would help."

Marie came around the counter and walked over to one of the far shelves lined with herb canisters and bottles of oil. "What kind of health problem is your mother-in-law having?"

"What kind? Oh, uh, appendicitis. Yeah. Bad case of appendicitis."

The girl's thin dark eyebrows pitched forward in a frown. "Appendicitis. I see." She glanced at the contents of the shelf, reading the labels for guidance. "Did you see Pete before you came in? He was just here."

"He was?" Butch really admired the way the young shop girl's black curls swayed around her waist when she reached overhead for items off the shelf. "Sorry I missed him. Was he with that pretty new friend of his? I can't think of her name right now."

"Cheryl Steadman? Yes, that was her in the car." Marie turned back to the shop counter and pulled out a sheet of parchment and a bottle of red liquid.

Butch watched, feeling an uncomfortable twitch between his shoulder blades when the girl started marking on the parchment.

"What's that stuff?" He pointed to the red liquid she was using.

"Dove blood ink," the girl said matter-of-factly, not taking her eyes off the design she drew. Butch shivered. "This should do it. It's for disorders of the organs surrounding the stomach. That should cover appendicitis."

Vowing to himself to trash the paper as soon as he hit the street, Butch slipped in all the questions he could think of about Pete Fontenot while the girl rang up his purchase.

It seemed the girl's boyfriend, Sammy, was one of Fontenot's prize employees. He was sort of taking the boy under his wing, helping him finish college. Sounded like just the kind of stuff Fletcher was looking for.

He also slipped in a few questions about the blonde, to see if he could find out whether the smooching he'd seen over the weekend was as serious as it had looked. With a guy like Fontenot, you never knew. He could always be playing around, just making time. But if it was more serious, Cheryl Steadman could be an even better piece of news to take Fletcher than the kid Sammy.

"So, until our next rendezvous—" she paused for the laughter she knew would come "—until then, remember my number one rule for getting along with visitors to the city: Don't kiss them unless they kiss you first."

The laughter reverberated through the room again, the rich, raucous laughter of a roomful of half-smitten men. Which was quite a feat, Tony mused, when you considered that they had all been wearing frowns and grousing under their breath when they'd walked in here three hours ago.

Cheryl Steadman had been nothing short of amazing. She had dispensed an uncanny mix of professionalism— just enough to win their respect—and flirtation—just enough to soften their hearts without losing their respect. Within ten minutes she had them laughing tentatively with her as she talked about the hazards of being a friendly face in a sometimes unfriendly environment. She had them convinced—hell, she had *him* convinced—that she must have driven a cab herself during some previous incarnation.

This was one classy dame shaking hands with some of the men as she packed up the overhead projector and the transparencies she had used for her three-hour presentation. In fact, Tony had seriously begun to consider the possibility that she might be unattached.

Until he threw a few looks in Pete's direction. He knew then that he was already outclassed. He grinned and slapped his cap back over the thinning spot on the back of his head. *What's one more time?* he thought philosophically. Pete was a millionaire while he worked until midnight most nights chasing down city councilmen for their opinions on sewer lines. Such was life.

Who knows? he consoled himself. With Pete's reputation, he could be tired of her in another month, and maybe she'd be ready to slow things down with a poor but sensitive newshound.

He had noticed something about Pete besides the hunger in his face when he had followed Cheryl Steadman's tour de force in front of the class of cab drivers this afternoon. He had noticed the abruptness in his voice when they had greeted each other at the top of the program. He had noticed the way Pete stiffened when one of the men asked how Fats Peychaud was getting along, the way his jaw muscle had worked.

Tony knew how Pete looked when he had the hots for a dame. And he knew how Pete looked when something was bugging him. And right now, something was bugging him.

Fats Peychaud. He wrote the name down at the top of a column on his reporter's pad and slipped it into his back pocket.

CHAPTER EIGHT

THE SECOND DAY of the class for cab drivers, a pewter apple appeared on Cheryl's desk at the Chamber. The card read "World's Best Teacher."

She knew, even without a signature, where the gift and the sentiment originated. It could only be Pete.

On the fourth day of class—a bone-chilling January day of the type that always reminded New Orleanians they lived on the waterfront—hot apple cider and fresh, warm pastries from Madelaine's were delivered midway through the class.

The cab drivers loved the special treat. And Cheryl told herself she loved the thoughtfulness of the man behind the treat.

And the first day of class for a new round of fifty drivers, Pete showed up before class started to mingle with the drivers and set them at ease. When Cheryl took the floor, he watched quietly for a few minutes and then eased out the back door.

His last, lingering look before he let the conference room door close behind him almost wiped Cheryl's agenda for the class out of her mind.

But she simply loved, she told herself, his thoughtfulness.

And she missed his nearness. Now, absently scribbling notes in her accounting class, Cheryl would have traded all the thoughtfulness in the world for another chance to press close to him and drown in one of his torrid kisses. Just the memory was enough to reduce her to dewy readiness. When he'd left the meeting room earlier in the day, his eyes on hers had brought aching peaks to her breasts and a shimmery tingle to her thighs.

But it wasn't to be, she told herself, raising her eyes to look at the notes of the person at the next desk, hoping to catch a clue to the point Fay had just made. Pete had hardly spoken to her during the past week, and all his gestures, she was certain, were simply his way of fulfilling his promise to make the Friendly Faces project a success.

She believed that. Sometimes. Other times, she believed the darkening of his eyes when their lips had met and the swelling hardness against her thigh when her body had been crushed to his.

That, she told herself brutally as the class drew to a close, was called being in heat. And she was not interested in a man who was simply in heat.

The new Cheryl, the un-Cheryl-like person whose presence she had ignored for the past week, gave the old Cheryl a knowing look. *Oh, really?*

As she and Fay walked across campus after accounting, Cheryl tried to drag her thoughts away from the emotional maze that had frustrated her for days.

"Say, I'm having lunch downtown Saturday," Fay said, pulling her furry Russian cossack's hat down over her ears against the evening chill. "How about it?"

Mentally reviewing her schedule, Cheryl nodded. A Saturday afternoon with Fay would be the perfect distraction. "Sure. Want to meet downtown? The Pearl?"

"Sounds great. How's the charm school for cab drivers coming?" Fay asked.

Shrugging and keeping her eyes straight ahead, Cheryl filled her in, carefully leaving out the details that were most important. The details that had to do with Pete.

"You're hooked," Fay declared. "Teaching is addictive, sweet thing. It's like sex. It's such a high you won't be able to do without it once you've experienced it."

Cheryl laughed, grateful for the dark, wondering if Fay was right. Was she learning, after all these years of apathy, that sex was addictive? Or was it Pete Fontenot?

SPOT COMPLAINED about his vantage point on the kitchen floor while Pete peeled the small shrimp he had boiled and cooled for *rémoulade*.

"How many times do I have to tell you, Spot, cats don't like shrimp," Pete said earnestly to the pink-nosed protester. He took another swallow of beer and looked down at the kitten, almost grateful that he'd had no calls in response to his newspaper ad about the missing animal. "Not buying it, huh?"

Lifting his face hopefully at the softening tone in Pete's voice, Spot walked over to rub against Pete's legs.

"Okay, okay. But only one. Agreed?"

Spot's squeaky reply certainly sounded like a yes to Pete. But as soon as the little beggar had inhaled the bite-size shrimp, his meows rose in intensity. It was apparent, Pete knew, that he had been caught in the lie. Cats did like shrimp, and Spot now knew it.

"Okay. One more. That's all. Period. No more. One. Got it?" Pete grinned down at the black-and-white kitten, who had filled out and cleaned his coat until it sparkled in the weeks since he had shown up in the flowerpot out front. Then he'd been a scrawny derelict with mournful yellow eyes, one darkened by black fur and the other brightened by white fur. Now, both golden eyes were continuously wide with kitten wonder.

"Because if we eat any more, there won't be enough for dinner tomorrow night," Pete pointed out as he continued his preparation. "And if you think boiled shrimp is good, wait until you taste *rémoulade*. A little creole mustard, spices, a little olive oil. Crispy lettuce. Ah, you're a lucky cat, Spot."

As he finished peeling the shrimp and tossing them with the tangy dressing in which they would marinate overnight, Pete realized he had far too much food—even allowing for Spot's weakness for Cajun cooking. Company, he decided. That's what he'd do. Invite company for dinner tomorrow night. It was a Friday night and he'd stayed in alone, except for Spot, every night this week.

Brooding. And waiting. Wondering when Kurt Fletcher would call again. But he hadn't. It had been almost two weeks since the last call, the day Tony had been in his office. With each day that passed without contact from the sleazeball his old partner had become, Pete grew a little more confident. His mind grew a little easier. Fletcher had changed his mind. He had found another patsy for his stupid drug deals.

Things were looking up, Pete decided as he wiped his hands and stashed the shrimp in the refrigerator, retrieving another beer as he did. Fats was on the mend. He had worked out a flextime schedule for Sammy to make classes easier. And Fletcher hadn't called.

Fats and Sammy and Fletcher were not the faces on his mind, however, as he contemplated the possibility of a dinner party the following evening. A dinner party. An intimate dinner party, at that, he thought. After all, there was too much shrimp *rémoulade* for one man and a roly-poly kitten, but not enough for the six who could sit around his dining room table.

The only face he could see across a candlelit table from him was fair and framed in white-gold hair. With a few stray freckles high on the cheekbones and a smattering on her nose.

With Fletcher out of his hair, why not? No reason to avoid her anymore.

He picked up the phone and was rewarded with her breathless voice on the second ring.

"Hungry?" He grinned at the withering expression he knew his question would elicit.

"Yes, as a matter of fact, I am," she said tartly. "I just ran up the steps from accounting class, and I haven't eaten yet."

"Accounting? You're really getting into this teaching business, aren't you?"

"I'm on the other end of these lessons. I'm in the M.B.A. program at Tulane."

"Ah. Well, if you think you'll be hungry about this time tomorrow night, how about dinner?"

Could he have imagined the little bit of music in her voice as she said yes? He certainly hadn't imagined the tightening in his groin when she ended the conversation with "I'll bring an appetite."

He hoped she did just that.

THE MOST DELICIOUS-LOOKING thing at the table was Pete. In the glow from the candlelight, Cheryl decided, he was devastatingly seductive.

His golden brown hair was combed back neatly off his forehead, which gave her the most incredible urge to run her hands through it and tousle it into its usual disarray. The black tie he had worn with the crisp white shirt and formal dinner jacket was neatly in place, which made her fingers itch to yank it free and loosen the buttons at his neck.

And his face was closely, recently shaved, which set her to thinking of staying until morning, when she could feel the roughness of a day-old beard against her lips. Her cheek. Her neck. Her . . .

"So why an M.B.A.? You planning to take Wall Street by storm?"

Cheryl barely heard Pete's question over the rush of his voice against her senses. Her brain, tonight, had moved to a back row seat, hidden from view behind a cluster of glowing, vibrating, noisily happy sensations.

"I just want to get ahead," she said. "I figured out years ago I could do that one of two ways—by riding on my father's coattails or by being good enough on my own. Without my father's name or his money. I want to trade on what I have to offer, not my father's reputation."

Pete paused, the silver fork of shrimp stalling on the way to his lips. "That's good. I like that."

She watched the shrimp as he popped it into his mouth. His lips moved slowly. She wet her lips, longing to taste his kisses.

"This is wonderful," she said softly, lusting after the touch of his hands as he refilled her long-stemmed glass with crisp, dry sauvignon. "I know it's a cliché, but you really shouldn't have gone to so much trouble."

"No trouble." The barest of smiles trembled at the edge of his lips. His eyes were intense. She saw the reflection of her own heated thoughts. "Spot and I eat by candlelight most evenings. We're just glad you could join us."

Cheryl's laugh was breathless. The oddly marked black-and-white kitten was curled up in contented slumber beside a now empty china salad dish, licked clean of any sign of sauce or shrimp.

"Does he like Napoleons, too?" she teased.

"Loves 'em."

The evening had been as elegant as any of the city's posh restaurants could have offered. Pete's town house was picture perfect and dimly lighted; his teak and chrome dining table was set with understated china so fine it was almost translucent. The wine was perfect. The food was perfect. And the host was much, much more than perfect.

In her favorite mauve silk sheath, with her fine hair braided with strands of baby's breath and delicate mauve ribbon, Cheryl felt like the star of a glitz-and-glamour TV miniseries.

And as soon as the hero finished clearing the table, the love scene would begin to roll. Old Cheryl had been left home tonight. New Cheryl was only vaguely nervous in a tiny part of her soul that was easily overwhelmed by the parts of her soul that longed to go the limit with this man made of the stuff of dreams.

Her only real reservation was that he had begun to touch her heart as well as the more readily accessible parts of her anatomy.

She could give that problem to the old Cheryl to deal with when the time came, she told herself as she roamed the living room.

The chrome Art Deco dining table and matching torch lamps were echoed in the adjoining living room. Expensive and subtle flair was evident in the low-slung white couch, the chrome tables and the hand-thrown pottery that served as accent pieces. Masks of all types—from frivolous peacock feathers and sequins to hand-painted, hand-carved wood from cultures as diverse as the Javanese and the American Indian—covered the walls. The recliner, which faced a sleek white wall unit that Cheryl would have bet hid a television and the sound system that had wafted mellow jazz across the room the entire evening, was functionally funky and blended with the cream-and-chocolate color scheme.

His elegant town house overlooking a small courtyard complete with fountain and intricately carved wooden benches was simply another example of his unfailingly good taste. It seemed Pete Fontenot never made a false move.

"Cognac?" His voice was close behind her before she realized he had returned from the kitchen.

"Where are the milk carton masks?" Fingertips brushed as she took the small snifter. He laughed.

"Long gone. They didn't fit the decor," he said dryly.

"I like what you've done." She wasn't sure she trusted her voice. Her smile felt wavy, wobbly.

"I copied it out of a magazine."

"What?" She turned to him, her impatience to feel his touch growing.

"The room. The furnishings. I saw them in a magazine and had the whole room done over. Except for the masks." His grin was rueful. "I wasn't sure I trusted my judgment to do it myself. And I didn't want some silly decorator coming in here and creating something I couldn't live with."

"It's lovely."

"But it's a fake."

"No, it isn't. How do you think any of us know how to dress or how to decorate?"

"You're born with it."

"No, we aren't. We just learn as we go along," she said as he led her to the couch. "I spent my whole childhood copying my father. His movements. His way with people. His ice-cold charm.''

''I didn't have anybody to copy,'' Pete said, and smiled sardonically. ''So I watched old Humphrey Bogart movies and practiced being a tough guy. My old man was...not real sophisticated. Hardworking. Hard-drinking. But not what you'd call sophisticated. And my mom...well, she was always pushing. Study harder. Stay out of trouble. Make something of yourself. So I tried to make myself into Bogie.''

They laughed together.

''Why don't you come to the Sparta parade with me?'' he asked suddenly. ''It's one of the early parades. Runs just a few blocks from the neighborhood. We always make a big party out of it. You can see what I mean about the folks.''

She nodded. ''I'd like that.''

The old Cheryl protested. Going home to meet his family was a bit much. The new Cheryl shifted slightly, turning her knees in his direction. She breathed in the cognac and with it the scent of his maleness. The cognac warmed her but didn't mute the sensations flowing through her.

He moved an arm to the back of the sofa. ''Did you succeed?''

''At what?''

''At learning to be like your father?'' He twirled a stray strand of her hair on his finger, then tucked it behind her ear.

The fire from the cognac met the fire low in Cheryl's loins. ''Sometimes I'm afraid I did.''

''Why afraid?''

His arm across the back of the couch whispered against her shoulders. Her nipples tightened. She knew without looking they were evident beneath the silk. "Because I learned how to be in control."

"Is that bad?"

"It is if you never learn how to let go of that control."

She knew her voice was growing hoarse with the tension building within her. If he touched her, she knew, he would find that the slow-burning heat low in her body had melted all the control she was boasting about. It was only a matter of finding the trigger that could release her.

If only he would touch her. Throw her down on the couch and plant his knee between her thighs and seek her tongue with his. A touch. That's all she needed. One touch from him would make it okay to give in to the uncontrollable desires that raged through her.

"Cheryl?"

She turned to look into his eyes. His smoky eyes. The question in her eyes would have to do as a response. Her voice didn't seem to be working.

"You know how to let go of the control. I remember."

Still she couldn't move. He took the snifter from her hand and set it, with his, on the table. She waited for his touch, never releasing him with her eyes. The touch didn't come. He raised his hand, but only to loosen his tie.

"Don't!"

Her soft command surprised her as much as it did him. With trembling fingers, she reached out to halt him, covering the softly furred hand at his throat.

"Let me."

She loosened the tie. Clumsily. Her fingers were numb with nervousness. He swallowed heavily as she grazed his throat. Perhaps he, too, was maintaining only tenuous control.

She slipped open the top two buttons while she was at it, then smiled tremulously. "There. That's better."

The words were barely a whisper, the soft whisper exchanged by lovers. What would he think of her? she wondered. That she was easy? That she must melt into helplessness with every man who waggled a finger in her direction?

"It's up to you, Cheryl."

The words were the gentlest challenge; she didn't know if she had the courage to meet it.

He lifted her hand and pressed it to his neck. His pulse raced wildly against her palm, keeping time with the erratic rush of her own. Then he moved her hand to his chest. Through the crisp shirt she felt the bud of his nipple and, again, the thundering beat of his heart.

"There's more, if you aren't convinced."

He wasn't grinning. He wasn't teasing. Cheryl wondered if it was only her imagination or if her breath was truly coming in shallow, rapid pants. She knew what other evidence of his arousal remained, and heaven help her, she wanted to know that proof, too, hot and heavy against her flesh.

"Then why don't you . . . why don't . . ."

His voice, which she suddenly realized was as hoarse with passion as her own, came to her rescue. "Because I want to know that you want me, too."

The low moan was from her own throat, Cheryl realized. "I want you, Pete. Oh, Lord, I want you."

Once she spoke the words, she couldn't turn them off. She might have spoken them all night had he not lowered her, almost roughly, certainly quickly, to the couch and covered her lips with his. Her shoes slipped off.

They writhed on the couch, instinctively moving to allow every part of their bodies to touch, to press, to be together. Their mouths were hot and seeking, drinking deeply but still hungering. He lowered his face to her breast and, through the silk, covered the taut bud he found with a hot, damp kiss.

He raised the hem of her dress, branding her thigh with the heat of his hand. She cried out.

"Please!" She breathed against his hair. "Oh, please!"

He looked up, his face a blur of passion. "Let's take it slow," he urged. "We've got all night."

"Next time. We'll take it slow next time." Her voice ached with desire. "I need you. Now."

She fumbled with his fly, the pressure of his erection increasing her urgency. Deftly, he helped, sweeping away her silken undergarments and opening his pants. His hard, silken flesh burned against hers. When he hesitated, she thrust forward to bring him into her.

It was all he needed. He thrust deeply, burying himself in her heat, then held still until her whimpering cries had stopped.

"Are you all right?"

His voice was a faraway dream. Her only answer was the pressure of her hands on his hips, urging him to movement. His fullness was more than she had expected, the sweet urgency was more than she could have dreamed for. Her frenzy built as she felt him growing harder, stronger. She shattered into a million tiny flashes of light and heat, straining to hold back the cries that rose up in her throat.

As she ebbed against him, she felt again the swelling, the growing frenzy of his thrust. She looked up; his eyes caressed her with naked clarity.

"Pete..."

She felt his explosion within her, an explosion he took no pains to hide. He called out to her.

When he collapsed, his face against her neck, she wrapped her arms around his back. The dampness beneath his shirt matched her own. Her silk dress was a mess; her hair was a mess. But before Pete had recovered enough to speak, she wanted him again. The old Cheryl had just died giving birth to a new woman, and, for the moment at least, this new Cheryl was gloriously, peacefully, gratefully content.

Not to mention aroused. *So this is what it's really like,* she thought, closing her eyes and drinking in the fragrance of their mingled bodies. *So this is why sex has everybody standing on their ears.*

At last, she understood.

She protested when he started to pull away from her, and Pete raised himself on one elbow to look down at her. "Are you all right?"

"Don't I look all right?" she murmured, forcing her heavy lids open. She almost moaned out loud at the intensity in his gaze. What had happened to the Pete of the snappy patter? The don't-give-a-damn Pete?

He leaned closer and kissed her. Softly, with a tenderness neither of them had been able to manage before. He trailed his tongue along the rim of her lips, and her nipples sprang to instant, aching life again.

"I didn't mean for it to be this way," he whispered, continuing to brush her face and lips with soft kisses. "I meant to take time. I wanted to make you feel like you've never felt before."

The breathy sound from deep in her throat was half laugh, half moan. "Oh, Pete, you did. You did."

His eyes crinkled in a smile. He hoisted himself off the couch, quickly adjusting the tail of his shirt to cover himself. He took her hands and lifted her to her feet. But instead of helping her smooth the silk sheath crumpled around her hips, he slipped it over her head and left her standing in the silk camisole whose partner had been tossed carelessly onto the chrome coffee table. Damp blond ringlets peeked from beneath the hem.

He cupped the damp curls, then touched the sleekness of her hip, sending a shiver through her. She felt strangely unembarrassed by the intimacy of his touch, by the blatantness of her passion, by the wantonness of her undress.

"Can I get you more cognac?" he asked, taking her hand in his.

"Yes, I want more," she said, holding his eyes with hers. She didn't mean cognac and didn't intend for him to misunderstand.

He left their glasses on the table and led her down the hall to the last door on the left. The brass lamp on the bedside table glowed warmly, dimly, casting a golden halo over the boldly patterned bedspread. In one swift motion, Pete left the spread on the floor at the foot of the bed, then pulled the sheets back.

With gentle fingers, he released her rumpled braid. Ribbon and baby's breath fell to the carpet. Weaving his fingers through the hair that fell to her shoulders, he cradled her head in his palms as if he held something dear. A tingle worked its way from the top of her head downward.

"Thank you," he whispered.

"Why?" Surely, she thought, the thanks should be hers. Surely she should be the one grateful to him for finally showing her that rigid control was not the be-all and end-all of life.

"For wanting me, too."

Before she could respond to the undisguised vulnerability in his words, he pulled the camisole over her head. Standing naked at last in the dim light, Cheryl was hit with her first attack of shyness. She knew her shortcomings; voluptuousness was not one of her attributes. Still, her breasts responded to the caress of his glance. His eyes on her skin were almost like a touch, bringing her to life.

His devouring look stopped and he raised his eyes to hers. She registered his alarm. "I forgot to ask about..."

"I'm safe," she said simply.

"You're safe with me," he replied.

She knew he meant what he said. And more. More, probably, than he knew.

"You lie down," he said gently. "I'll go bring your things."

"I don't need them," she said. "Stay with me."

When he didn't move, she finished the job of undressing him. The shirt peeled back to reveal a hard, lean chest and a flat belly. She feathered light touches over him, savoring the texture of his skin for the first time. He helped lower his pants, and she reached out to touch the part of him that had, for too short a time, been part of her.

He gasped and stirred against her touch.

"So soft," she breathed, feeling the response well up in her even as he swelled against her touch. "Your skin is softest where your body is hardest."

This time, they made love. The heat between them turned down now to a manageable level, they enjoyed the leisurely exploration of love that Pete had wanted the first time. His hands made every inch of her feel special; she learned that even her inexperienced hands could do the same for him. She discovered the taste of his skin and the mind-weakening wonder of his tongue seeking out every erotic nerve ending in her body.

And when their tender meanderings grew feverish, he filled her once more and she held tightly to the feeling of oneness between them.

As she drifted into sleep, cheek against his chest, damp thigh curled around damp thigh, she wondered if lust could, chameleon-like, metamorphose into love.

CHAPTER NINE

CHERYL WAS USUALLY ten minutes early for everything and never one minute late for anything, but she kept Fay waiting exactly eight and a half minutes Saturday.

Her luncheon date with Fay had been the last thing on her mind when she'd woken up in Pete's arms that morning. The first thing on her mind had been slinking quietly away and taking a streetcar home in her rumpled silk dress so she wouldn't have to face Pete with the evidence of their lovemaking still clinging to her skin. Her wanton actions appalled her in the light of day. She wasn't sure she could take the lazy grin that was sure to light his face when he opened his eyes.

The second thing on her mind, when her movement prompted a drowsing Pete to tighten his arms around her and pull her back tightly against his chest, had been the springy fur of his belly against her back, the rough tenderness of the hand that cupped her breast, the scratchy face against the back of her neck and the surging manhood prodding her buttocks.

The urgency of his erection had quickly become her own urgency. Her shyness didn't linger.

So she was late. She dashed into the diner and looked around, wondering what telltale signs she had forgotten to eradicate in her quick dash home to swap the evening's silk for cords and a sweater.

Fay sat patiently in a corner, reading glasses perched low on her button nose, lost in the paperback novel she had pulled from the arsenal of belongings she carried in her mammoth shoulder bag. Fay didn't complain about her tardiness. But she did study her closely enough that Cheryl knew she thought it odd. And even odder that Cheryl's fair skin darkened in a blush.

By the time their salads arrived, the awkwardness had evaporated in a round of talk about whether spring would arrive in time for Mardi Gras, how much an M.B.A. would help Cheryl if she stayed in public relations, and Fay's attempts to ward off a visit from her high school sweetheart in Pascagoula, who was in the final throes of a painful divorce.

"I may be going through a dry spell," Fay said, waving a kosher dill for emphasis. "But I do not want to pick up a balding, overweight optometrist on the rebound."

"Maybe he's tall, dark and handsome," Cheryl countered, thinking that was far less intriguing than the thought of someone lean and blond who was trying to outcool Humphrey Bogart.

The beret perched on Fay's red curls quivered with her laughter. "Who are you kidding? He was balding and overweight in high school!"

Cheryl enjoyed the camaraderie with Fay but not enough to talk about having a new man in her life—an experience she knew women were supposed to share avidly with their closest friends. Although Fay was closer than anyone, Cheryl had been a loner too long to open up easily. She was too new to friendship. And, more importantly, she was too new to the business of having a lover. Her tongue tied just thinking about Pete.

They finished their salads and headed for the counter with the check. As they waited for change, Fay eyed her sternly. "Okay, we have an important mission today, and I don't want any argument from you."

"What?"

"We have to find you a Mardi Gras costume." She held up her hand to halt the protest. "I'm your professor. My words are pearls of wisdom. You'll take that to heart. *If* you expect to pass this accounting course."

Actually, although she had opened her mouth automatically to say no, Cheryl could think of no reason not to get into the spirit of the celebration. Pete seemed to be changing everything about her, even her aversion to roaming through crowds of rowdy merrymakers.

She was growing to love his city as much as Pete did. And she couldn't think of any good reason to shut herself off from the experience.

So she followed Fay from one little shop to another, looking for something that would satisfy her own need for subtlety and Fay's desire for flamboyance. Everything Fay picked up was either skimpy or revealing or downright bawdy. And everything Cheryl picked out was, in Fay's opinion, dull as dishwater.

"You will not go as a clown," Fay stated firmly as they marched down a narrow French Quarter street. "Or a teddy bear. I don't see what was wrong with being a fan dancer."

"Fay, that costume only had three fans," Cheryl reminded her.

"So? One in the back, two in the front." Fay shrugged. "What more do you need?"

"Not to get arrested?"

"Honey, you'd have to prance naked along a parade route to get arrested on Fat Tuesday." They turned into another store. "Come to think of it, that might not even do it."

They finally agreed on a harem costume, a filmy bit of satin and gauze that paid only lip service to hiding Cheryl's curves.

"Are you sure this isn't a little too...much?" Cheryl asked hesitantly as the shopkeeper rang up her purchases.

"What have you got against being sexy, Cheryl?"

Cheryl blushed again. Judging from the night before, nothing at all. She did wonder, however, if she could repeat her performance and continue to live up to Pete's expectations. He must travel with some pretty hot numbers. And Cheryl Steadman, in spite of her actions the night before, was not a hot number.

FLETCHER DIDN'T LOOK as happy with the information as Butch had expected him to be. Not only had Butch come up with the kid, Sammy Reilly, but this dame, Cheryl Steadman looked like a sure thing. A guy like Fontenot was one of those white-knight types who'd go ape if you messed with his woman.

But here Fletcher sat, his face just as sour as it had been before Butch walked through the door. Go figure.

"Good job." There was no real appreciation in his voice as Fletcher crushed a cigarette under his foot. The damp, cold room reeked of the cigarette butts that littered the scarred wooden floor.

"So whadda we do now, boss?" Butch shifted from one foot to the next impatiently, trying not to look around. He'd always figured his place wasn't much to write home about, but *this* was a real hellhole. Cold and dark—one bare bulb in the middle of the ceiling gave off the only light—with a rusty green refrigerator. One table leg was shorter than the other three and propped up on a can of tuna fish. Butch was eager to blow this joint.

He was also eager to put some hurt on this Fontenot guy. It was sort of his religion—hating people who had that much going for them. And he had sweated all night, imagining the goings-on in that dark bedroom in Fontenot's ritzy place in the Quarter. He was looking forward to wiping the smile off that lucky stiff's face.

"Take another one of his drivers out. Not Reilly. Anybody else." Fletcher's eyes narrowed as he thought through his next step. "Then give him a warning call. Tell him the danger's gonna strike closer to home if he doesn't make up his mind on a pending business deal."

Butch was ticked off now. Here he'd figured out exactly how to stick it to Fontenot, and Fletcher was going to keep messing around pulling small stuff? It didn't make sense. "But, boss, what about—"

"Leave the thinkin' to me!" Fletcher snapped. "Now get your butt out there and take care of one of Font'not's drivers. We ain't got till bloody Christmas."

"NO, MA." Clutching the phone to his ear, Kurt mouthed the foulest four-letter word he could come up with. His mother. Now he had his old lady on his back, too. "I ain't gonna have time for dinner tomorrow, Ma."

He listened to her rave on about how long it had been since he'd been home for Sunday dinner and how weak the old man was getting. And how Mary Margaret was struggling to make ends meet now that the worthless piece of garbage she'd married had finally flown the coop. And how all of them could sure use the help of their best and only son and brother.

He didn't want to hear it. He certainly didn't want to go and have to spend an hour looking into their faces over fried chicken and mashed potatoes. His ma would look gray and tired and too old, just as she had the last time.

His old man would be even skinnier than before, and his hands would shake just a little bit more when he passed around the gravy boat. Mary Margaret's brats would squall and raise hell and knock over furniture, and Mary Margaret would look more like Ma than she had the time before.

And it all depressed the hell out of him. They kept looking to him for help. Hell, it was all he could do to keep Monteleone's thugs off his back. Who appointed him the Fletcher family savior, anyway?

"Ma, I don't think I'll make the Sparta parade, either. I got too many things shakin' here in the office." He looked around the ten-by-ten room that became his office when he shoved the bed back into the wall. Office, he thought bitterly. That was a joke. His old lady would cry if she could see this dump. "I know the old crowd always shows up, Ma. But . . ."

He paused for another round of whimpering and nagging. The old gang would be there, all right. Including Font'not, with that classy new broad he was shackin' up with. That SOB certainly wasn't making life any easier for him.

It's your own damn fault, he told himself as his mother's voice droned on. *You're bein' too soft on him.* Even Butch had seen that, even thickheaded Butch.

But every time he decided it was time to lay it on heavy, something stopped him. It wasn't like he was afraid of his old buddy, although he'd seen Pete mad enough times to know that his temper wasn't something to mess with. Pete had been plenty mad when he'd found out Kurt was siphoning off some of the company's money to do a little betting on the side. Hell, it wasn't like stealing. He would have put some of his winnings back into the pot. But Pete was too damned mad to listen to that. Had practically shoved a check down his throat and told him to clear out of his office. Threatened to turn him in if he didn't take the money and run. And a couple hundred thou had seemed like a lot then. But it had gone fast. Too fast.

Yeah, when Pete got mad, he could go crazy.

Pete had always been like that. He'd had this streak of righteousness that had started to bore Kurt. They'd always swiped stuff from old man Rouquette's market. But when Kurt had wanted to break out of the kid stuff into something bigger—bust a few stores for the cash in the safe, just to get a little pocket money—Pete had laid down the law. And, hell, once Pete laid down the law, Tony rolled over and died. And that just left Kurt. Wouldn't have been any fun alone.

Still, the old days—before Pete got so particular—had been fun. The three of them must've put a million miles on those three old bikes.

That's no reason to lighten up on him, he chided himself.

"All right, Ma. Tell you what. Next Sunday. I promise, I'll be there next Sunday."

If Monteleone's men hadn't taken him out of the game by then, he thought as he hung up the phone.

SAMMY WISHED he could shrink to the size of a bug and slither through a crack. Come to think of it, that's about how he felt. The size of a bug.

Nobody else's woman came into the garage and gave them heck while everybody else stood around and listened. Oh, they were pretending not to pay any attention. But he knew they were grinning behind his back and calling him henpecked and thinking that Sammy Reilly had a lot of growing up to do.

Even Pete, standing over with the dispatcher, was hearing all this. That's probably what bugged him the most. More than anything in the world, he wanted Pete to respect him. He'd never had an old man. Not that Pete was old. But, well . . . it would just be nice to have somebody like Pete think he was okay.

And now here was Marie, causing a ruckus right here in the garage. Sammy always used to be proud when Marie came round to bring dinner on the night shift or stop by to ride the bus home with him. But right now . . . well, he would have been glad to be a bug so small nobody would notice.

"I won't let you work another shift tonight," she concluded, her voice rising in anger, her long curls quivering with her intensity.

The garage, always roaring with engines and the beep of horns as cars rolled into or out of the gate, was silent. Except for Marie. Sammy wished fervently for the noise that had suddenly abandoned him when he needed it. "Marie, it's not—"

"I don't want to hear it," she interrupted adamantly. "You've got a class tonight. And you can't miss it."

"But we can use the money." Sammy lowered his voice, wishing Marie could be convinced to do the same. Convincing Marie of anything was something he had trouble doing, however. "You got Shanna's doctor bill yesterday from the time she had the flu, and—"

"You let me worry about that. I'm her mother. You worry about college."

That stung. He might not be Shanna's father yet, but he sure wanted to be. "I'll take care of college. But I'd like to take care of you and Shanna, too. Let's get married, Marie."

She crossed her arms tightly and glared at him through the stormy slits her dark eyes had become. "We're not gonna talk about this again, Sammy. When you finish college. That's when we'll get married."

"Darn it, Marie. Why don't we get married now? Then we wouldn't always have to be fighting about it."

"We're not fighting." Marie's statement was delivered as if it were the final word. "I'm just telling you how it's going to be. You're not going to be worrying about money and college and me and Shanna. You worry about college. Not money."

"Maybe I'll just have to find a way to get more money than I can get driving cabs," Sammy countered, grasping at straws. He was trying to gain control of an argument he'd never stood a chance of winning. "I'll find us enough money that I won't have to worry about doctor bills and paying rent. Then you'll have to marry me, and I won't have to worry about you and Shanna being alone for the next two years, either. That's what I really worry about!"

Marie glared. "You just go to class tonight," she commanded, then turned and stalked out of the garage.

Sammy shook his head. Sometimes he didn't know why he wanted that hardheaded woman, anyway. She was just like his mother. Always bossing him around and flying off the handle and yelling at him. But they always made up. He almost smiled when he thought of how sweet she was when they made up. She wasn't ever mean, just hotheaded. Just like his mother.

Maybe he would go to class tonight. It was only his second class, and it would put him way behind to miss it.

And then maybe he would try to figure out some way to make more money. Maybe then Marie would marry him, even if he did still have two years of college to finish.

PETE HID HIS GRIN as he walked from dispatch back to his office. Sammy and Marie were quite a pair. Sammy pouted like a little boy every time Marie wouldn't agree to marry him, and she fussed over him like a mother hen. Life in the Reilly household, if Sammy ever convinced her to tie the knot, would never be dull.

Although, come to think of it, love was never dull, he told himself as he slid into the leather chair at his desk.

You'll never know anything about love, Pete Fontenot.

The taunt came to him out of the blue, as clear and biting today as it had been the day Eleanore threw it at him. One more measure of hurt to mete out before she left; one more way to get back at him for breaking their engagement. The words had hurt less than letting her go. She would have been happy in that knowledge, if she'd had any way of knowing.

But Eleanore had never had a clue when it came to figuring out Pete Fontenot. She'd figured that having a woman with the right background and the right breeding on his arm was all he needed. She'd figured that was a perfect trade-off for the life of wealth she could have as Pete Fontenot's bride; the perfect trade-off for getting her family's faltering finances back on track. Love didn't even enter the equation.

Pete hadn't been interested in a business proposition that included a two-carat rock on her left hand and a lifetime of wondering.

You'll never know anything about love, Pete Fontenot.

He'd thought at the time it must be true, or he never would have fallen for Eleanore's smooth-as-glass act.

And maybe, he thought, toying with the letter opener on his desk, it was still true. Maybe he was just falling for the same old routine, act two.

But no matter how cynical he tried to be about Cheryl Steadman, he just couldn't see her in the same league as Eleanore DeVrie. They might both be leggy blondes with upper-crust upbringings. But that's where the similarities ended.

For one thing, Cheryl had floored him with her talk about making it on her own, without a leg up from her old man. Maybe she'd been blowing smoke, but the set of her chin had reinforced the determination in her voice.

For another thing, nobody could fake the kind of passion he'd discovered in Cheryl this weekend. She had completely blown him away. Pete felt his office heat up just remembering. Her complete lack of inhibition, so at odds with her carefully modulated control, was unexpected. Even to her, it seemed.

When she'd dashed out so quickly on Saturday morning with that flimsy excuse about meeting a friend for lunch, Pete had entertained the thought that she might have used him to take the edge off her appetite and planned to move on. After all, what interest could she really have in someone like him?

But she had called that afternoon to thank him for dinner. To thank him! She had sounded so unsure of herself, so hesitant, as though she weren't absolutely certain he would want to hear from her, when all he'd been doing for the past hour was staring at the phone, wondering if he should call. Wondering if calling after her hasty departure would just be leading with his chin.

Then the phone had rung and it was her. Coy and tentative and sensuous and just bordering on too innocent to be believed. Pete couldn't remember another time when a simple telephone call had aroused him so instantly and so thoroughly.

So they'd packed a moonlight picnic and headed out to a quiet spot on Lake Pontchartrain. A very quiet spot, fortunately, for their final course had not come out of the wicker basket.

But it had been the best part of the picnic.

Saturday night's picnic had segued into Sunday morning's breakfast and a tour of a plantation about an hour's drive out of town.

Spot had complained about being left alone all day when Pete returned home late Sunday night. And Pete had had to admit, as he'd turned out the light and crawled between the sheets alone, that Spot had a point. He *was* spending a lot of time with Cheryl.

But it didn't necessarily have anything to do with love, Pete decided, frowning at the year-end financial reports Elaine had put on his desk for review. And probably not. Not if he was smart.

His telephone buzzed and Pete reached for the receiver. "Fontenot."

"We're not gonna mess around forever, Font'not. Next time, look for somethin' closer to home."

The line clicked and went dead before Pete could open his mouth. He hadn't recognized the voice, but he certainly knew a threat when he heard one. His heart dropped to his shoes. He'd thought Kurt Fletcher had found better ways to waste his time. Though this voice hadn't belonged to Fletcher, Pete was willing to bet that his ex-friend was responsible for the threat.

He didn't know what the hell to do about Fletcher, short of using the same kind of bullying tactics that his old partner was employing so ineffectually. The police were no help in dealing with thugs like him. Especially if Fletcher was hooked up, as everyone in the old neighborhood said, with organized crime. If that was the case, he might just as well call in the Boy Scouts as call in the police. Like mosquitoes, police buzzing around would do nothing but irritate the crime bosses.

When the bosses got irritated, they brought out the big guns. Right now, Fletcher was not a big gun. Right now, Fletcher was nothing more than a mosquito, himself. And Pete didn't want to run the risk of bringing any *real* wrath down on himself and all he'd worked so many years to build.

Maybe he'd look up Fletcher. If debts were Kurt's problem, maybe he could buy him off. It was better than having to beat the living daylights out of him. Pete looked down at his fist. He hadn't used it for years. He didn't want to have to start again. He'd tried too hard to leave all that behind him. He'd be damned if a loser like Kurt Fletcher was going to drag him back down into the gutter.

His office door burst open.

"Pete!"

Elaine's face was deathly pale and her eyes were frightened. She pointed to the blinking line on his phone.

While he walked around the desk and led a trembling Elaine to the sofa, Pete answered the phone. The cord stretched taut as he patted her hand.

"Mr. Fontenot. This is Captain Anderson, NOPD. There's been an accident, Mr. Fontenot."

CHAPTER TEN

THE ACCIDENT was no accident.

Two young girls who had witnessed the wreck had left no doubt about that. The long, black Lincoln Continental had taken more than one swipe at the cab. Unfortunately, the parkway at dusk had been too dark for the wide-eyed girls to get the plate number of the hit-and-run Lincoln.

The taxi driver, with only a broken wrist and a mild concussion, was already kicking up a fuss about leaving the hospital. Which was more than could be said for Fats Peychaud, who probably wouldn't be strong enough to leave the hospital for another couple of days.

It might also be more than could be said for the next driver, Pete thought as he stared numbly at the watercolor of the Louisiana bayou hanging on the wall facing his desk. The soothing scene brought no peace of mind today.

Kurt Fletcher meant business. There was no doubt about that. He had been a fool to think Fletcher would drop it. Even as kids, Kurt hadn't been the type to pull back, even in a hopeless situation. Pete could remember too many times when, confronted with indisputable evidence of their pranks, Kurt Fletcher had lied right to his mother's face.

No, Fletcher didn't give up. So no matter what kind of personal danger it might bring to Pete, he had to do something. He couldn't stand by and let Fletcher's goons pick off his drivers one by one. If Fletcher wasn't stopped, it was only a matter of time before he killed somebody.

Elaine buzzed him. Pete stared at the blinking line, held back from answering by a lethargy that was uncommon for him. He had been at the accident site and the hospital until the early hours of the morning. Too late to call Cheryl. Too late to do anything but stare into the darkness for the two hours that remained until daylight. So he had stared. Out of the darkness, the same two images kept coming back to haunt him. The first was the mangled taxi wrapped around an oak tree.

The second was Cheryl. Cheryl. Cool as ice water and hot as pepper sauce. Cheryl. As the hours between four and six faded into daybreak, his yearning grew. A yearning to pillow her head on his shoulder and spill out his dilemma to her.

Cheryl Steadman, however, was the last person he planned to involve in Kurt Fletcher's sordid business. He was certain she would hightail it out of his life and back to safe territory so fast he'd be knocked over in the tail wind.

No, Cheryl was the last person to look to for help with a problem like this.

At last, he picked up his phone and buzzed Elaine.

"Can you make an excuse for me, Elaine?" he asked wearily. "I just don't want to talk to anybody right now."

"It's Captain Anderson."

Pete winced. The tall, black NOPD captain who had shown up at the accident shortly after Pete arrived the night before had been as intimidating as anyone Pete had ever met. He had a voice like a bullhorn and a disposition to match. Pete, who was very little over average height, had found it disconcerting to look up into the man's disapproving face.

If he didn't talk to him now, he was just putting off the inevitable.

"Thanks, Elaine."

Wishing he was the type who could grab a little quick courage from a bottle, Pete punched the furiously blinking telephone line.

Captain Anderson wasted no time on pleasantries before barking into the telephone. "Fontenot, I want to know what's going on."

"What do you mean, Captain?" Pete fought to keep his tone even; the last thing he needed was to drag this cop down on his case.

"Don't play dumb with me, mister. This isn't the first close call you've had. And the last one was just a couple weeks ago. What gives? And why didn't you think that was important enough to bring up last night?"

"It just didn't cross my mind."

Profanity sizzled across the line. "Don't hand me that garbage. Who've you crossed lately?"

"I honestly can't imagine why anyone would be doing this, Captain Anderson."

Pete knew he was a bad liar. Now so did Captain Anderson. The silence grew long and menacing before the rumble of the captain's voice came back at him.

"Listen, smart guy. I don't know what kind of people you're playing games with. And frankly I don't care. But if you start taking your problems to the streets, I get riled. I don't like to get riled. You won't like it if I get riled. Think it over. If you're smart, you'll get your butt in here with some answers before I find the answers on my own."

A crash in his ear signaled to Pete that his interview with the captain was over.

Pete didn't like the idea of making an enemy of Captain Anderson. But he knew better than to put a man like that on the tail of somebody like Fletcher. The law sniffing around would accomplish nothing. It would simply force the people who were pulling Fletcher's strings to step up the violence.

FLETCHER'S MOTHER seemed embarrassed—almost flustered—at not being able to tell Pete how to get in touch with her son.

"I'll tell him you called," she promised, fidgeting with the frayed collar on her blue print housedress. She smelled of talcum powder and onions, and she looked decades older than Pete's own mother. The sharp, pointy face she had passed on to Kurt had settled into fatigued old age.

"Please do, Mrs. Fletcher."

"Oh, I will. He's coming to dinner on Sunday." She looked, to Pete's eyes, pitifully pleased with the news, as if the prodigal did not return with regularity. "I'll tell him then. He'll be so glad."

"I'm sure he will."

He walked the streets of the neighborhood, sticking his head into the barber shop and the garage where he and Kurt had made pests of themselves during the years when they longed to make the leap from pedaling bikes to double-clutching hot rods. He even stopped in to see old man Rouquette and shoot the breeze, although he never thought for a minute that the aging grocer would know where to find his ex-partner.

Everyone greeted him fondly. And everyone, when he asked about Fletcher, grew silent and looked disbelieving or disappointed.

Even Louis Rouquette, to whom he didn't mention Fletcher, seemed to share the neighborhood's opinion of

Pete's quest, word of which was clearly traveling through the neighborhood more quickly than Pete was.

After a few minutes of catching up on gossip, the grocer turned his sagging eyes on Pete and said sternly, "You got a good business now, son. Good future. You watch out. Don't go draggin' yourself down just to rub elbows with no-accounts again. You hear me?"

Pete smiled. He would have loved to shock the old man with a bear hug as thanks for all the help he had given him when he was growing up. As much as he had learned from his father and his mother about the work ethic, it was old man Rouquette who had first insisted that his adolescent delivery boy live up to that work ethic.

Pete didn't hug him; he couldn't bring himself to. He told himself the white-haired old man wouldn't much appreciate his getting sloppy about things, anyway.

"I hear you."

As he headed out the door, Rouquette's voice stopped him and he turned just in time to catch the cigar tossed in his direction. "You're old enough now, I expect."

Pete laughed out loud, knowing the grocer got a charge out of finally letting him know that he hadn't been nearly as clever as he'd thought all the times he'd snitched smokes from behind the counter.

Having had no luck in the old neighborhood, Pete finally did the last thing he could think of to reach Fletcher. He drove to the docks and found the one person he knew who was up to his eyeballs in drug running and the numbers racket and asked him to pass along a message.

He ignored the flicker of surprise in the eyes of the warehouse chief at his words. "Tell him Pete's ready to deal."

THE ARRAY OF NEWSPAPER clippings spread out on the Chamber's boardroom conference table clearly made Dave Arnaud a happy man. Grinning broadly around a cigar clenched between his teeth, he waved a fistful of letters and telephone messages in Cheryl's face.

"Steadman, I told you this was a hot idea," he said gleefully. "Look at this. We got four letters yesterday from other cities interested in doing the same thing. Atlanta. Phoenix. Omaha. And—" cigar ash drifted onto the letters as he riffled through them looking for the right one "—Vegas. How'd you like a trip to Vegas to brief them on the Friendly Faces project, Steadman?"

"No, thanks," Cheryl said as she studied the clips. The story was being picked up off the wire services all over the country, and there was a half-page spread on Pete that had appeared in the *Times-Picayune*. Cheryl knew that article almost word for word now; a copy lay spread on her dining room table at home, where she had absorbed the story of Pete's struggles more than once.

She looked up from the clips into Dave's sparkling eyes. "I've got a few more weeks of this, Dave, then my career as a teacher comes to a halt."

"Don't be in such a hurry," Dave said. "The president of the Merchants Association called this morning and asked if we'd consider expanding the project. Waitresses, chambermaids, busboys. The whole nine yards. We might have to add staff just to keep Friendly Faces going."

The all-too-familiar gleam in Dave's eyes was a clear signal that this was another notion he wasn't willing to drop.

"While you're adding staff," Cheryl said, looking him as squarely in the eye as possible from the advantage of her three-inch heels, "find yourself a new teacher, Dave. I'm glad we've got a winner here, but I didn't come all the way to New Orleans to teach manners to people who work with tourists. I've got brochures on hold and an advertising campaign that needs pulling out of the ditch because half my time right now is tied up in these classes. I'm ready to get back to work."

Dave studied her features, his grin frozen in place. "But they love you. You're a natural."

"No. I'm a natural when it comes to planning and organizing publicity campaigns," she said pointedly. "That's why you hired me and that's what I plan to be doing."

She turned back to the clips and gave her words an opportunity to sink in. Dave pulled out a chair and sat, pushing it back from the table far enough to stretch his stubby legs out and prop his feet on the edge of the polished wood. Using his cigar for a pointer, he gestured thoughtfully in her direction.

"You know what, Steadman? You could be right. I'm thinking you're going to be too busy to be doing that kind of grunt work, anyway."

"Too busy?"

"Yeah. Director of publications. I like that title. How about you?"

Cheryl's adrenaline kicked in, but she kept her face expressionless. "Dave, we don't have a director of publications."

He shrugged. "Hey, I'm the executive director of marketing. If I say we need a director of publications, we need a director of publications. Unless you don't like the idea of a promotion and a raise."

"Are you serious?"

"Well, I don't exactly have the boss's blood oath on it yet," Dave admitted. "But with the kind of publicity we've been racking up for him, I think he'd just about kiss my fanny on Jackson Square if I asked him to.

"Of course, it would mean you would have to give up all the special projects work," he added, all seriousness. "No more hobnobbing with talk-show hosts. You'd have to turn all that over to somebody else."

"I'm willing to make the sacrifice," she said wryly, feeling almost giddy with the excitement. If this came through in time, it would be a great little bit of news to feed up to Huntley Steadman with his before-dinner drink a couple of weeks from now. "Thanks, Dave."

He waved off her appreciation. "Thank me when it's official. Besides, I'm just tired of arguing with you. I'll bet that new copywriter won't be so damned disagreeable when I give her such great opportunities."

Cheryl floated on the possibility of a raise and a promotion for the next two hours. Her Friendly Faces class that afternoon was the best yet. Afterward, as she packed up her overhead transparencies and stashed them in her briefcase and straightened the room before leaving for the streetcar stop, her bubble burst.

She hadn't heard from Pete, she suddenly realized. Not today. Not the day before. Not since he took her home Sunday night, leaving her at the front door with a kiss so breathtaking she had forgotten to turn out the light over the aquarium before drifting contentedly into the bedroom. Not since Sunday, when she had tried so hard to keep mushy sentimentality out of her eyes as she looked into his eyes. Not since Sunday, when she had warned herself against even thinking of love in relation to a man who had picked tough guy Humphrey Bogart as his role model.

The night before, she had gone to sleep uneasy but still trying to hide from herself the reason for her unease.

They'd had a wonderful weekend. They had been together almost every waking minute—and most minutes when they weren't awake—since Friday night.

But nobody had said a word about carrying their little weekend fantasy into the real world, Cheryl reminded herself, weaving through the crowds in the Canal Street crosswalk.

Nevertheless, she had expected him to call. Hadn't he been attentive through the first two weeks of class, even before they became lovers? she asked herself. Little gifts, reminders that he was pulling for her? And now that they were lovers, nothing.

The thought came to her as she stepped up into the streetcar. *Maybe you aren't lovers.*

She dropped the coins she had ready to pop into the fare box and fumbled for them. Finding a seat against the window, she stared numbly at the after-work crowds bustling down the sidewalks.

Maybe a weekend together didn't mean the same to him as it meant to her. Maybe he'd satisfied his curiosity about the hard-nosed publicist from the Chamber of Commerce and was ready to move on to new territory. Maybe...

The "maybes" haunted her all the way out to the Tulane campus. By the time she arrived, she had miserably resigned herself to having enjoyed the kind of fling that every woman should experience once. Holding her head high, she tried to effect a stance that would tell the world she wouldn't lose any sleep over Pete Fontenot.

She was so caught up in her efforts to be as nonchalant about Pete as he apparently expected her to be that she almost overlooked the young redhead in the Bayou Taxi jacket looking perplexed and lost in the middle of the campus.

"Sammy?" He swung his head in her direction; his eyes were filled with uncertainty. "You may not remember me," she said. "Cheryl Steadman."

"Oh, hi, Miss Steadman." He stared down at the card in his hand.

"Do you need some help?" she asked, amazed at how old it made her feel to be addressed so formally by someone who was not that much younger than she.

"Well, I have an appointment with a career counselor. Only, I've forgotten which building to go to. Pete brought me out here the first time, and I wasn't paying much attention to where we were going," he admitted.

Cheryl discovered that hearing Pete's name hurt more than it should have for someone who was appropriately sophisticated about weekend flings. She also discovered that she wasn't surprised to learn that Pete had been supportive of Sammy getting into college.

"Come on. I'll show you." She felt like a den mother with a lost Cub Scout as she led him across campus and told him where he could get a campus map. Although Sammy seemed tongue-tied in her presence, Cheryl chatted about everything except what she really wanted to talk about: Pete Fontenot.

Her restraint ran out at the sidewalk leading up to the administration building. "How are things at work?"

Sammy frowned. "Okay."

He wasn't very convincing. "Are you sure?"

"Sure, I'm sure."

He was even less convincing. His ruddy complexion grew even ruddier. A thread of worry wove itself into her consciousness.

"Something's wrong, isn't it?"

"One of our drivers had another...wreck."

A spark of something shamefully like relief flickered in Cheryl's heart. "I'm sorry. Was he badly hurt?"

"He's okay." Sammy seemed to squirm uncomfortably under the interrogation, like a kid caught at something he knew he wasn't supposed to be doing. "He had a concussion, but I think he'll be okay."

"I guess Pete's been pretty worried." She all but held her breath waiting for the answer. Could it be that all her "maybes" were nothing but paranoia, after all? She remembered how concerned Pete had been the last time one of his drivers had been injured—just a couple of weeks ago, wasn't it? Wasn't it likely he hadn't forgotten her at all but had just found himself tied up with other, more pressing problems?

"Yeah. He wasn't even in all day," Sammy admitted.

Cheryl permitted herself a little bit of hope. Pointing out the right room to Sammy, she headed for her accounting class.

Maybe, she thought, he would call as soon as things settled down for him at work.

PETE'S EYES were sandpaper rough. He closed them briefly as he left the stale, stuffy hospital for the cool darkness of the winter evening. Maybe tonight, he thought, he'd get a little sleep. Pete was grateful to be free of one of the burdens hanging over him. Fats was feeling much better, and both his drivers were going home the next day, so he wouldn't have to spend any more time in the hospital.

The company car was parked directly under the golden glow of a lamppost in the hospital parking lot, so Pete could tell long before he arrived at his car that a visitor waited for him. He was sitting on the long, sleek hood of the limo, his feet propped on the sports car blocking its path.

As he drew closer, Pete made out the wiry frame of Kurt Fletcher. His heart started to thud. He'd asked for it, all right. But still he didn't relish the idea of having it out with Fletcher. Gunfight at O.K. Corral might be Fletcher's style, but it wasn't Pete's anymore.

"Heard you're still having problems with clumsy drivers," Fletcher said as Pete approached the cars. "Thought I'd deliver my condolences personally."

"Cut the garbage, Fletcher. I want you off my case and I want you off it now."

Fletcher raised his eyebrows in surprise. "I heard you were ready to deal, partner."

"I am. On my terms."

Fletcher's face curled into a snarl. "You don't have much bargaining power where I come from, Font'not. What terms?"

Pete paused. If Fletcher didn't bite, he'd be right back where he started, struggling with whether or not to bring the police in.

"I don't do business with hoods, Fletcher. You know that. But you and I go way back. I don't forget that." Pete took a long, slow breath. The words came hard. The memories they conjured came even harder. "And if you need help, I'll help. If you've got debts to pay, the money is yours. No questions asked. Just tell me how much. But don't expect to reel me into any of your shady deals just to bail you out of whatever mess you've got yourself into."

Fletcher jumped up from the hood of the car and faced Pete. "I ain't one of your charity cases, old pal."

"Just think about it," Pete said. "Think of it as a loan. Pay me back when you can. We'll work out whatever details make you happy. But I'm not putting my neck on the line to save your butt. And if you give me any more problems, I'll go to the police. I don't operate on your side of the fence. Just remember that."

Fletcher glared at Pete for a moment, then wheeled around and flung open the door of his sports car. Slipping into the seat, he looked up at Pete with a smile.

"Thanks for the offer, old pal. I'll think it over." He revved the engine to life. "By the way, that's quite a dish you're seeing these days."

The words roared in Pete's ears, drowning out even the thunder of Fletcher's sports car as it sped away.

CHAPTER ELEVEN

PETE REELED as reality ate into his consciousness.

Kurt Fletcher knew about Cheryl. Knew enough to realize that she was the most potent weapon he could use against Pete.

Propping clenched fists against the hood of his car, Pete cursed himself for not taking Fletcher's scrawny neck in his hands when he'd had the chance. It was clear Fletcher didn't understand loyalty; perhaps self-interest was the only concept that registered on a mind like his.

Cheryl. Just thinking of someone like Fletcher looking at Cheryl, watching her, letting his thoughts run rampant with the kind of degenerate fantasies that Pete knew must occupy his mind... It made Pete crazy. If the coward hadn't driven off in such a hurry after dropping his bomb, Pete would have pulled him out through the open car window and beaten his sneering face until even his mother wouldn't recognize him.

"What was that all about?"

Pete whirled at the voice, his fist readied for releasing the fury rising up in him. But it was just Tony, who, obviously sensing the fury, stepped back.

"Whoa, pal. What's the problem?"

"What are you doing here?" Pete demanded. In the old days, Tony would have been one of the first people he confided in. Now, he was instantly leery. Was Tony here

as one of the gang from the old neighborhood? Or as a
reporter for the *Times-Picayune?*

"I heard about the wreck. When I couldn't track you
down, I played a hunch that you'd be here." He shoved
his cap back on his forehead to look Pete in the eye.
"Something tells me Fletcher wasn't here to express his
sympathy."

"Why are *you* here?"

Grim exasperation on his face, Tony waved his empty
hands in the air, then pulled back the lapels of his tweed
jacket. "Look, Ma, no recorder. No notebook. Pete, I'm
your friend. That's all."

Pete took a deep breath, trying to quell the impotent
anger he felt toward Fletcher and himself for making
Cheryl vulnerable. "We all used to be friends."

"Don't shut me out because I'm a reporter, Pete."
Tony's words were gruff. "If I'm interviewing you, you'll
know it. I don't use my friends."

Frustrated with his own newborn suspiciousness, Pete
turned away and once more leaned his fists against the
sleek surface of his car. He didn't know what to do. He
couldn't play in Fletcher's league anymore. And in trying
to be Mr. Cool, he might have set Cheryl up. He simply
hadn't been thinking. Damn it!

"Tony, you don't want to get mixed up in this," he
said, straightening and reaching into his pocket for the
keys to the car.

Tony grinned and clapped Pete on the shoulder in one
of the few expressions of warmth either allowed himself.
"I'm sure of that. Why don't you spill it, Pete? Maybe I
can help. Does Fletcher have anything to do with these
accidents?"

Pete hesitated. "Are you the only one who knows that?
Or did somebody put you onto it?"

"I'm a good reporter, pal." They both grinned this time. "So what's his game?"

"He wants a partner on one of his deals." Tony's look was incredulous. "A partner with plenty of discreet transportation."

A short expletive was Tony's only response.

"I don't think you want to know any more than that."

"Why haven't you gone to the police?"

They exchanged a look and Tony nodded. "You're right. Fletcher's co-workers don't play nice when the cops come snooping around."

"Listen, Tony, I appreciate your concern. I really do. But stay clear of this. You don't want to get into it. I'll work it out." Pete unlocked his car door and stared Tony squarely in the eye. The look carried thirty years of understanding. "But I don't want to worry about whether I'm going to drag anybody else I care for under with me."

CHERYL EXAMINED the fresh coat of shell-pink polish on her nails and pushed the redial button on the phone one more time.

It was way past the hour when she usually called it a night, but she was determined to reach Pete before she went to bed. Surely he would be home soon. She had read next week's accounting assignment and started outlining the research paper that would be due before the end of the term. She had cleaned the refrigerator and planned a menu for her father's visit, which was getting closer than she cared to think about. And she had given herself a manicure.

If he didn't answer this time, she told herself as she glanced at the clock over the kitchen sink, she might have to put off her mission until morning.

He answered on the third ring. His voice was sharp. There was nothing friendly or welcoming about it. Cheryl had second thoughts.

"Who is this?" he barked into the momentary silence created by her hesitation.

"This is Cheryl, Pete. Is everything okay?" She decided the news about her possible promotion would have to wait.

Now Pete was the one who created the silence. "Everything's fine."

No apology for his abruptness. And still no welcome in his voice. No desire. No teasing. Not a whit of friendliness. Maybe the host of fears she had built up on the streetcar had been valid, after all, she thought. Maybe the accident had nothing to do with his not calling.

"I ran into Sammy on campus," she said cautiously, a little too formally for someone who had trailed her tongue along his jawline and memorized the exact spot on his back that drew a moan when she raked it gently with her nails. "He told me about the wreck. I called to see if the driver's okay...if I can do anything."

"Thanks. You don't need to do anything," he said brusquely.

She felt as if he'd slapped her. And as if she'd done something wrong without realizing it. "Oh."

"I've had a long day. I think I'll turn in now."

"Wait!" She couldn't let him hang up like this. In just another minute she would say the right words and unlock the mystery of his inhospitable reception. "I...you've had a rough couple of days, Pete. How about if I treat you to lunch tomorrow?"

"I don't think so, Cheryl." Was that a wavering of the firmness in his voice or was it her wishful thinking? "I have a pretty busy day tomorrow. I'll see you around, okay?"

He didn't even wait for an answer. The line went instantly quiet, the stillness broken only by the dull thud of her heart against the wall of her chest.

KURT WATCHED IMPATIENTLY as the baby-faced redhead playfully swatted the toddler's backside and scooted her into the shop with her mother. Kurt chewed on the end of his toothpick and started a slow amble toward the cab parked out front.

Before Sammy opened the cab door, Kurt was beside him.

"Sammy? Sammy Reilly?" He twisted his face into a grin as the young man turned a wide-eyed questioning smile in his direction. *Perfect,* Kurt thought. *Too gullible for words.* "Aren't you Sammy Reilly?"

"Yes, sir."

Kurt clasped the young man's tentatively offered hand as warmly and sincerely as he could manage. Not much handshaking went on in his world. Most people kept their hands in their pockets, wrapped around a pistol for safekeeping.

"Sammy, you don't know me, but I'm Pete's old partner. Kurt Fletcher. We used to own Bayou Taxi together. We've been pals since—" he shook his head as if remembering "—since before we could reach the pedals on a bicycle."

Sammy's face brightened. "Yes, sir. It's nice to meet you, sir."

"Pete and I go way back, Sammy. So I care a lot about my old pal. You can appreciate that, I'm sure. I'd do anything for him."

"Sure. Everybody feels that way about Pete."

Distaste almost marred Kurt's friendly facade. What made Pete Fontenot so damned special, that's what he wanted to know. If Pete hadn't screwed him out of his half of Bayou Taxi, he'd be a millionaire today, too.

"I know that, Sammy," he answered, his expression changing to one of deep concern. "I also know that Pete's having some problems. Some serious problems that have him deeply worried. You know about that, don't you, Sammy?"

Sammy hesitated, a frown creasing his ruddy forehead.

"It's okay, Sammy. You're a friend of Pete's and so am I. We can be frank with each other, don't you think?"

"Y-yes, sir."

"The reason I wanted to talk to you, Sammy, is this. I want to help Pete out of this jam he's in. And I think you can help. Wouldn't you like to help Pete?" He paused while the words sank in.

"I'd do anything I could to help Pete, Mr....uh..."

"Just call me Kurt, Sammy." He put a hand reassuringly on the boy's shoulder. Technically, Sammy might no longer be a boy. But in Kurt's circles, he was still no more than a youngster. He and Pete and Tony had had more street smarts than this kid by the time they hit the double digits. "I have a plan to help Pete out of his jam, and you're just the man to help. And while you're at it, you could pick up a nice chunk of change for you and the—" he gestured toward the shop "—the little family. Set you up real comfortably for your first year of married life. Whaddaya think, Sammy?"

Sammy's eyes were wide. He didn't think to question how Kurt knew so much about him. He could hardly contain his smile. "That sounds wonderful, sir. Kurt."

Kurt wrapped an arm around Sammy's shoulders and squeezed. "That's great, Sammy. I knew you were just the one to talk to, because I know you care just as much about Pete as I do. Why don't we walk around the corner, have a short Sazerac, and I'll explain the deal to you. Just between us, okay?"

"Sure, Kurt."

The tightness in Kurt's gut began to loosen for the first time in more than a month.

PETE'S CODE of fair play was the only thing responsible for Cheryl's presence at the parade of Sparta trailing along Saint Charles Avenue. She realized that now.

She took no delight in the enormous floats drifting by. There were dozens of them, each filled with dozens of masquers—members of the Krewe of Sparta who dressed in costume and footed the bill for all the floats and the trinkets that were thrown to the spectators. The parade was discordant and gaudy and high-spirited. Cheryl saw it only through a mist of misery.

Pete had called to see if she still wanted to go because he had already asked her and it was now the only gentlemanly thing to do. That much was clear to her now as she stood on the sidewalk with only Pete's family for company.

After almost two agonizing weeks of unexplained silence, he had called about the parade. Cheryl had rejoiced. Whatever had kept him away would finally be resolved. He, like her, had found it impossible to stay away. He would look into her eyes and be unable to stop himself from sweeping her into his arms. They would laugh and he would tell her all the inside stories about the Sparta parade that he knew from thirty-plus years of Mardi Gras, and she would once again feel the world opening up before her, vibrant and alive and more fun than the first trip to the circus.

It wasn't unfolding that way at all.

Pete stood stiffly to one side, keeping a careful distance between them, making sure their shoulders never touched and their eyes never met. And Cheryl understood the truth.

He had called because he was a gentleman. Because Bogie would have called. Because he was obligated. Not because he wanted to.

At first, Cheryl let the parade trail by unnoticed. The only thing she could manage to focus on was the lump that had lodged in her throat, threatening to dissolve into tears.

Then, as Pete's family chattered around her, as family friends swept up with big smiles and merry greetings, Cheryl remembered her upbringing.

Composed and smiling, she would enjoy the parade if it killed her. Pete Fontenot would never know that she ached on his account. He would never know that she expected any more out of him than the sullen silence she was getting. She would win the hearts of his plump, smiling mother and his somber, wiry father and the nieces and nephews and brother and sister and in-laws whose names and faces were a jumble. She would be, once again, the ever charming daughter of Huntley and Amanda Steadman.

Pete Fontenot be damned.

"What in the world is that?" she asked brightly as Lou, Pete's younger brother, unfolded a tall stepladder with an orange crate nailed to the top.

He grinned. Pete's grin. Her heart ached. She grinned back.

"You people from Cincinnati don't know much, do you?" he teased as he hoisted the smaller of his sister's two children into the orange crate.

"Cleveland," she corrected, looking up as the youngster giggled happily from her bird's-eye view of the passing parade. "And you're right, we don't know much."

"How in the world can you get through childhood without Mardi Gras?" Angie asked. Her silvery eyes were Pete's without the brooding. "That would be like going through life and never having anybody tell you about Christmas."

Cheryl laughed. Neither Christmas nor Mardi Gras held much magic for her right now. She had gone through twenty-six years without passion and excitement; she hadn't missed it, either. Until now. "I suppose you don't miss it if you don't know it exists," she said, dazzling them with her orthodontist-perfect smile.

"One tip, in honor of your first Mardi Gras," Lou said, pointing toward the passing float. "When they throw the doubloons, don't reach for them. Wait for 'em to hit the pavement, then stomp on 'em. Don't worry about anybody's fingers. Just stomp. It's a cutthroat business. Remember that and you'll be okay."

Everyone laughed, knowing that the battle to take home the worthless prizes was part of the tradition of silliness and unreality that marked Carnival season in New Orleans. Cheryl laughed, too, and joined everyone in reaching for a fistful of plastic necklaces flying through the air in their direction.

Surely, she thought, Pete would notice and remember that she was gutsy and not bad to look at . . . and worth at least one more weekend of lovemaking. That would be enough. If she knew it was the last, she'd pay closer attention. She'd capture every detail and hold it close and it would be hers forever. Every moment of soft pressure from his lips. Every rough brush of day-old whiskers. Every teasing bite that brought her breasts to achingly full attention. Every swelling throb of his silken flesh as she stroked with a skill born not of experience but of—

She shut off the unvoiced thought. Frantically, with just a bit of panic. That was one thought that wouldn't haunt her as the rest of the details did.

The taste of his skin. The heat of his glance.

Let me know just once more, she prayed. *It will be enough. I promise. Just once more and I'll never ask again.*

She turned away, reaching up to grab a strand of yellow plastic beads floating in her direction from one of the masquers on the float. Her fingers closed around the plastic. It felt as phony, as transparently phony, as heartbreakingly phony as the smile on her face and the pact she was making with whatever mystical force was granting wishes this particular day.

One more weekend would never be enough.

But if it was all she could get, Cheryl would take it. And she'd count on her upbringing to see her through the desolation that would follow with the good grace that came with good breeding.

AS THE FLOATS of the Sparta parade trickled slowly by, Pete called himself every foul name he had learned since the day he first heard gutter language. He was grateful for the words, although none of them seemed vile enough just at the moment.

His nephew, sitting on Pete's shoulders, kicked his short, chubby legs excitedly every time trinkets were thrown in his direction. Pete welcomed the punishment.

However, the pint-size running shoes didn't hurt nearly as much as watching Cheryl having a great time without him. From the corner of his eye, he could tell she wasn't even glancing in his direction. She was too busy adding her voice to the throngs that shouted "Throw me something, mister" every time another float passed. She had caught on to the spirit of Mardi Gras quickly. He would never have predicted it the first time he saw her a month ago.

Cheryl was real people.

And he wouldn't see her hurt, no matter how much it was hurting him right now. Granted, he hadn't heard from Fletcher since that night at the hospital. But he now knew better than to assume his onetime partner had found other fish to fry. Fletcher was biding his time. Making him sweat.

In the meantime, Pete hoped, Kurt would also be figuring out that he'd been wrong in assuming Cheryl Steadman was anything more than a one-time conquest.

The thought made Pete's head hurt.

"What's the matter, pal?" Tony's voice plucked Pete out of his reverie. "Losing your touch? You don't have a single valuable souvenir."

Tony had rolled up his cap and shoved it into his back pocket so he could pull his multicolored necklaces over his head. His broad neck was hung with a tangle of bright plastic, like almost everyone else in attendance at the tacky, noisy parade.

"I'm serving a more important function today," Pete said, pointing to the giddy youngster astride his neck.

"Ah, yes. Furniture." Tony looked around. "And escort to the lovely and talented Miss Steadman, I see."

Pete ground his teeth tightly together. Was it his imagination, or did Tony sound a little more than casually interested in Cheryl? "Right."

His clipped response drew a calculating appraisal from Tony. "Looks like she's a big hit with the Fontenot clan. Your mom seems crazy about her."

Cheryl and Elsie Fontenot were sharing a laugh over something.

"Maybe I'll go talk to your mom. I haven't seen her since I started shaving every day," Tony said casually. Too casually, it seemed to Pete.

He watched, on edge, as Tony sidled up to the street corner where Pete's family had huddled. Tony's stocky arms resting along the shoulders of both women linked the trio together as they talked. Pete wondered if he hadn't set himself off a little too far from his family and then wondered why no one had seemed to notice. Cheryl seemed to be providing sufficient entertainment for them this afternoon. At least, sufficient for Tony. They talked. And laughed. Tony bought cotton candy and she ate it, licking the sticky pinkness off her fingers and lips.

Pete looked away. It wouldn't do to watch.

But within minutes, his gaze was drawn once again to the friendly knot of people from whom he had intentionally excluded himself. They were having fun. The way they were supposed to.

And he was kicking himself harder than the preschooler locked around his neck was.

He asked himself why Cheryl hadn't made any attempt to talk to him, pull him into the group. It was bad enough his own mother didn't seem to notice his absence. But he had expected to have to fight to keep Cheryl away from him.

Dreamer, he chided himself bitterly.

Tony slipped a plastic necklace over Cheryl's head. Her sunshine-blond hair was done in a French braid, the way it had been on the night they first made love. Although he had loosened it and let his hands sift through it the way he'd dreamed of, he hadn't fully satisfied his urge. There had been too much else to distract him: the endlessly long expanse of creamy white thigh; the small perfection of her breasts; the triangle of dark gold that kept drawing him closer, tempting him to the sweetest passion he'd ever known.

Now, Pete was sorry he couldn't loosen the braid again. A dozen different shades of sunlight and silver blended temptingly, cinched with a hot-pink ribbon that was little-girl chaste, big-girl taunting. It begged to be pulled loose.

Tony was looking at it, too. Pete couldn't help but notice.

"Come on, Keith," he said suddenly, tugging playfully on the ankle of his rider. "Let's see how your big sister is doing."

"Bet I've got more stuff," Keith piped up.

With as much gregariousness as he could muster, Pete passed off his nephew to Lou, who was standing next to the ladder to make sure it stayed steady. Then he turned to Tony, Angie and Cheryl, who were harmonizing poorly to a high school band's version of "Saints."

"I see you've finished your stint as uncle," Angie teased.

Cheryl turned, her face registering surprise.

"I'm too old to put my neck through that for much longer," Pete said. Easily, he hoped. Casually, so as not to give away the furious beat of his pulse. He realized suddenly that he'd said the words without taking his eyes off Cheryl's face. That wouldn't do. He looked away.

Smiled at Tony. Wanted to growl at him. Warn him that Cheryl's hot-pink ribbons were none of his business.

"Don't be talking ugly about yourself," Tony said cheerfully. "When you talk about getting old, you're taking my name in vain, too, don't forget."

Pete's gaze drifted to Cheryl again. She hadn't spoken. He longed to hear her voice. He wanted her to smile again, the way she had smiled all afternoon while he watched across the yards that had stretched between them like barren, endless miles.

He could think of nothing to call forth that smile, no clever words that would loosen the stiffness that had suddenly overtaken her face. His mind was blank of everything except the thought of kissing her, of taking her in his arms and feeling the thrust of her small, perfect breasts against his chest, burning him.

"Having a good time?" The question was all his mind, weakened with the fever of wanting her, could come up with. His tongue flicked out to moisten his dry lips. He wondered if hers were still sweet from cotton candy.

"Wonderful."

He didn't notice how toneless her voice was. He didn't notice that Tony and Angie had drifted discreetly away, turning their attention back to the parade. All he noticed was that her eyes were troubled. Did her lower lip tremble? He almost reached out to still the tremble with the brush of a fingertip.

Fear held him back.

By now, he was as afraid of his own emotions as he was of anything Kurt Fletcher could do to him. He was in too deep. That much was clear.

Sweeping her long, lithe body once more with eyes that hungered so deeply she felt their touch, Pete turned away and left her standing alone in the crowd.

CHAPTER TWELVE

CALLING FAY had seemed like the thing to do. After all, what did Cheryl know about seduction?

Fay, on the other hand, would have the right instincts. After a decade in New Orleans, Fay seemed to have more than a little of the vamp in her.

But now, with half the contents of her closet strewn across her bed and the other half in a pile on the floor—a pile that Fay had labeled "librarian material"—Cheryl wondered if taking a half day off work and calling Fay had been the right decision.

"You've been living wrong," Fay pronounced, looking doubtfully at the conservatively cut silks and wools and linens. "We don't have a lot to work with here. Let me ask you this. Do you want to be a campy seductress? Or do you want to seriously rattle his cage?"

Sitting cross-legged on the rug, Cheryl stared at Fay from behind her glasses. "Oh, this is dead serious."

Fay opened her mouth to speak, then walked over and pulled Cheryl's glasses off. "Can you see without these?"

"Not on your life." Cheryl grinned, fumbling for the glasses. "But I do have contacts."

"I won't even ask why you wear the glasses all the time."

Shaking her head, Fay looked carefully at the clothes lying around the room. "Okay, you want to rattle his cage. Then we have to keep your ice-queen image intact.

That'll make it even more devastating when you come on to him.''

Fay looked up dubiously. "Are you sure you want to go through with this?"

"Ice queen?" Cheryl ignored the question, a hurt expression on her face.

"You know. Blond. Classy. Blue eyes, pale skin. Always in control. You're the type that drives 'em wild because they always imagine they'll be the ones to break you down."

Cheryl blushed. So that's what had attracted him. "Oh."

As Fay culled a suit skirt and jacket from the floor, Cheryl wondered how much she had missed by being such a loner all her life. Although she had been embarrassed when Fay showed up and pumped her for information about the mystery man she wanted to seduce, Cheryl had actually ended up enjoying the giggly gossip session that had followed her confessions about Pete Fontenot.

Was she sure she wanted to go through with this? Fay's question was a good one. The look in Pete's eyes at the parade yesterday had been, she thought, a dead give-away. He still wanted her; he just didn't want her to know he wanted her. In fact, he'd been downright jealous of the fun he thought she was having with Tony. When she suggested that Tony drive her home to save Pete the trouble, she had thought for a moment that he was going to throw her over his shoulder caveman-style and drag her back to the car.

The notion had its appeal.

And she had ended the day determined to confront Pete Fontenot and let him know he wasn't fooling her for a minute.

Besides, she confessed to herself, her ego needed the consolation. If she could just get the interest he had tried so hard to conceal to surface, her bruised ego could begin to heal.

"This is it," Fay pronounced.

"It's just a suit," Cheryl said skeptically.

"Trust me."

Fay settled into the rocker to finish the last few paragraphs of Tony's story on Pete while Cheryl dressed. The suit was winter white in a soft wool, with charcoal buttons and the same dark piping at the pockets and along the deeply cup lapels of the jacket. A lace-edged silk teddy and cream-colored stockings came first.

"Wow." Fay folded the section of newspaper and put it back on the top of the chest of drawers. "He sounds like the patron saint of the underdog. And he's rich. And not too bad on the eyes. How come you get all the luck and all I get's an optometrist with middle-aged spread?"

"Luck? Lucky is not the label I would put on my relationship with Pete Fontenot so far."

When Cheryl pulled on the skirt, Fay rolled it up at the waist to bring the hemline just to the top of her knee.

"Which blouse?" Cheryl asked as Fay held out the suit jacket.

"No blouse."

"No blouse?"

"Just put on the jacket."

She did. The lacy edge of her camisole peeked out from the V of the jacket. It could have been the neckline of a blouse. It gave just enough coverage that her cleavage wasn't blatantly visible where the lapels came together. And it was just flirty enough to make him wonder, Cheryl realized. Her stomach swirled uneasily.

Next, Fay ordered her to replace the glasses with the contacts. Then Fay retwisted the tight knot of hair at the back of her head, leaving it softly loose as she pinned it back in place. A strand or two floated at her cheek and along the back of her neck. It looked as if it could fall apart any moment.

The only change Fay made in her makeup was to bring a deep vermilion lip gloss out of her own purse. Cheryl's lips gleamed.

Cheryl's highest heels and a pair of prim pearl earrings completed the picture. Fay made her turn slowly in front of the full-length mirror. She didn't look much different than she looked every morning when she went to work. Not enough to put your finger on, but enough. She was not quite naughty but no longer so unrelentingly nice, either.

Still, she would never have had the nerve to face Dave Arnaud looking like this.

"What did you do?" she asked Fay.

"Just think of me as your fairy godmother," Fay said with a smug grin. "Except, if you decide to stay out past midnight, you won't turn into a pumpkin."

"Oh, no," Cheryl said firmly. "He's not getting the full course today. Just the appetizer. Enough of a taste to make it impossible for him to keep up this ridiculous game he's playing."

"Oh, to be a fly on the wall," Fay said longingly. "And to think, all I've got to look forward to is the optometrist."

Fay offered a lift to town, and as they headed to her car, Cheryl stopped cold in her tracks at the top of her stairs.

"Fay? How am I going to know what to say?"

Fay looked up, smiling again at her creation. "Use your instincts."

"I don't have those kinds of instincts," Cheryl protested.

Fay took in the willowy blonde two steps up from her, her vermilion lips settled in a wet pout, her hair looking as if she had just spent two hours tossing on a satin pillowcase.

"Oh, yes, you do. You may not know it yet. But you definitely have those kinds of instincts."

KURT SAT as tall as he could manage between two moose-size thugs in the back of the car. Determined they wouldn't see him squirm, he did his best to square his narrow shoulders and keep his head up. They seemed equally determined to squeeze him between them, to reduce him to a thin, shivery package heading along the Lake Pontchartrain Causeway to who knows where.

From the window of his one roomer, he'd recognized Monteleone's thugs right away. His first impulse had been to climb out the window and down the fire escape and run to... where? That had been the question. Where the hell could you run from Monteleone? Timbuktu wasn't far enough. Especially if it was doubtful you could get across town without getting picked up and dragged back like a squealing pup.

And once they'd seen you scared, it was all over.

He had stayed put, opening the door and inviting them into the dank, gray room. He'd gone cheerfully when they'd asked him to come along for a little ride. He'd swallowed hard as they headed for the causeway over the lake, knowing he could be fish bait before the day was out.

He tried hard to remember the words for a few Hail Marys. He wondered if close would be good enough to do the trick for him. It had been a while since confirmation.

Kurt heaved a sigh when they veered off the causeway and headed away from the water. He swore to himself and whatever Providence was watching over him that he would learn all the words, if he could only be spared from wearing cement shoes tonight.

The single lighted window of the cabin didn't shed much light on the bayou darkened in the late afternoon by Spanish moss and other overgrowth and a sun that was low in the west. Kurt willed his legs to walk steadily across the ground he could not see to a future that was even murkier.

Monteleone sat at a rustic wooden table in the sparsely furnished cabin. Fishnets and poles hung from the pine walls. A mounted fish arched in shimmering blue over the stone mantel. Two faded armchairs sported cushions deeply notched with years of use. He didn't look up when Kurt entered; he was cleaning fish, the shiny blade of his knife flashing.

The two thugs stood by the door and gave Kurt a little shove farther into the room. Monteleone finished filleting the fish he was working on, then tossed it with a slap into a pan of water on one end of the table.

"I had a good day," he commented, expertly slicing the head off the next fish. "Best catch I've had in a while. I'm in a good mood."

He didn't look to be in a good mood. Jowly and tanned, his face was set in the constant sneer of displeasure that kept everyone hopping to please New Orleans's most infamous crime boss. Kurt hoped he was telling the truth. He tried to pull his eyes away from the knife Monteleone handled so deftly.

"I got only one thing spoiling my good mood tonight," he said, still not looking at Kurt. "You know what that is, Fletcher? Sure you do. It's you. You're the only thing spoiling this otherwise perfect day of fishing. Ain't that a shame?''

Kurt opened his mouth to speak, wondering even as he did so whether the words would come out or stick in his dry, tight throat.

Monteleone waved the hand that held the knife to ward off Kurt's words. "Don't talk to me, Fletcher, unless you're gonna tell me when this old pal of yours is coming in on our deal. Can you tell me that, Fletcher?"

Finished at last, Monteleone tossed another fish into the icy water and picked up a stained towel to wipe the blade of his knife.

"It's, uh...one of his drivers is making a run for us this week." His voice sounded thin, reedy. A long silence followed his words.

Monteleone pushed back from the table and propped his feet up, balancing his straight-backed chair on the two back legs. "One of his drivers? One of his *drivers*, Fletcher? One of his drivers ain't good enough. Use the driver if you have to. Set 'im up for a fall, if that's what it'll take to get Fontenot in on this. 'Cause I've got too much stuff coming through this town for one piddling cab driver to handle." He linked his fingers over his belly. "I need Fontenot working for us. I need his fleet behind us or we're going to have a lot of powder sittin' around drawing attention instead of earning money for us. You got that, Fletcher? I need Fontenot."

"I, uh...he's..."

"You've been dragging your feet. And I'm getting fed up. I'm also getting fed up with carrying your debt. If you can't handle this job in time for that big shipment I've got coming in on Fat Tuesday, I'll take care of Fontenot myself. And we'll have to find another way of taking care of what you owe me. That sounds fair, doesn't it?" Monteleone looked over at the two hulking men by the door. "Sounds fair, doesn't it, boys?"

"By Fat Tuesday," Kurt repeated, trying hard not to babble. He felt senseless words bubbling up inside him, excuses and promises that he knew would only irritate the man who now cleaned his nails with the knife. "I can do that. I'll set up the run with his driver this week and we'll . . . yeah, we'll set him up to take a fall. Just like you said. That'll get Fontenot's attention. He's like that. He—"

The knife clicked sharply shut. Kurt knew he'd babbled. He quickly shut his mouth.

"I don't care how you do it. Just do it. By Fat Tuesday. Or the boys here'll take you on a one-way tour of the bayou. Right boys?"

PETE GLANCED at his watch. Half past four. Good. He could send Elaine home soon and shut down the switchboard. No more dodging calls from Captain Anderson.

The man had become a royal pain. He'd somehow seen the two Bayou Taxi accidents as his chance to make a name for himself by linking one of the city's most prominent businessmen to something shady. He obviously didn't have a clue what. But this was Anderson's big chance and he didn't want to blow it, that much was clear.

His snide comments about Pete's start in the gutter finally coming back to haunt him, and his innuendo that the underworld connections who had made Pete's rise possible were now exacting payment had just about earned Anderson a punch in the nose.

Getting the cops off your case, Pete had discovered, could be as impossible as getting rid of a two-bit crook like Fletcher. It didn't help that he half believed everything Anderson said. He *had* come up from the streets. He *had* been Fletcher's business partner. The fact that he had never spent a dime he hadn't earned the hard way didn't count for much right now. The fact that he had bought Fletcher out the minute he realized that his partner wasn't dealing from the top of the deck didn't make his connections to crime any less real.

He'd tried to walk away from his roots. To buy his way out. To buy his parents out. And as many of his friends as possible.

It just hadn't worked.

He thought with remorse of the shabby way he'd treated Cheryl at the parade Sunday. Dragging her down there, all in the name of being a gentleman, only to turn his back on her and ignore her. It didn't excuse him for one minute that he'd only called her because he couldn't last another minute without at least seeing her. Without at least having her near enough that he could hear her voice, watch her move, maybe breathe in the flowery scent of her hair.

Breeding shows, buddy, he chastised himself. *You acted like a jerk. Who could blame her for going off with Tony?*

He had tried to tell himself, as he choked down Cajun fried chicken at his folks' house after the parade, that it had just been a friendly gesture on Tony's part. That Cheryl had done nothing more than grab a welcome opportunity to escape.

It hadn't helped.

Pete stared at the estimates for repainting six cars in his fleet. He needed to make a decision and get the ball rolling on the job. The numbers didn't make much sense to him. He was tempted to tell Elaine to make the decision. The thought that he might be losing his grip on the company's day-to-day operations scared him. Could he lose it all? In spite of his holier-than-thou attitude with Fletcher, could he end up watching it all sink around him?

Thanks to Fletcher's persistence, everything he'd worked for, lost?

He reviewed the numbers on the painting estimates once again, then reached over to buzz Elaine just as she was buzzing him.

"Pete, a Ms. Steadman to see you."

"Tell her I'm in Seattle today, can't you?" he growled.

"Certainly, sir," she said sweetly, a sure sign that she was overruling his foul temper. "I'll send her right in."

"You're fired," he said, almost smiling in spite of himself. Elaine knew him better than he knew himself. And liked him anyway.

"Hold your calls?" she said, her voice all saccharine innocence. "Why, certainly, Mr. Fontenot."

Something about the way Cheryl looked when she walked into his office and, with deliberate care, closed the door behind her, tripped an alarm in Pete's brain. She didn't look like herself. He couldn't put his finger on anything—she was dressed in one of those all-business suits she always wore, hair up, prim and proper. But something wasn't quite right.

"Hello, Pete."

Was her voice a little more sultry than usual? A little more purposefully seductive? *Don't be a fool,* he told himself. That was wishful thinking. If anything she was probably getting ready to lower the boom on him for being such a horse's—

His thoughts came to a halt as Cheryl walked, in what surely must have been slow motion, toward his desk. She captured his eyes with hers, never releasing them as she walked around the edge of his desk, shoved a stack of papers carelessly to one side and slipped herself onto the desk. Nonchalantly, she lifted one long, smooth leg and propped her foot on the arm of his chair. The other leg dangled dangerously close to his thigh. He caught a glimpse of shadowy thigh as her knee-length skirt hiked up ever so slightly, and dared not look any closer.

He felt trapped. Like a wild animal, his first instinct was to run. Also like a wild animal, he found himself frozen to the spot.

"Rough day?"

Her voice was silk against his nerve endings. What was she doing? Something was up; she wasn't acting like Cheryl.

"Not bad." His own voice sounded strained. That was it. Her hair. Usually so severe, so patted-in-place perfect. It was just a little . . . loose. He recalled how it had fluffed softly around her face after they made love. It was like that now. He could have groaned. He looked around for escape, but she was in his path. One false move and her legs would be all over him. He cleared his dry throat.

"You look a little ragged around the edges," she said softly, sympathetically. Her eyes were all tenderness. He allowed himself a sigh of relief as she slipped off his desk, giving him one last glimpse of long, slender thigh as she did so. Instead of moving away, she moved behind him. "Let's see if we can get rid of some of this tension."

Her hands were strong and gentle, kneading the muscles along his neck and shoulders. But she worked in more tension than she worked out. A tapering fingernail grazed his skin as she ran a hand up the back of his neck, then buried it in his hair. A chill shook him.

"You're not relaxing, Pete." She leaned closer to whisper in his ear, a breathy whisper that accompanied the heat of her breasts against the back of his neck. Just the heat of their presence, a hairbreadth away, sent prickles of desire tickling along his back.

He jumped to his feet. If he didn't escape her touch soon, he would be feeling the shock waves of her nearness through his entire body. He would be throwing her down on his desk and slipping that skirt up to her waist and . . .

Or would she be throwing him down? He sucked in a shocked breath as she stepped in front of him to block his path again. Her whole body was now just inches from his. He noticed, for the first time, the hint of lace that flirted temptingly with him from above the lapels of her all-business jacket.

She took his tie in her hands and held on playfully, letting the backs of her hands rest against his chest.

"Now, Pete, you're not going to play hard to get again, are you?"

There was no doubt, now, about the seduction in her voice. She loosened his tie and slipped it slowly from around his neck. She turned her palms to his chest and sought out the hard buds of his nipples.

"Cheryl, I don't think—"

A slender finger over his lips stilled the words. "You don't have to think, Pete."

She unbuttoned the top button of his crisp white dress shirt. He took half a step backward before running into his desk. She moved forward. And then closer. She touched her tongue to the hollow at the base of his throat. He gasped. She laughed softly.

"You know what I'm wondering, Pete?" she whispered, letting her body brush over his.

He couldn't even answer. All the longing he'd tried to squelch for the past two weeks had rushed to the surface. He was hard against her thigh. The sway of her body against his told him she hadn't missed that fact, either.

"I'm wondering if you've ever made love in your office."

He closed his eyes. But the vision of her dark, wet lips just inches from his face remained behind his closed lids. He breathed deeply, but the calming breath turned on him as he inhaled her scent of wildflowers and womanhood.

"Cheryl, if you're trying to..."

"As a matter of fact, I am." One hand played along the side of his neck. The other trailed down his chest and the hard planes of his belly. "I'm doing a pretty good job of it, wouldn't you say?"

Mustering all the strength he had, Pete reached up to still the hand at his neck. "No, I..."

He was too late to capture the other hand. It slid provocatively lower, burning through the pleated front of his trousers. He leaped against her, hot and beyond his control.

She murmured appreciatively. "Oh, yes, I am, Pete."

Giving up his losing battle, Pete reached for her, intending to take the kiss—and more—she had been offering since she walked in the door.

She backed swiftly out of his grasp.

His eyes shot open in surprise.

Her eyes were no longer fuzzy blue. They glistened sharply. Her lazy smile had stretched into a thin, rigid line.

"Not. So. Fast." Each word was a distinct threat that kept him from moving toward her. His arousal died on the harsh edges of her voice.

"I want you, Pete," she announced boldly. "I don't think I've ever done anything to hide that. And I thought you wanted me, too. Until yesterday. I came here today to find out if I was wrong about that. It turns out I wasn't."

The seductive smile returned for just a moment. "I was dead right about that, I'd say."

He opened his mouth to protest, but she bulldozed over the unformed words. "When you're ready to quit playing games and tell me what's on your mind, let me know. Until then, you can wonder every time you walk into this office what it would be like to toss me onto your desk and make love until neither one of us can walk straight."

Cheryl closed Pete's office door firmly behind her. She stopped to smile at his secretary and to compose herself. Then, to finish out the play, she pulled Fay's vermilion lip gloss from her bag and slicked it over her lips one more time, fluffed her hair casually and said goodbye to the wide-eyed woman at the desk.

She smiled all the way home.

CHAPTER THIRTEEN

CHERYL'S SMUGNESS had started to wear off by lunchtime the next day. Hair once again sleeked back smoothly, her lips a subtle shade of pink, a silk scarf tied snugly at her neck, she felt her courage falter.

Had she really acted so brazenly? She closed her eyes to shut out the embarrassing memory. Oh, yes, she definitely had. In fact, the palm of her hand had burned all the way home. The memory of Pete, alive and urgent against her, had seeped beneath her calm exterior. The agitation wasn't entirely unpleasant. At least, as long as her confidence in her seductive powers had remained intact.

But in the cold light of her office, with the realities of printer's deadlines and media callers slowly letting the air out of her balloon, Cheryl wondered. Had she merely made a fool of herself? Or had she ensured that whatever had kept Pete away was now set in concrete and would keep him away for good?

"Hey, Steadman. Got a minute?" Dave bounded through her open door, catching her staring at the blinking green cursor on her computer screen.

"Sure, Dave. What's up?"

"Not much." The grin he could barely hide told her that was far from the truth. "Just wanted to see if the Chamber's new director of publications had time for lunch."

"What? You're kidding."

"Look at this face," he said with mock seriousness. "Do I look like a kidder?"

She jumped up and surprised herself by giving him a big hug of gratitude for going to bat for her. "That's wonderful!"

The hug, from the woman who had always taken care to keep her physical distance before, flustered him. Cheryl suddenly wondered what she had gained for herself in all those years of being Miss Unapproachable to her friends and co-workers and family. She might have made a fool of herself the afternoon before, she told herself, but at least she'd elicited a response.

At least she'd felt alive.

"So how about lunch? I'll go over the details."

"I wish I could, Dave," she said, sincerely meaning it for the first time since she'd started working for him. "But I've got less than an hour before the Friendly Faces class. How about tomorrow?"

"Sure. Let me go ahead and fill you in on a few things right now, though."

Closing the door for privacy, Dave outlined the substantial raise that would come with her new title, as well as the different responsibilities and a special benefits package now that she had moved into the category of administrator.

Then he turned to leave, pausing at her door to turn back with a devilish smile. "Now don't go getting pregnant on me, Steadman."

She laughed good-naturedly, thinking that only Dave could find a way to turn such good news into a sexist poke in the ribs. Then she looked up to see someone standing behind Dave as he opened the door and headed down the hall. Pete. Her head grew suddenly light. Pete! She made a valiant effort not to blush, either at the implications in Dave's remark or because of what had passed between Pete and her the afternoon before.

"You're a dangerous woman behind closed doors," he said, casually walking through the door and closing it once again. He wasn't smiling.

Cheryl's heart began to thud. What if he had come to turn the tables on her? He certainly looked the part of the seducer. His charcoal wool suit was shot through with just a hint of teal, a color picked up in the silk tie half-knotted at his throat. His hair was tousled, his sunglasses hung carelessly from his breast pocket, and his face hadn't seen a razor in more than twenty-four hours.

But then, Pete Fontenot always looked the seducer, didn't he? Whether in an old T-shirt and leather jacket with a pair of jeans saved from the rag heap or in a dinner jacket that hung on him with easy elegance. Pete always looked capable of turning even the most unconcerned heads.

"You should know," she retorted, forcing herself to smile.

His jaw remained rigid. "Yeah. I should know."

She propped herself against the edge of her desk, looking more casual than she felt, and gestured to a chair. He didn't move. She was glad the chair was between them. Was he angry? She couldn't tell.

"What were you trying to prove yesterday, Slick?"

So we're back to "Slick," she thought. If he wasn't angry, he at least had every intention of keeping her at a distance—physically and emotionally, she suspected.

"I think you know very well what I was trying to prove," she said, placing her hands on her hips and daring him to deny it. "I was trying to prove that your shabby treatment of me had nothing to do with how you really feel about me. I think I succeeded.''

He leaned forward, elbows locked, hands gripping the back of the chair between them. ''Yeah. I guess you did.''

''So, did you come down here to tell me what all your game playing is about? Or just to assure yourself that you can be in the same room with me without getting turned on?''

Now he almost grinned. *You can play in his league, after all,* Cheryl told herself. The realization restored the confidence that had been ebbing slightly all morning.

''I came here to tell you to stay away from me.''

The words knocked the air out of her. It was all she could do to keep from crumpling right there in front of him. *So this is the price you pay for feeling alive,* she thought wryly. ''Then you'll have to tell me why. Because I don't believe that's what you really want.''

Pete swore softly. ''You're a tough one. You know that, Slick?''

''No, I'm not, Pete.'' She raised her chin another notch. ''But I'm learning to be.''

The words seemed to take him aback more than all the false bravado she'd thrown at him so far. He shoved his fists into his pants pockets, but not before Cheryl noticed that his knuckles were white with the effort to control his emotions. She was almost sorry for whatever she was putting him through.

But whatever it was, she told herself, it was no worse than what he had put her through during the past two weeks.

''I'm going to give it to you straight. And you'd better be smart enough to pay attention,'' he said harshly. ''I'm in trouble. I've got people from the wrong side of the law breathing down my neck. They wouldn't stop at much to get what they want out of me. Snapping your pretty little neck wouldn't rob them of one minute's sleep. Is that clear enough?''

Cheryl looked at him, puzzled. Whatever she had expected to hear, this wasn't it. This made no sense to her. It was as if someone had suddenly spliced a frame or two from a bad movie into the middle of her life.

"What are you talking about?" she asked incredulously.

"I'm talking about crooks, sweetheart," he said impatiently. "Hoodlums. Organized crime. The bad guys."

She folded her arms across her chest. "Do you really expect me to believe that?"

He tossed back his head and laughed, but there was no humor in the sound. "I guess not. Things like that don't happen to rich kids from Cleveland, do they?"

"Pete, do you really expect me to believe that you want to turn our relationship into a one-night stand because some gangsters are trying to strong-arm you?" She shook her head. "Can't you do a little better than that?"

"Believe what you want. Just keep your mouth shut about this." He pointed a finger at her. "And keep away from me. I won't have you on my conscience. Clear?"

When it was clear she had no intention of answering, he wheeled around and stalked out of her office.

Cheryl operated the rest of the day on automatic pilot. She visited the print shop to view a press proof of a new industry brochure. She taught the Friendly Faces class. And she drafted a memo outlining her proposal for a new format for the Chamber's newsletter.

She carried on with everything she was supposed to be doing, because that was how a Steadman coped. But she didn't believe what Pete had told her; she was more frightened by the thought of her father's visit, scheduled for the next evening, than the gangsters Pete had fabricated to scare her off. The idea was perfectly ludicrous. He'd watched far too many Bogie movies, she told herself.

But if not that, then what? What else would motivate him to throw her out of his life so forcibly, so indisputably?

The question haunted her all the way home, in spite of her efforts to focus on the menu for the dinner party with her father. Huntley Steadman was a connoisseur of great food, a man accustomed to the best, prepared by chefs who were artists in their field. What could Cheryl, with her open-a-box, microwave-it experience, do that would possibly impress him?

With Fay's guidance and the loan of her best New Orleans cookbook, Cheryl had settled on something simple. Cajun barbecued shrimp for an appetizer. Red beans and rice—the poor man's dinner that had been elevated to the status of a New Orleans gourmet specialty—with crisp salad, crusty French bread and pastries she would pick up from Madelaine's at lunchtime tomorrow.

Madelaine's, she thought, hanging on to the back of a wooden streetcar seat to maintain her footing as the contraption clattered to a halt. Madelaine's. Or some other French bakery. Surely there was another one, one that wouldn't be a slap in the face when she walked in the door. For Pete would surely be there—his voice, his eyes, his taste—when she walked in the shop and placed her order with the woman behind the counter.

Fresh pastries from somewhere, she amended her menu as she trudged up the stairs to her apartment. *If he can stand to order me out of his life, I can certainly stand to get on with mine without mooning over him. But Madelaine's . . . Madelaine's can wait awhile.*

Briefcase tucked under her arm, Cheryl fished in her purse for her house key. But when she reached for the door, key outstretched in front of her, the door creaked slowly open.

Astonished to think that she could have walked out that morning without securely locking the door behind her, Cheryl pushed it open wider. She had been preoccupied, certainly; but it wasn't like her to be that scatterbrained. Or scatterbrained at all. A prickle of uncertainty skittered through her.

Everything registered in an instant of slow-motion horror. The slashed couch, its stuffing strewn across the hardwood floor. The shattered pottery. The clock, its steady heartbeat stilled with the impact of crashing to the brick hearth. The aquarium, shattered and spilled, its inhabitants lying motionless on the soggy rug.

With a short, strangled cry, Cheryl dropped her briefcase to the floor with the rest of her life's debris and dashed back through the door.

She stood on the street, so disoriented she could only stare at the colorful plastic beads still hanging from tree limbs, a reminder of the gaiety of the weekend parade. Then she heard the streetcar rumbling in her direction. She moved toward it and jumped on without thinking, without planning. She simply needed to get as far away as possible from the violence.

Cheryl coached herself into composure as the green wooden car headed back toward town. She was past Terpsichore Street when she saw the policeman, leaning against a lamppost and talking to a florist who had stepped out of his shop. She stood, thinking if she got off at the next corner she could run back to him. He would help. He would find the people who had broken into her apartment—mischievous kids, no doubt—and make her feel safe and whole again.

Before she reached the back exit of the streetcar, Pete's words filled her head.

I'm talking about crooks, sweetheart. Hoodlums. Organized crime. The bad guys.

She stopped, a hand flying to her mouth.

Snapping your pretty little neck wouldn't rob them of one minute's sleep.

Cheryl's knees trembled weakly. She sank into a vacant seat and let the streetcar rumble on toward town. Her outrage over the destruction in her apartment turned suddenly to panic.

Could the danger Pete had warned her of, that she had dismissed so flippantly, be real? Had her involvement with Pete unwittingly drawn her into something life threatening? Something that her carefully guarded life in Cleveland hadn't prepared her to imagine, much less handle?

The thought that someone might have made a conscious decision to vandalize her apartment—had picked her with deadly purpose—was much more terrifying than the prospect of someone randomly choosing her place to pick up a VCR or a microwave.

Cheryl wasn't sure, as the streetcar reached the end of the line and she got off, that she could handle knowing someone was after her. That someone might be watching her. No one she knew could handle something like that. No one except Pete.

Her eyes darting constantly in search of any threat, Cheryl dashed through the Quarter without thinking. Busy shops and bustling streets streamed by without capturing her notice as she headed for the quieter residential sections of the Vieux Carré. Without explaining her reasons, even to herself, she rang the bell on the intercom outside Pete's gate. All the while, she watched over her shoulder, alert to a danger she wasn't sure she would recognize if she saw it.

Hadn't she let herself be lulled into thinking that Pete wasn't dangerous?

His voice answering her ring startled her. He'd said he was in trouble. What kind of people did Pete Fontenot know, anyway? Wasn't just showing up here dangerous?

But where else could she go?

"Pete, it's Cheryl. You have to let me in." Her voice wavered, threatened to crack. "Please, they've broken into my house."

Pete's immediate answer was the buzzer admitting her to the courtyard. Cheryl closed the gate carefully, making sure it latched before heading through the garden toward the entrance of Pete's town house. He met her halfway down the stairs, his eyes angry and frightened.

"Are you all right?" He took her by the shoulders, peering deeply into her eyes for a sign that she had been hurt.

She nodded, her breath coming in unsteady gulps. Now that she was here, she felt safe enough to give in to her fear. He pulled her up one step to his level and swept her into his arms. She collapsed against him, almost knocking her glasses off as she buried her face in the crook of his neck.

"Pete, they broke in and tore up everything." The words were torn from her throat, ending in a sob. "The couch was slashed, the fish are dead, the clock. Everything. Why, Pete? Why?"

He held her close, soothing her with a warm hand at her back. She was too preoccupied with her own fear to notice the tightly coiled control he had tensed himself against losing.

"I'm sorry, Cheryl. I'm sorry. I was too late. I wasn't using my head."

He led her into the town house and, still holding her under his arm, poured her a glass of brandy and drew her to the couch. He made her sip the brandy until her trembling began to subside.

"Why, Pete? Who did this?"

He pushed a streak of silver-blond away from her forehead. "Have you called the police?"

She was still so stunned she didn't notice that he hadn't answered her question. "Not yet. I was afraid to stay. I didn't know if they were—" she took a deep, shuddering breath "—still there or not. I didn't know what to do. I just . . . came here."

"That was the right thing to do," he said softly. "I'll call the police. I'll deal with them."

"I can. That's not . . ." A look of fresh dismay crumpled her slowly recovering face. "Oh, Pete! My father! My father's coming tomorrow night. Oh, Pete, what am I going to do? If he hears about this, he'll . . . he'll think I can't take care of myself."

"Don't worry about your father right now," he soothed, taking one hand in his and stroking it calmingly. "We'll take care of your father."

"No, you don't understand," she protested, her blue eyes stormy and dark. "He never has . . . He thinks I shouldn't be here, anyway. Pete, he just thinks I'm being silly, trying to make it on my own. I'm twenty-six and he still thinks I'm just a headstrong kid."

Pete regarded her sympathetically. "You're twenty-six and still trying to prove yourself to Daddy."

She opened her mouth to disagree but realized she couldn't. After a long moment she murmured in quiet despair, "Right. And it looks like I won't be proving anything this time, either."

"Leave that to me, too," he promised. "You'll be ready for your father's visit."

"How? You haven't seen the place, Pete. It's . . ."

He squeezed her hand in his. "Trust me. I'll take care of it."

She nodded numbly. "Okay. But I can handle the police."

"No. I'll do it."

She looked up at the sharpness in his voice. His words from earlier in the day came back to her again. *I'm in trouble.*

"Why did this happen, Pete? What kind of trouble are you in?"

He hesitated, then took her nearly empty brandy snifter and walked to the liquor cabinet and poured another splash of the amber liquid.

"Why, Pete? I think I deserve to know." She took the glass her thrust toward her.

He didn't sit beside her again. He paced to the window, where Spot rubbed against his legs as he stared at the garden below. Absently, he picked the leggy kitten up and held it to his chest as he stared. She knew it wasn't the fountain or the benches or the greenery he saw.

"Kurt Fletcher was my partner," he said at last. "We each owned a cab and started pooling our profits to buy more. We started Bayou Taxi on a shoestring. We weren't rich, but we were—" He laughed softly. "Who am I kidding? By our standards, we were rich."

"What happened?"

"I bought him out. About four years ago."

"Why?"

Spot squirmed out of Pete's hands. "I found out he was skimming money off the top to support his gambling. Later, after he was long gone, I found out he'd been playing with drugs, too."

"What's he got to do with your trouble now?"

Pete turned back to her, as if suddenly realizing he had been speaking to her. "Cheryl, the less you know the better. He's behind it. He decided you'd make a great target, a great way to get me to bend. I'm sorry."

"Was he right?" She walked over to him and looked into his troubled eyes. "Am I a great way to get you to bend?"

The silence stretched out too long, until an answer wasn't necessary.

"Why didn't you just call the police? Tell them what's going on?"

"No!" The word exploded from his lips. "And you can't tell them, either. Siccing the police on these people is like . . . like signing your own death warrant. You don't know the kind of people Fletcher runs with, Cheryl."

"And you do?"

"I grew up on the streets. Remember? I know what I'm talking about. Calling in the police just makes them mad."

"Well, I'm mad, too," she declared firmly. "They've destroyed my home. They've frightened me. They've used me. And if you think I'm going to stand by quietly and not say a word, you're crazy. I didn't grow up on the streets. I grew up in a civilized—"

"Crime isn't civilized." He interrupted her tirade with the simple statement. "Crime doesn't play by your rules, Cheryl. Let me take care of this. My way."

"And if your way doesn't work?"

"It will."

Reluctantly, she let his arguments wear her down. She agreed, after he called the police and arranged to meet them at her apartment, to let Pete do all the talking. No doubt, she told herself, he was right. This was a world she knew nothing about. She had known that from the start and let herself get swept into it, anyway. And what had she gotten for failing to listen to her own good judgment? Mixed up with who knows what kind of people.

And Pete. Did she really know Pete? Did she really *want* to know the kind of man who had once been business partners with someone who could—without losing one minute's sleep—snap her pretty little neck?

She shuddered.

When she walked into her apartment again, behind the police, carefully avoiding the steady hand Pete offered, she steeled herself against the violation she felt. She walked gingerly among the ruins, touching nothing, while Pete and the police officers talked. She answered calmly when one of the officers questioned her and looked on dispassionately as technicians from the crime lab walked in to begin their work.

The part of her that had grown up confident in her safe, secure world had been swept away. She mourned it quietly, in silence.

Mourning for her fairy tale romance with Pete would come later.

She avoided looking at him as he calmly talked with the police, avoided seeing how easily he lied. How easily he dealt with destruction. How complacently he faced violence.

She avoided looking at him, but she couldn't avoid the longing that welled up—a hopefulness timid in the certainty that it would be struck down. His voice was a balm to her nerves. His quiet authority restored some of the peace to her troubled mind, in spite of the logical voice trying to remind her that he was the reason for her troubled mind in the first place. She remembered, without trying, the instant comfort of his arms around her.

When the questions were finished, the crime lab remained behind to finish its work. Fingerprinting. Other procedures she knew nothing of—and didn't want to know.

"It'll be a while before they're finished," Pete said. "Let's go."

"You go," she said. "I'll stay and get started cleaning up. I have a lot to do."

"You can't stay here tonight."

"I don't have anywhere else to stay."

"Stay with me."

She quivered like a plucked violin, every string taut and aching with unreleased music. "I can't, Pete. I thought you wanted me out of your life. So I'll be safe."

She couldn't help the bitterness in the last words.

His gaze faltered, dropped. "It's too late for that."

Wearily, she nodded. He reached out to touch her cheek. "Just stay with me. So I won't worry. I won't . . . You don't have to . . ."

She reached out to touch his cheek. Her heart leaped at the feel of rough stubble there. She felt it against her skin, intoxicating enough to whisk away the residue of everything else that had happened today. To make her aware only of sensations. Not fear or uncertainty or bitterness. Only warmth. The smoothness of skin. The tautness of muscle.

"Yes, we will." She smiled. And remembered her promise. One more weekend. One more night. She hadn't realized, then, how prophetic that might be. One more night with Pete was all she could allow herself. Because a lifetime with a man from Pete's world was too frightening to contemplate.

And any more than one night might make a lifetime without him impossible to face.

THE RAGE in Pete's soul began to subside the moment she stepped back into the living room, carefully covered in a silk, man-tailored sleeping shirt she had brought from home. The creamy fabric, a reflection of the satin paleness of her flesh, began to eat away at his fever for revenge and replace it with a new, far more compelling fever. The drive to end Kurt Fletcher's power to haunt him melted slowly into a compulsion to lose himself in her softness.

Her hair floated around her shoulders, as he always wanted it to, dropping a soft shadow along one side of her face. Her dimple disappeared behind the curtain of corn silk. She stopped in front of him, her rosy nipples casting the faintest of shadows on the front of her shirt.

Raising his hands to her face, he pulled her to him for the tenderest of kisses, weaving his hands through her hair. Her lips were softly pliant, molding to his with a flicker of the tip of her tongue along the edges of his teeth. Her hair sifted through his fingers, liquid moonlight, as cool and smooth as every inch of her inviting body.

Releasing her lips only slightly, he murmured, "Cheryl, I'm sorry. I want you to know how sorry—"

She stilled him with a fleeting kiss, then whispered against his lips. "Sh. I don't want sorry. I want..."

She hesitated. He heard the censored word. It was what he wanted, too, but like Cheryl, he knew it had no place in their future.

"I want you," she finished.

The savage passion that had brought them together the first time was tempered now by the draining emotions of the evening. She eased close to him and he drew her closer still, his arms protective and strong against her back. Her long legs pressed to his, not urgently, but lovingly, savoringly. He allowed himself the luxury of roaming her subtle curves.

When her breathing gave way to soft sighs and gentle moans, he eased loose each button of her nightshirt while he explored the inner sweetness of her mouth. The silk slipped away easily. Her skin glowed in the dim circles cast by the torch lamps. He lifted her and covered the dusky peak of one breast with his mouth. It was hard against his tongue. And soft. Her gentle moans grew more urgent as he teased her breast, bringing it to a taut pucker. She tugged at his clothes, freeing flesh to her touch.

When they both stood, flesh to flesh, their clothes in puddles at their feet, he took her by the hand and led her into the bedroom.

"Are you sure?" His finger followed the curve of her back. Feeling her vulnerability in the tremble of her supple muscles, he felt fear rising in his chest again. "Tonight's been... If you'd rather..."

"I need you tonight."

He heard the vulnerability in her voice, now, saw it in her troubled eyes. And again, heard the words she didn't say. She needed him tonight; it was no longer possible to think of tomorrow nights.

He knew she was right, even though the hunger for more was strong in him. He wanted more than tonight. But he had no right to ask for it, not with such uncertainty hanging over him.

She lay back on the bed, waiting for him, reaching out to draw him close. He perched on the edge of the bed, beyond her reach, and leaned over to kiss her ankles. He nibbled at her instep, inflamed by her surprised gasp and the groan from deep in her throat. His mouth trailed up her smooth, slender calf, and he lifted her leg to whisper a kiss along the back of her knee. She whimpered, then stilled as his kisses continued along her thigh. With gentle fingers, he parted her flesh and set the final fire with his moist, seeking tongue. Her fingers ached toward him, grazing his shoulders, and still he caressed her, teasing at the throbbing bud, pressing his lips to her until her thighs contracted convulsively and she arched to meet him.

He rested his face against the smoothness of her belly, drinking in her warmth, waiting for it to calm the anxiety in his heart. He raised himself above her. Her chest and cheeks were flushed, but the clarity in her blue eyes struck him like a blow. She, too, was counting on their physical nearness to dissipate the emotional gulf created by their fears.

"We're together, Cheryl," he whispered, running a palm over one nipple, still puckered so tightly it seemed to be aching for relief. She moaned weakly in response and clutched him to her breast, as much for comfort, he sensed, as for satisfaction.

Wanting her to be ready, he kissed and teased her nipples until he felt her hands move to his back and urge him toward her. As he thrust into her, slowly, gently, she cried out again and arched against him, urging him to join her as she rode out another crest of pleasure.

He waited, willing himself to enjoy the look of abandon on her face, the tiny sighs that were his name on her lips, before he started to move. With each languorous thrust he dropped another kiss on her lips, her neck, her shoulders, a breast, moving until the sight of her, the taste of her, the scent of her overcame him completely.

AT MIDNIGHT, when her sleep was so deep he felt he could rise without disturbing her, Pete slipped out of bed and went into the living room. Pouring himself a shot of whiskey, he stood by the window, looking out on the placid garden nestled beside the fortress of civilized restraint he had bought for himself. The fortress that was to keep at bay all the evils he had worked so hard to rid himself of. All the evils of poverty.

Evils that no designer furnishings, no carefully landscaped garden, no tailor-made suits could banish.

For the first time in many years, Pete Fontenot cursed the fate that had always left him looking through the glass from the wrong side.

He wondered if he could reach down inside himself and find the courage to take to the streets again. Returning to the law of the streets was the only answer to dealing with someone like Kurt Fletcher. He had enough money now that he wouldn't actually have to get his hands dirty.

But could he do it? Could he really turn his back on what he'd worked so hard to become?

He thought of Cheryl. Her soft flesh, her trusting eyes, the tender heart that had been bruised, first by his treatment of her, then by the reality that Pete Fontenot was not who he pretended to be.

For her sake, he had to do it. He couldn't let her become one of Fletcher's victims. The victim of his own past.

Also for her sake, going back to the laws of the street to handle his problem with Kurt would mean putting her out of his life forever. Irrevocably and unconditionally.

CHAPTER FOURTEEN

PETE WAS SO SHORT-TEMPERED the next morning that Elaine didn't even attempt to tease him into a civil mood. When he barked out the news that he was going out and might be gone a while, her response was a heartfelt, "Good!"

He had called his mother first thing to ask if she had a couple of staff members who could clean up Cheryl's apartment. When Elsie Fontenot learned what had happened, she was horrified and insisted on overseeing the work herself. After making that call, Pete occupied himself with rounding up a new couch and rug and delivering a new aquarium.

Cheryl had left for work nervous that morning, lacking faith that he could deliver an apartment free of signs of vandalism by the time her workday ended. And lacking faith that she could return to the apartment alone, cook dinner and wait patiently for her father's arrival.

"Please come with me," she had pleaded. He had hated the uncertainty in her eyes. An uncertainty he had put there. "Have dinner with us. Just help me through tonight."

He had wanted to protest. Knew he should. But he couldn't deny her one last thing. Didn't he owe her that?

Now, staring at the telephone number he couldn't call, he asked himself if he didn't owe it to her to clear out of her life.

Getting the number hadn't been hard. A few quick stops on the way back to the office from Cheryl's apartment. A carefully placed question, a couple of hands plied with the right amount of dough. Pete remembered exactly how the street operated.

Remembered too well, he chided himself, for someone who's stayed on the right side of the law.

Had everything been moving in this direction all along? Was it fate, after all, that he end up living down to all the expectations for kids like him—kids with no money, no education, no opportunities? Where would this leave him? Belonging nowhere? Still pressing his nose to the leaded-glass window but no closer to getting inside than he'd ever been?

A month ago, he would've said he was on the other side of the window. But now...

He stared at the phone number. A quick call would set it all in motion. The thought roared in his head, struck him suddenly with a blinding headache. He looked down at his hands, remembered Cheryl moving beneath his palm. How could he?

Sitting in on Fletcher's deal would be better than sinking to this, he thought. Except that sitting in on one deal with Fletcher would never be enough. Once Fletcher had him, he had him for good. Whatever he wanted, Pete would be obliged to do or risk being set up for a fall.

This way, he told himself, would be clean and simple. Men like Fletcher died every day without anyone turning a hair over it. Who would notice if Fletcher suddenly disappeared?

Pete picked up the telephone and punched in the number. A woman's voice, thin and sharp with a vaguely exotic accent, crackled across the line. She had to prod him twice before the words he had been given would come out of his dry throat.

"I know where the Pony can get some action tonight." The voice wasn't his. It fell from his lips, but it wasn't his. "Tell him I'll see him at Le Bistro, half past eleven."

"Says who?" she barked, fishing for the final code word.

Pete took a long, deep breath. "The Duke says."

"What'll the Pony look for?"

"I'll be wearing a brown leather jacket. Jeans." *And about a gallon of nervous sweat,* Pete thought bitterly.

CHERYL ENTERED HER APARTMENT warily. In spite of Pete's assurances, she still expected to find ample evidence of the previous night's disaster.

There was none.

"Oh, Pete." She looked around in amazed appreciation. A quick glance at the living room revealed nothing suspicious, nothing out of place. A new rug and a new couch—as nearly like the old as possible—were in position. Every book was in its place, every magazine stacked neatly, every candlestick straight. Two silver-dollar angelfish, three tiger barbs and two black mollies swam amid bright coral in a new aquarium, the same fish in the same quantities she'd had in the old aquarium. He hadn't seen them more than twice, but he had remembered.

"Pete, I can't pay for this," she said, surveying the room, in awe of his ability to make things happen. "Not until my insurance—"

"This only happened because of me," he protested. "It doesn't let me off the hook, but it eases the guilt. Please."

"But…" she faltered, not wanting him to feel guilty but finding it difficult to ignore her independent streak, too.

"No time for buts," he said, taking her briefcase and purse and pointing her toward the kitchen. "We've got cooking to do."

It was the first time he had touched her since they made love the night before. The emotional shield he had constructed was almost palpable, but she was determined it wouldn't be enduring. He had slept most of the night—when he wasn't pacing the living room—rigidly on his side of the bed, taking care not to touch her. He had agreed to come tonight, but she knew him well enough to know that he had agreed only reluctantly.

Her pride should have hurt—would have hurt just a few weeks ago, before old Cheryl and new Cheryl met and agreed to coexist on a neutral territory that felt more and more like home. Old Cheryl would never have gone to the Sparta parade after almost two weeks of silence; new Cheryl had been willing to test him out. Old Cheryl would never have set out to seduce him into revealing his desire for her; new Cheryl had relished the experience. Old Cheryl would never have flown to him in panic the night before.

New Cheryl has pride, she told herself as they pulled ingredients from the refrigerator and cabinets, *but not so much false pride that she lets it get in her way.*

Pete didn't have to love her or even touch her. Just help her through this night. Tomorrow, she could worry about getting on with her life. Tomorrow, she could worry about whether that would be possible without Pete.

They worked companionably, Pete tucking a kitchen towel around his waist and Cheryl tied into a bibbed apron that read Kitchen Closed Due to Illness; I'm Sick of Cooking.

She talked about her promotion and filled him in on the last of the Friendly Faces classes, which had been held that afternoon. He asked polite questions and answered hers about the recovery of his injured drivers. They talked about Sammy and Marie. She told him about Fay. The conversation was neutral and pleasant, allowing each to forget what seethed in their brains.

Cheryl didn't worry about her father. And she almost forgot, for the first time that day, that strangers had ransacked her apartment the day before.

They were sitting on the new couch listening to a Dukes of Dixieland album when the doorbell rang at seven-thirty. Giving the room one more appraising look, Cheryl headed for the door.

Their greetings were formal. Hello. A handshake. No laughter, no welcoming gleam in anyone's eyes. In spite of a thirst for her father's approval that had fueled most of her ambitions and dreams during her twenty-six years, Cheryl conjured a reserve to match Huntley Steadman's. She had mastered the trick long ago and was far better at it, she had always thought, than the slack sons from whom he never withheld approval.

She introduced her father to Pete and thought how different this reunion must seem to him from the hugs-and-kisses joy with which his family had come together before the Sparta parade on Sunday. The two men shook hands and measured each other's worth. They would circle, Cheryl thought, most of the night.

"Fine place you have here, Cheryl," Huntley said, taking precise, clipped strides around the living room while she poured a gin and tonic for him and wine for herself and Pete. "You've definitely got your mother's eye for decorating."

Cheryl knew, as she handed him a frosty glass, that the room looked small, even cramped, to him. The combination living room and dining room would sit quite nicely in their dining room at home. And the knickknacks he weighed with a casual glance were nice collectibles, but beside the priceless antiques and objets d'art strewn so casually through the Steadman home in Cleveland, they must seem little more than garage-sale bargains.

She almost grinned. Not that Huntley Steadman had ever been within ten blocks of a garage sale. Not, come to think of it, that his daughter had ever been to one, either. She made a mental note to ask Fay about a Saturday of garage saling some weekend soon.

"I take it you're a native of the Crescent City, Pete," Huntley said convivially. "Fontenot has the sound of a good local name."

"Yes, I grew up here," Pete said.

"What line is your family in?"

"My parents have a cleaning service."

Pete's words were a subtle challenge, a warning to Huntley Steadman that he wasn't from thoroughbred stock.

Huntley's own impeccable breeding allowed him to receive the news with no noticeable reaction. Only Cheryl knew what to watch for—the flick of his thumb over the smooth surface of his gold wedding ring. It was the only nervous tick that ever gave Huntley away, an all-purpose gesture that served to signal disapproval or impatience or dismay. It was a gesture Cheryl had seen many, many times.

"I'm sure there's a great demand for reliable help in that area," Huntley said, his gaze wandering to the shelf of candle holders. "Are you involved in the family business?"

"No. I run a cab company."

"A cab company. I see." Huntley Steadman's nose was long and straight, perfect for looking down.

"He owns the company," Cheryl inserted.

Huntley's ice-blue eyes grew a little more appreciative. "Is it a large operation?"

Cheryl knew the numbers already. More than two hundred cabs. Fifty limousines. Twenty specialty cars, including a Jaguar and the antique roadster Pete liked best.

Huntley raised his eyebrows to show he was impressed. But not too impressed. "How did you get started, Pete?"

"By rebuilding a piece of junk that was the only transportation I could afford and calling it a cab," Pete said. "That was thirteen years ago."

"A self-made man, I see."

"All of us are, one way or another, Mr. Steadman."

Cheryl watched as her father pondered that, clearly growing interested. She wondered if he ever paused to think about what kind of man he'd made of himself, what kinds of men his sons had made of themselves.

"Interesting observation, Fontenot. Then you don't believe our environment is the ultimate molder of our character?"

"No. No, I don't believe that." As Pete spoke, Cheryl saw the stubborn set of his jaw that she had seen so often. She realized that his belief in the words he was speaking to her father was what had made the difference between the Pete Fontenot she saw tonight and the Pete Fontenot who could have been. "How about you, Mr. Steadman? Are you a self-made man?"

Cheryl tried to hide a grin and reached, without thinking, for the gris-gris Pete had given her. The movement caught his eye; they stared at the tiny flannel pouch that Marie had mixed to give her power over people. She wrapped her fingers tightly around it and Pete winked. She grinned back.

Power over Huntley Steadman, she thought. Not very likely. Still . . .

Huntley swirled his glass in his hand as he considered the question Pete had used to put the attorney on his own witness stand. "Am I a self-made man? In the traditional sense, no. The Steadman family has deep roots in Cleveland. By your definition, however, I suppose I must be, in one way or another, self-made."

The two men stared at each other, the unasked question unnecessary. What kind of man had Huntley Steadman made of himself?

"If you'll excuse me, I'll check on dinner," Cheryl said, grateful that her small apartment meant she wouldn't have to miss a moment of the tentative sparring between the two very different men.

While she put on rice to simmer and prepared a tray of appetizers, the two men backed into more neutral territory. When Huntley brought up the subject of the city's tourist industry, Pete started in on the impact of Cheryl's latest project.

"I've never felt that a good product had to be marketed," Huntley said, spearing a barbecued shrimp from the cut glass tray Cheryl proffered.

"That's an interesting observation from a man who's spent his entire life marketing himself," she said. The tray hit the table a little more loudly than it should have. Huntley glanced up at his daughter. "You just call it something different. Politicking. Playing the game. Meeting the right people in the right places at the right time."

Huntley looked as if he didn't quite know what to make of the unexpected words. "I hardly think it's the same thing."

"Of course it's the same thing," she said, quelling the heated irritation that had welled up in her, striving for the reasoning calm she had learned from her father. "People need to know that Huntley Steadman is the best corporate attorney in Cleveland. So you take the message to the country club and the Rotary and the board of the Opera society. You make sure they hear you and see you and know that you're a force to be reckoned with."

"But tourism...public relations..." Huntley floundered for words.

Cheryl didn't wait for an answer. "Did you know that boosting the tourism and convention trade is seen as the best route to financial stability for this city? And without my efforts, we might not make it? Without my efforts, unemployment might continue to rise? My efforts are the equivalent of hobnobbing at the country club and exchanging educated opinions at the Rotary luncheon."

When Huntley stared at her in silence, Cheryl smiled her best social smile and decided it was time to end her civilized tirade. Her voice turned sweetly pleasant. "On a different scale, of course."

"Of course," Huntley said, taking a long swallow of his gin and tonic. "Well, you've certainly given me plenty to think about. Have, uh, has your mother sent the latest pictures of Kevin's two? I, uh, I have pictures right here, I think, if you haven't seen them."

Breathing deeply to calm her overactive pulse, Cheryl allowed him to change the conversation to his grandchildren while they finished the appetizer. The encounter was now over. Cheryl wondered if she was entertaining her father at her own home for the first and last time. His sons, she was sure, never challenged him so aggressively.

Dinner was a stiff affair, with the simple food obviously not impressing her father in spite of its link to the traditions of the city. In fact, he seemed to perk up only when pressing Pete for more details about his rise from being the owner of one disreputable cab to being the brains behind one of New Orleans's most successful and respected transportation empires.

"I still don't see how it was possible to finance your efforts that quickly," Huntley pressed, clearly wondering if Pete had resorted to making the bulk of his money in a less legitimate way than simply the sweat of his brow.

"It's really quite simple," Pete said, looking Huntley squarely in the eye. "You work sixteen hours a day. You eat peanut butter and jelly for supper and corn flakes for breakfast. You pay less for rent than some people pay their grocer every month. And you don't spend a single penny just because you want to. You spend it because it'll get you where you want to be."

"Were you that sure of where you wanted to be?"

"You have to be that sure. Of where and when."

Huntley looked up at Cheryl sharply, recognition in his eyes as he took in Pete's words. He was remembering, she realized, that he had heard the same words before. From her.

"So you had a timetable? Did you stick to the timetable?"

Pete grinned. "No. I beat it by two years."

"What about setbacks? You must've had setbacks."

Pete's grin evaporated. "Just one. So I worked eighteen-hour days for a while."

Huntley wiped his fingertips delicately on his napkin and pushed back slightly from the table. Then he stared at Pete for a long while; it was his summation stare. Cheryl recognized it; the stare intended to indicate just how seriously he was considering something. A stare intended to give weight to the words that followed. Juries were always quite impressed by Huntley Steadman's summation stare. Most people were, in fact.

This time, however, her father's summation surprised her.

"I'm quite impressed with you, young man. I almost wish my own children had had the gumption to turn themselves into self-made successes, as you have."

Pete returned the long look he had just received. His response was as surprising to Cheryl as her father's stinging statement. "One of your children has, Mr. Steadman."

Huntley looked, at first, confused. Cheryl knew he was searching his mind for what Pete Fontenot could possibly know about Allen and Kevin that he didn't know himself. With a pang of disappointment, Cheryl realized he hadn't overlooked her meager accomplishments in mentioning his own children; he simply hadn't even considered her in measuring their accomplishments. Cheryl was a girl; girls didn't count.

She should have been used to it, but even at twenty-six, it hurt. Even at twenty-six, she would have given almost anything to hear him say he was proud of her. To hear him say to her, as he just had to a man who was virtually a perfect stranger, that he was impressed by her.

"Yes, certainly," Huntley responded, his look of uncertainty changing to guilty surprise as he glanced in Cheryl's direction. "You're right about that. Cheryl was always determined to make her own way."

Although he had never considered that a positive statement before, Cheryl could see that, for the first time, he might be viewing it differently. If he could admire Pete Fontenot's gutsy determination, why not his own daughter's?

"Why don't you tell him about your promotion, Cheryl," Pete suggested, dropping his napkin on the table and rising. "And I'll get the dessert."

Pete insisted that no one left New Orleans without bread pudding and *café brûlot*, a flaming coffee with cinnamon, cloves and liqueurs that he wasn't willing to trust to the hands of a novice. So, reluctantly, Cheryl gave her father the sparse details of her new responsibilities at the Chamber.

"You've done well," Huntley said. "You've done well picking a young man, too. Pete's . . . well, he's not exactly someone you would have met at the country club back home. But I like him."

"Maybe he's better than someone I would have met at the country club," she countered. "Someone like Geoffrey."

Huntley flicked at his ring. "Geoffrey's a good person. I was sorry that didn't work out. But Pete... He's got gumption. A few rough edges, maybe. But gumption."

"I'm glad you like him, Dad." *Now when are you ever going to like me that well?*

"I think he's...ah...rubbing off on you, too." The look in his eyes told her that Huntley wasn't sure if he liked the results or not.

Pete's bread pudding was a hit, and the after-dinner conversation was mellowed by just the right amount of brandy in the *café brûlot*. Updates on the family and a discussion of Mardi Gras experiences filled a respectable hour between the time they left the table and the time Huntley announced he needed his rest for an early meeting the next morning.

Pete insisted on calling for a cab and, when a discreet knock at the door ten minutes later signaled it had arrived, Huntley was suitably pleased when he walked downstairs to a shining silver limousine.

"Why, thank you, Pete. How very considerate of you." Their parting handshake, Cheryl could tell, was firm.

"My pleasure, sir. It's yours for the rest of your visit, if you need it. Just give them your name. I'll tell them to have a limo waiting, courtesy of Bayou Taxi."

Huntley beamed, then turned to Cheryl for their goodbyes. He reached out and patted her on the shoulder. "Thanks for a delightful evening, Cheryl. I'll have to get your mother down here soon so she can see how well you're doing."

Cheryl longed for him to grab her in his arms and hug her. Wasn't that how fathers were supposed to act toward their daughters? she asked herself, knowing it was too much to expect from stiff-necked Huntley Steadman.

But not too much from the new Cheryl, she reminded herself as he turned toward the limo.

"Dad!" Calling out just in time to catch him before he slipped into the car, she closed the distance between them and threw her arms around his neck. "I'm glad you came, Dad."

It was as much intimacy as she could muster this first time out. As she backed away from the car and waved, she knew she had taken a first step that would be easier the next time. Had that been a tear glistening in his eye as he turned toward the limo?

Not very likely, she told herself as the limo purred to the end of the driveway. But then, Steadmans had been known to do some very unlikely things under the influence of New Orleans.

A SELF-MADE MAN. Pete pondered the phrase while he and Cheryl stashed dinner plates in the dishwasher. Had he meant what he said to Huntley Steadman, that everyone was self-made in the sense of choosing his or her own directions? And if he had, how much of what he had done to make himself the man he was today did he want to toss out the window?

In spite of the sparring with Huntley Steadman, he hadn't been able to clear his mind of the rendezvous he had planned. Throughout the evening, he had mentally rehearsed his stop by home to swap his dress slacks and gray tweed jacket for faded leather and denim, a quick-change that would transform him from the businessman who was helping a friend survive a difficult evening to someone who had skated deliberately over the line from the legitimate to the criminal.

He glanced at his watch. Just minutes after ten. If he intended to make his appointment with the Pony, he would have to excuse himself any minute. Casting a glance at Cheryl, he knew he had to take care of Kurt Fletcher. There was no way he would let Kurt reach her again, no way he would let him get off scot-free with what he had done already.

But did he intend to lower himself to Fletcher's level to rid himself of the problem? Was that all he had learned in almost twenty years of fighting to overcome what he was born to? To lash out? To fight lawlessness with lawlessness?

Meeting Huntley Steadman explained a lot to Pete. He was aloof to the point of coolness, yet so socially correct, so amicably proper that no one could accuse him of snobbery. The ramrod up his back was shoved up his psyche, as well, keeping him cautiously distanced from anything and everything that might dirty his fingers. An attorney, Cheryl had said. Mostly corporate work, no doubt. Nothing as messy as divorces or crime.

And this was the man Cheryl had spent her young life trying to emulate in an effort to wrench some emotion from him.

It explained a lot. Her childhood had been rigid and controlled and filled with a prosperity that doubtless hadn't made up for the lack of laughter and hugs and kisses. Even flinging herself into the arms of a father she hadn't seen in months had been an act of courage, a moment of reckless abandon in which she had risked rejection. It was a way of life he couldn't imagine. And it was a way of life she was slowly managing to put behind her. He had seen evidence of that every day they'd been together. She was a different person, in so many ways, from the young woman Huntley Steadman had raised her to be.

And she deserved better than a man who couldn't leave the streets behind him.

The thought startled him. Since when, he asked himself, did he intend to become the man she deserved, anyway?

He looked over at her face, enjoying the relieved relaxation in her eyes. Seeing once again the light dusting of freckles that made him think of innocence and freshness.

Maybe since the first moment he'd looked into that face, he told himself. Maybe it was then that he'd fallen in love with her. It had just taken a month for him to figure it out.

The kitchen clock stared down at him. Ten-fifteen.

"I've got to go," he said as they closed the dishwasher. "Spot's getting hungry for his dinner."

"Oh." The disappointment flitted over her face almost too quickly to see. But he knew her, he realized, well enough to see it anyway. He had a decision to make.

But suddenly, there seemed only one possible decision.

"He asked if you'd come, too."

"He did?"

He leaned over and kissed a freckled cheek. "He certainly did."

WHEN THE DIGITAL CLOCK on Pete's bedside table flicked to eleven-thirty, he reached across to kiss the bare shoulder where her freckles were heaviest.

"I'm disappointed," he said softly, brushing his cheek against her breast on the trip back from her shoulder.

"You are?" Her languorous words told him she didn't believe it for a minute. "Me, too."

His eyes widened. "You are? Why?"

She laughed teasingly, then ran her nails over his smooth jaw. "Because you shaved to meet my father. I like it when you're scratchy."

"You'll just have to wait for morning if you want scratchy." He pulled her closer.

"Now you."

"Now me what?"

"Why are you disappointed?"

"Because I hoped you'd have freckles all over."

She groaned. "All over? Aren't they bad enough already?"

"You may not know this," he said, all seriousness. "But freckles are a known aphrodisiac."

"You have a freckle fetish?" She pulled away and feigned horror. "Pete, how could you let things go this far without telling me you have a freckle fetish?"

"Please don't hold it against me," he pleaded. "It goes back to Mardi Gras, the year was…19-something. A long time ago. While you were still in bobby socks."

"I never wore bobby socks," she protested. "That was before my time."

"See what I mean? It was a long time ago. Probably 1967."

"You've been chasing freckles that long?"

He nodded. "Absolutely. Her name was Shea Darensbourg. She was quite a vixen. There we were—"

The ringing of the telephone interrupted him. He was instantly tense, his heart thudding. It couldn't be the Pony. He hadn't left his name. No one could link him to that call.

Blood racing to his head, Pete reached across her for the telephone.

"Pete?" Sammy's hesitant voice was a welcome relief. "Pete, I'm in big trouble."

CHAPTER FIFTEEN

CHERYL HADN'T REALIZED a police precinct would smell bad. As she sat, stiff and upright on the pockmarked vinyl chair, her eyelids drooped more visibly as each long hour ticked by. She grew accustomed to the smell of bad coffee and cold pizza and humanity that hadn't seen to matters of hygiene for longer than was advisable.

It was hard to believe, as she sat there, that her father spent some of his long days in such an environment.

Cleveland, she thought as she suppressed a yawn, must be different from New Orleans. A thought that seemed instantly, ludicrously self-evident, even to her befuddled brain.

It seemed as if days had passed since she and Pete waved her father off to his hotel in one of Pete's limos. Huntley Steadman would be in serious danger of suffering a coronary if he could see her now; Amanda Steadman would faint dead away.

Pete had spent hours locked up with that glaring captain, who had been summoned from his slumber after the officers in charge listened skeptically to Pete's story. Occasionally, a sound of loud anger erupted from the office where Pete and the captain had disappeared, usually when someone eased through the door with a new supply of coffee.

Cheryl's eyes blurred; she hoped her glasses hid the burning redness she felt. Pete had no doubt been right when he suggested she stay at his place and sleep. But curling up in the cozy warmth of his bed while he sweated it out here hadn't been an option. She wanted to be with him.

"Be reasonable," he had pleaded as he pulled on a pair of jeans. "I'll be there half the night trying to sell them on this story. Maybe all night."

"It doesn't matter," she had protested, dragging herself from between the sheets to dress. "You were there for me when I needed you."

She put a hand on his shoulder and forced him to look into her eyes. "And I think you need me, whether you admit it or not."

Pete hadn't opened his mouth, but she saw the evasiveness in his eyes that was all the confession she needed.

"So," she said, playfully poking a finger at his chest, "I'm along for the ride, whether you like it or not. Besides, we shouldn't be long. All you have to do is spring Sammy."

In spite of everything that had happened, he had grinned. "'Spring Sammy,' huh? You've been watching too much TV, Slick. If all I had to do was plunk down some bail and spring Sammy, we'd still be there forever. The wheels of justice crank pretty slowly when you've been busted for hauling drugs. But it isn't even that simple. I've got to convince them to let him go, free and clear, by laying out this whole business with Fletcher."

"That should simply make it easier," she said logically.

"Right. You haven't met Captain Anderson. He's a real sweetheart. He'd love to nail my butt to the wall."

She had pressed close to him and cupped his jeans-clad rear in her hand. "He'll have to fight me for it first."

He kissed her soundly. "That wouldn't slow him down a bit, Slick."

Covering another poorly stifled yawn, Cheryl looked around the squad room for some sign of a coffee machine. Pete had been right. The wheels of justice weren't exactly spinning along at a rapid clip tonight. But she had meant what she said. She was along for the ride. In the past few days, she had discovered that she had—as her father put it—more gumption than she had dreamed of. And she was ready to use it. Because she liked the person she became when she was around Pete Fontenot.

Just as she was wondering if they would arrest her for vagrancy if she fell asleep and slipped to the floor right here in the lobby of the precinct, the front door opened. Marie whirled in, looking around frantically and heading for the front desk. Cheryl jumped up and grabbed her by the arm.

"Miss Steadman!" Marie was breathless, with only a crocheted shawl to protect her from the early-morning chill of late February. "Oh, thank goodness, Mr. Fontenot must be here."

"He's with the captain right now," she said, putting an arm around Marie's shoulders and leading her to another pitted vinyl chair, whose stuffing was spilling out of a big rip in the seat.

"Then Sammy can go home soon?" Her young face looked hopeful.

"We hope so, Marie."

"Oh, Miss Steadman, what has happened?" Her flawless forehead puckered in a worried frown. "I know Sammy would do nothing wrong. He would rather die than do something to lose Mr. Fontenot's respect. He's a good man, Miss Steadman. I know he is."

Cheryl took a deep breath, wondering if it would be wise to tell the young woman the whole story. That, she decided, should be Pete's decision. "Why don't we go find some coffee," she said, taking Marie by the hand.

"No." Marie shook her head and looked toward the many doors leading out of the station room, as if expecting to see Sammy walk through one and into her arms any minute. "I better wait for Sammy. Do you know what happened, Miss Steadman?"

"I think there was some confusion. Over some drugs. But I'm sure it was all a mistake. I'm sure Pete will get it straightened out." She felt the strongest urge to cross her fingers when she spoke the words. What would she do, she wondered, if Pete couldn't get this mess straightened out?

"Drugs!" Marie almost squealed the words, then stopped to cross herself. Looking around and discovering that her outburst had drawn no attention whatsoever, she nevertheless lowered her voice to a worried whisper. "It couldn't be! Sammy wouldn't have anything to do with drugs. Unless..."

She turned suddenly pale.

"What is it, Marie?"

Tears sprang to the young woman's eyes. "He said if I wouldn't marry him, he would find a way to get plenty of money. Then I wouldn't worry anymore and maybe I'd marry him. What have I done?"

Cheryl comforted the young woman with all the reassurances she could think of and managed to forestall any serious falling of tears. After Marie was calm again, Cheryl distracted her with questions about Shanna.

About an hour after Marie came in, Pete came out of the office, followed by the disgruntled-looking captain. Pete nodded his reassurance to the two women while the captain barked some incomprehensible orders. Cheryl placed a hand on Marie's arm to keep her from rushing toward the two men. Something told her a near hysterical young woman wouldn't do much to improve the captain's mood.

They waited nervously and, about half an hour later, Sammy did, indeed, appear at one of the doors. His head hung down sheepishly, and he hazarded only a quick glance up at Pete before hanging his head again. Cheryl watched as Pete reached out to clap Sammy on the arm and speak words that eased the anguish in the young man's face.

As they walked toward Cheryl and Marie, Cheryl heard the captain snap at their backs, "I want this mess resolved, Fontenot. I expect full cooperation this time, or I'll personally lock you up and throw away the key."

"I understand, Captain."

Marie threw herself into Sammy's arms, oblivious to the fact that Sammy remained stiff. "Sammy! Are you all right?"

"I'm fine." His voice was subdued as they headed out the door toward Pete's car.

Marie's eyes pleaded with him for reassurance. "You didn't do this thing, did you? Make drug deals?"

"Yes." His answer was almost inaudible. "The guy told me it would help Pete. And I could make some money while I was at it."

Pete turned to the young couple again. "It was all a misunderstanding, Sammy. You're not to worry about it right now. I think I can get it all straightened out."

"You wanted to make money so I would marry you," Marie said, now as downcast as Sammy and paying no attention to Pete. "That's it, isn't it?"

"I told you I'd find a way," he mumbled, then looked up at Pete. "But, Pete, the guy said he was a friend of yours. He said you needed help. I didn't even know what he was putting in the car. He just said it would help you. Honest, Pete. That's what he said. If I'd known it was drugs—''

"I know, Sammy. It wasn't your fault."

Marie suddenly stopped in the middle of the parking lot. "We're going to get married."

Everyone turned to her. There was silence in the rosy darkness of early morning.

"I mean it," she said firmly. "Tomorrow. Or the next day. As soon as possible. We're going to get married."

"Oh, no, we're not," Sammy protested, bringing shocked surprise to her face.

"What do you mean? All you talk about for months is getting married. You even start pushing drugs so we can get married. And now you say no?"

His chin jutting out stubbornly, Sammy shoved his hands into his pants pockets. "I'm not having you married to any jailbird. You don't want that kind of father for Shanna."

Cheryl had never seen anyone as thoroughly miserable as Sammy looked at that moment. From what Pete had told her about the couple, all Sammy had wanted for months—besides the pride of being able to call himself a college man—was to become husband and father to Marie and Shanna. And now, when Marie had finally changed her mind and agreed, he no longer felt worthy.

The fiery anger in Marie's dark eyes met the wounded stubbornness in Sammy's hazel eyes. Sammy might be hard-headed but something told Cheryl that his will was no match for Marie's spicy temper.

"You're not a jailbird, Sammy Reilly!" Marie jabbed his chest with her finger. "You're the best person I know. You're gonna do great things. But not without a good woman behind you, making sure you don't get yourself into another mess like this one. Tomorrow, we go get a license.''

"Marie..."

The wavering protest in his voice sounded distinctly like wedding bells to Cheryl. She smiled at Pete, but he wasn't smiling back.

He didn't smile during the entire trip across town to deliver their passengers to Marie's front door. He didn't smile at Marie's insistence on deciding the details of an impromptu wedding later in the week. He didn't smile as she talked about the dress she would wear and whether Shanna was old enough to attend without disrupting the ceremony and whether they would be able to marry in the church on such short notice. He didn't smile as she extended an invitation to the two of them, with Sammy arguing all the way.

And he didn't smile as he drove toward Cheryl's apartment instead of back to the French Quarter. In spite of Cheryl's attempts to find out what had happened during the hours he'd spent locked up with the police captain, Pete had very little to say. Brusquely, he said the captain had been skeptical at first, then livid that he hadn't come to the police with the story in the first place. He had agreed to drop the charges against Sammy, but only if they could bring in Kurt Fletcher on charges that would stick.

"So what happens now?" she asked as he pulled up in the cobblestone driveway, leaving the car running.

"So now I cooperate with the police," he said sharply, reaching across her to open her door. "Why don' you try to get some sleep?"

She stared at him, wondering if it was only her imagination or if he had actually avoided looking her in the eye ince they left the police station.

"Cooperate how?"

"It's late, Cheryl."

"No, it's early. Cooperate how?"

He smiled, a bone-weary smile that said he would have een grateful for one less hassle tonight. He stared over e steering wheel, still not looking at her. "Cheryl, go to ed."

"Are you going to shut me out again? Is that it?"

He said nothing. She waited, listening to the low growl f the engine punctuated by the song of crickets in the arden. She contemplated trying to wait him out but de- ded he would be much more agreeable the next day af- r a little rest. She stepped out of the car.

"I'll see you tomorrow," she said, waiting for his re- ly before she closed the door.

"Good night, Cheryl."

The words sounded much more decisive than a simple ding to the evening, Cheryl thought as she climbed the airs to her apartment. *It's not going to be that easy,* she owed silently, willing a warning in his direction. *I may ot have flashing black eyes, but I'm as stubborn as Ma- e. You're no match for me, Pete Fontenot. Not when ve made up my mind.*

ETE FELT as if every move were being made underwater, battle against the tide. His arms and legs were like lead, s head a thick mass of rubber that held no room for inking clearly or making decisions. The weariness, he lt certain, came more from the stress of the past twenty- ur hours than from his sleepless night.

"How about a drink?" Even Tony's voice seemed to come to him through a fog.

The two friends had been trying to track down Kurt Fletcher all day. Pete knew he had to find Fletcher, and soon, or Sammy's fears of saddling Marie with a husband with a record would be more than pessimism. And Sammy wouldn't be the only one. Captain Anderson had made that more than clear during their discussion the night before.

That had been the worst part, the part Pete couldn't share with anybody. Bile rose up in his throat each time he remembered the distaste in Anderson's eyes, the sneering distaste that came from dirtying one's hands. Dealing with Pete Fontenot had clearly dirtied Anderson's hands. The captain had the playboy entrepreneur all figured out: two-bit hustler from the wrong side of town who'd made his fortune by flouting the law; a low-rent con artist who would now, at last, be discovered and, if Anderson could manage it, exposed.

Anderson had relished the thought. And probably washed his hands as soon as they finished talking, Pete thought bitterly. He'd seen that kind of reaction before. But not in a long time. Not in so long that he'd almost forgotten it. Sometimes, in recent years, he had even wondered if he had only imagined those kinds of looks from people who knew with righteous certainty that they were better than him. He would never wonder again.

"If I had a drink, I'd end up with my face on the desk," he said, dredging up a smile for Tony. Thank goodness for Tony. His old friend had called as soon as he came across the police report on Sammy while working his beat. After he heard the story, he had been at Pete's office in less than half an hour, offering to help.

"I'm a reporter," he had insisted. "Flushing out information is what I do best, Pete. Let me help."

And he had. But so far, all of their contacts had led to nothing but dead ends. Kurt seemed to have vanished from the face of the earth. Everyone clammed up when asked about him. Even flashing a fistful of money hadn't pried open lips that were usually loose when oiled with enough green stuff.

"Why don't you get some sleep. We can work on this again tomorrow."

"Tomorrow. I don't have many tomorrows." He rubbed the back of his neck. "Sammy gets married the day after tomorrow, and I want to be able to give him some kind of assurance before then that he won't have this thing hanging over his head. Besides, Sammy said Fletcher told him that Mardi Gras was the magic day. He said he had something big going on that day. If we're going to nail him, that's when we can do it. But Fat Tuesday is less than a week away."

"One more night won't make any difference," Tony insisted.

Elaine's buzz came at almost the same instant his office door burst open. Cheryl stood in the doorway, her shoulders square in a charcoal herringbone jacket and red silk blouse. The outfit cried no nonsense. So did the look of determination on her face.

"You've been avoiding me all day." Her accusation left no room for denial. "I want to know why."

Tony shifted uncomfortably and looked at Pete with a question on his face. Pete gestured for him to stay where he was.

"I haven't been avoiding you," he said without much conviction. His instructions to Elaine had been clear: screen his calls. The only person he wanted to talk to was

Kurt Fletcher; the one person he absolutely refused to talk to was Cheryl Steadman.

She smiled humorlessly. "I still say you must be a lousy poker player. Tony, can't you teach him to bluff?"

Rising from his seat sounded as impossible to Pete as rising to the bait Cheryl dangled in front of his nose. He didn't have the strength right now. Maybe Tony was right. He'd be better able to handle this tomorrow, after a good night's sleep. Maybe some of their calls would start to pay off by morning, too.

He mustered his last reserve of energy and stood to face her. "Cheryl, I want you out of this. I don't want you within a hundred miles of me when this thing falls into place. Just keep away. If you aren't smart enough to do it for yourself, do it for me."

Deep color seeped into her cheeks. Pete hated himself for talking to her that way, but he had to do something. He was willing to go down fighting if that's what it took to get Fletcher off the streets and Sammy off the hook. He wasn't willing to take Cheryl down with him.

Cheryl straightened the extra half inch it took to bring her eyes level with his. "If I'd been raised on the streets, I'd slap you for a cheap shot like that."

Abruptly, she turned her attention to the reporter, who was fingering the rim of his cap as if oblivious to the drama being played out under his nose.

"Tony, I want to help, except Mr. Macho here doesn't seem to think it's proper for his woman to worry her pretty little head about things like gangsters and drug busts," she said sharply. "You talk some sense into him. First he can't go to the police with the truth. Now he can't come to me. If he won't tell me what's going on, I'll find out other ways."

She turned to leave, but Pete grabbed her by the arm. "You don't know what you're getting into. This isn't Cleveland. This isn't the kind of gentleman's crime your father is used to dealing with. Just stay out of it."

"Don't underestimate me, Pete. I'm not stupid and I'm not a softy."

She wrenched her arm out of his grip and stalked through Elaine's office and out the door.

"That's some woman, Pete," Tony said appreciatively as Pete stared at the empty space where she'd stood, all ice-cold determination.

"She's crazy." He pounded a fist on the door, venting a frustration born of helplessness. Then he turned back to his desk and punched Elaine's number on the interoffice line. "Elaine, get me Dave Arnaud at the Chamber of Commerce. I've got to get her out of the picture, one way or another."

Tony shook his head. "Don't do anything rash, Pete. I don't think she's kidding when she says she's no softy."

"And I'm not kidding when I say she doesn't know the league she's playing in. I won't see her hurt again just because she's too damned stubborn to use her head and listen to me."

A SINGLE PINK ROSE in a porcelain vase waited in the center of Cheryl's desk when she arrived at work the next morning. She circled her desk, staring at the hand-painted piece of delicate china. Only one person would have sent the rose—she had seen too many just like it delivered to her mother—and she was afraid to take the card out of it's silver-embossed envelope.

Her fingers fumbled as she removed the card, still looking at the flower as if it might disappear if she took her eyes off it. The angular handwriting was instantly recognizable, although she realized it had been years since she last saw it.

> Cheryl,
> You've become a fine woman—a self-made woman, perhaps I should say. And I expect that you've only just begun.
>
> Dad

Cheryl sank into her chair and shielded her eyes with a slender hand, struggling for composure. She'd never committed the unpardonable sin of crying at work, and she didn't plan to start now, simply because she'd received a smattering of long-withheld approval from her stiff-necked father.

The few words weren't exactly gushing pride, but they were a start. They were more than she had come to believe Huntley Steadman would ever utter. And it did feel good. Oh, Lord, how good it felt. It swelled up in her chest and left her feeling ready to burst. She savored the only good thing that had happened to her in the past forty-eight hours.

Last night had been sheer misery. Pete's degrading words had haunted her all the way home, followed her into the kitchen while she picked over a salad, crept into bed beside her. They weren't a warming presence. She felt so isolated, so abandoned. She wanted to cry into someone's arms. But the only arms she could imagine giving her comfort were Pete's. And Pete had shoved her out of his life—again—with a vengeance.

Sniffling only slightly, Cheryl replaced her dad's card and set the rose on a corner of her desk, next to the spider plant that reached tendrils of green over the edge of the highly polished pine.

Well, she had outmanuevered Pete Fontenot before and she could do it again, she told herself confidently. As soon as he'd finished playing cops and robbers, she would make sure he understood just how dangerous it was to assume he could push her around. He had underestimated her and—

Her office door crashed open and Dave Arnaud stormed in, gesturing wildly at her with his cigar. Sweet-smelling smoke whirled in the wake of his frantic arm.

"What kind of crazy stuff have you been pulling, Steadman?" The door crashed shut behind him. He walked to her desk and thrust his face close to hers. "I go to bat for you, and you get yourself mixed up in a bunch of crazy business."

"What in the world are you talking about?" She stood, using the inches she had on him to her advantage.

"I heard all about this mess with gangsters and drug busts." His tiny, round eyes glinted with his lightning-flash anger. "I'm not having it, Steadman. We've had too much good publicity lately. I'm not having you get us all balled up in a bunch of bad press. You stay away from Fontenot. You hear me? You stay away."

Understanding suddenly dawned. "Just where did you get your information, Dave?"

"Fontenot called me," he said, his words firm with the conviction of his rightness. "You hear me? You stay out of this mess. Is that clear? Until your promotion goes into effect next month, you work for me. And I'm tellin' you, stay out of it."

"Dave, you don't know what you're talking about," she began, lowering her voice in the hope of bringing him down to a more rational level. Pete's version of the truth had obviously stirred up her boss's volatile temper. "I'm not—"

His cigar crumbled into ashes and tobacco on her desk calendar as he clenched an angry fist. "Don't make excuses. Just do what I'm telling you."

Cheryl placed her hands on her hips and looked him square in the eye. "I'll quit first."

His mouth gaped open. "You'll what?"

"You heard me."

She picked up her briefcase and headed toward her office door. Dave followed her. "Now, wait a minute, Steadman. You've got no reason to go off half-cocked. All I'm saying is—"

"When your temper tantrum is over, call me."

Her heart was in her throat as she marched through the door. *And if he doesn't call?* she chided herself.

The sound of his conciliatory chatter as she walked through the open elevator door relieved some of her fears.

Just wait, she told herself, *until I get my hands on Pete Fontenot.*

PETE RUBBED his burning eyes as he considered the contents of the cabinet. Nothing fit for human consumption, much less nourishment for a growing kitten, he thought as Spot brushed against his shins.

"Baked beans?" He looked down at Spot, who looked up reproachfully. "Getting picky on me, huh? Okay, how about I rustle up some rice. Twenty-three secret herbs and spices? Whisker-lickin' good."

Spot stopped his affectionate rubbing and lay down next to his feeding dishes.

"That settles it. Rice."

Pete took a pan out of the cabinet and started reading the instructions on the back of the box. "Bring to a boil..."

The telephone rang as he was reaching for the measuring cup. Pete stared suspiciously at the instrument on the wall. He would have let it ring if he could have been sure it wasn't Kurt Fletcher on the other end. The prospect of tangling with Cheryl again didn't promise good things for his digestion. He only prayed that hotheaded boss of hers had the good sense to cover up where he'd heard about her involvement in this mess. He'd hated doing it, had hated exposing her to problems at work.

But if it saved her life, it was worth it.

He picked up the telephone, praying for the only good break he'd had all day. Sammy sounded breathless and conspiratorial.

"He called, Pete. That Mr. Fletcher called, just like you said he would. He wants me to meet him on Fat Tuesday. He's got another deal, Pete. What do I do now?"

CHAPTER SIXTEEN

PETE HAD A HUNCH what Captain Anderson would say about Sammy's call from Fletcher, and he was prepared to fight him on it.

Nobody, but nobody was going to get hurt because Pete had been unlucky enough to grow up in the same neighborhood with Kurt Fletcher, unwise enough to throw in with an old friend when it came time to do business. If anybody ended up over a barrel on this, it would be Pete. Not Sammy. Not Cheryl. Pete.

So he had his answer ready when Captain Anderson peered at him skeptically across his tidy but overloaded desk in the police precinct early the next morning.

"Glad to see you're using your head for a change, Fontenot," Anderson snapped. "When Reilly goes out to meet with Fletcher, we'll put a wire on him and—"

"Sammy's not meeting with Fletcher."

The muscles tightened in the tawny face over the uniform. Pete didn't flinch from Anderson's challenging glare.

"What the hell do you mean, the kid's not meeting with Fletcher?" Anderson tapped a cigarette out of its pack and lit it. "Unless you want me to drop a felony rap on the both of you, that kid had damn well better meet Fletcher. Wearing a wire."

Anderson leaned over the desk, punching the air with the red tip of his cigarette. "And we'd damn well better hear what I want to hear on that wire, big man, or you and your little Irish buddy will be setting up housekeeping behind bars.''

''The kid's not meeting with Fletcher,'' Pete repeated, without changing expression or otherwise giving away the fury building in him. ''I'll meet with Fletcher.''

Anderson exploded out of his chair. ''Are you crazy? You must be crazy. Fletcher's dealing with Reilly. You show up and he'll haul out of there so fast all we'll smell is burning rubber.''

''No, he won't,'' Pete insisted quietly. ''It's me he's wanted all along. Sammy was just a decoy, a way to get at me.''

Anderson looked skeptical, but he also looked less inclined to shove his boulder of a fist through Pete's face.

''Sammy's got one cab,'' Pete continued. ''I've got a whole fleet. That's what he's looking for. Why do you think he let Sammy take the fall in the first place? To get to me. Fletcher knows me. He's expecting me there. He knows I won't let Sammy deal with him again.''

Anderson crushed out his cigarette. ''Okay. If that's the case, why didn't he call you last night?''

''Because I've turned him down too many times. He knows I'd do it again, if I was the only one he was hounding. But he knows if it's a choice between sending Sammy or coming myself, I'll be there.''

Anderson smiled, an unpleasant sneer. ''You're a regular fairy godmother, aren't you, Fontenot?''

Pete didn't answer. Any of the answers that came to mind were only likely to stir up Anderson's anger again. He frankly didn't give a damn whether Anderson thought he was a nice guy or not. All he cared about was taking responsibility for his own mess.

"You probably walk little old ladies across the street, too, don't you, Fontenot?"

The taunting tone grated on Pete's nerves. He ground his teeth together and answered Anderson's phony smile with one of his own. "No. I charge 'em for a cab ride, Captain. Remember?"

"Don't be a smart mouth, Fontenot. I'll slap you behind bars right now if you mess with me."

"You've got nothing to hold me on, Anderson. And Sammy is small potatoes. You want Fletcher. You want the big bust on Tuesday." He stood, planting his hands on his hips. "And I'm your best link to Fletcher."

"I've got the kid."

Pete shrugged. "You've talked to Sammy. You really think he can deliver what you want from Fletcher on that tape? Sammy's a good kid. And that's the problem. He's just a kid. Right now, a nervous kid."

For the first time, some of the starch went out of Anderson. He seemed to be considering Pete's words and realizing that the businessman might have a few cards worth dealing with, after all.

"Why should I trust you?" He hurled another challenge at Pete. "Maybe you're already in bed with Fletcher. How do I know?"

The two men glared at each other, neither wanting to give in, neither wanting to give the other the upper hand.

"You don't," Pete stated flatly. "All you've got is my word."

Anderson grunted. "Your word. How much is that worth?"

"What's it worth where you come from, Anderson?" Pete snapped. "I'll bet I could pinpoint your old neighborhood within a few blocks. Not too far from mine, if I had to bet. And I'd also bet, if I had to, that the biggest reason you don't like me is that you know me too well. I'm just like you."

The captain made no move to protest Pete's words.

"You and I made it out, didn't we? We tried to leave it behind us. And neither one of us likes getting our hands dirty again. We don't like to be reminded. That's why I want to be the one to nail Fletcher. And it's why you'd like to nail me. Am I right?"

The silence was a long one. Anderson stared out the glass window into the squad room, where a vagrant had lowered his head to a desk during booking and a clean-cut kid in handcuffs was being escorted out of the interrogation room.

Anderson turned back to face Pete. The sneer had disappeared. "You ever wear a wire, Fontenot?"

CHERYL WASN'T SURE what she was doing in the small chapel, one of less than a dozen people waiting for the quickly arranged wedding to begin. Except that Marie had asked her. Marie, who had also asked if she thought the ecru lace dress she'd bought but never wore for high school graduation would be okay as a wedding dress. Marie, who had asked if anyone would think it was strange that she didn't wear a veil, since they were so expensive. Marie, who had wondered out loud if Shanna was too young to be in the wedding.

Cheryl had, it seemed, become the young woman's confidante and adviser in the past few days, a big sister whose opinion had become sacred. Cheryl smiled. Helping Marie had been the only thing that kept her from dwelling on her heavy heart.

Dave had called, offering apologies and waving a white flag. He even told her to take Monday off to relax. The call had been a relief. She had been more apprehensive than she cared to admit about her high-handed reaction to his high-handed orders. She might not be quite as valuable an employee as she liked to think. So his suggestion that they forget about the whole thing had been welcome.

Cheryl had stayed away from Pete, and it hurt. But it didn't hurt nearly as much as the fact that she was staying away because he had made it perfectly clear that he wanted her to stay away. He was wiping her out of his life.

She battled against the hurt. *I won't think of him now,* she told herself. *I'll concentrate on the wedding, instead.*

She looked up just in time to see Sammy and Pete step out of the side vestibule, resplendent in tuxedos that Cheryl was certain Pete had provided. Sammy looked nervous, shifting from one foot to another. His best man looked like . . . well, like the *best* man, at least to Cheryl's eyes.

Pete's face was set in stone. A slight frown seemed to have formed a permanent crease between his brows. His eyes were cold steel, staring straight ahead. Only once did they stray, searching the crowd. And landing on Cheryl. The eyes softened, then hardened again to tempered metal. Or maybe she had imagined it.

The organ music segued into the wedding march. Reluctantly, Cheryl tore her eyes away from the man who had filled her thoughts so unrelentingly for the past days, the past weeks, the past month.

Shanna toddled down the aisle first, tossing rose petals onto the floor with a less-than-delicate overhand pitch. Cheryl grinned in spite of herself as the chubby girl in the pink flounces went about her task so seriously, with three-year-old concentration that would be lucky to last the length of the short aisle.

Then came Marie. Cheryl almost gasped aloud. The ecru lace dress, left over from an abandoned high school graduation, had once again been abandoned. Marie, who had insisted she wanted a small, no-fuss wedding, floated on a cloud of cream-colored satin and lace. Even through the veil, which drifted ephemerally around her dark beauty, Cheryl was certain she could tell that Marie's eyes were misty. A dream wedding—the kind of wedding she had certainly given up dreaming about the day she discovered a new life growing within her sixteen-year-old body—was coming true for Marie.

And Cheryl had no doubt who was the magician behind the dream come true.

Just imagining Marie's excitement was enough to bring tears to Cheryl's eyes. *Don't be a goose,* she chided herself, blinking rapidly to hold back the welling tears. *You don't cry at weddings. You have never cried at a wedding.*

Wistfully, she watched as Marie took her place beside Sammy in front of an arch of exotic flowers. The small wedding had become as wondrous as the dreams the young couple were bringing to it.

Cheryl had never longed for a big wedding, the kind of elaborate, show-stopping affair she knew her parents would want to stage for their only daughter. A fairy-tale wedding that would cost more than Sammy and Marie would live on for a year. But in these few moments of watching the young couple's dreams come true, dreams of her own were born. Happily-ever-after dreams. Knitting-baby-bootees dreams. Growing-old-together dreams. Hopelessly, hurtfully impossible dreams.

"Dearly beloved, we are gathered here..." The solemn words signaled the beginning of the ceremony.

As she listened to the vows she could barely hear repeated even in the small chapel, Cheryl felt an emptiness. She didn't want the extravaganza her parents wanted for her; she'd never dreamed of a wedding of any kind. But right now, she would have given anything to be the one standing in front of a judge saying the words Marie was whispering more timidly than she'd ever said anything in her life.

She wanted to make those words her own. And as she listened to the words—truly listened—she knew she could repeat each one wholeheartedly. Fervently. Unquestioningly.

Studying Pete's back, Cheryl wondered what was going through his mind as the deep silence of the chapel resonated with the words. Wondered if he had ever longed for that kind of commitment.

Cheryl's wishful thinking suddenly evaporated as she watched Pete pass the ring on to Sammy. He probably bought that, too, she thought bitterly. He could spend his money lavishly, see to it that the people who cared about him had everything their hearts desired. Except the little bit of Pete's heart that would have meant more than all the material things in the world.

Wasn't he just like Huntley and Amanda Steadman in that regard? Didn't he believe that his money could replace running the risk of involvement? Hadn't he been more than willing to write as many checks as it took to set her apartment right again after the break-in? Then he pushed her out of his arms at the first sign of difficulty.

Cheryl's emotions boiled as the ceremony drew to an end and the few spectators headed for the small reception hall behind the chapel. She was so distraught, she was tempted to bypass the reception and go home. Feed her fish. Read her accounting text. Run the dishwasher. Go

o bed early. Anything sounded better than having to face
eople aglow with love and the magic of a wedding.

Anything sounded better than running the risk of
oming face-to-face with Pete Fontenot.

But as she looked around at the sparse crowd, she knew
he couldn't disappoint Marie by not showing up at the
eception. Only family and a neighbor friend from high
chool had been invited to the small wedding, and Cheryl
new that her absence would be conspicuous.

She paused at the door of the reception hall, where a
ristine white cake dominated the lace-covered table in the
enter of the room. Pink punch and nuts and mints and
hose little finger sandwiches that no one liked waited at
a long table to one side.

Planning a quick congratulations to the young couple,
Cheryl headed toward the cluster of people near the cake
able. Everyone was babbling cheerfully; she heard the
unmistakable sound of sniffles coming from the two older
women who must have just become mothers-in-law.
Shanna was giggling gleefully from the arms of one of her
new aunts. And Sammy and Marie stood shyly at the
center of attention, arms linked.

When her time came, she gave both Marie and Sammy
a quick hug and graciously murmured the words she had
earned were appropriate for weddings. But her thoughts
weren't on the young couple, no matter how infectious
their happiness and enthusiasm. Her thoughts were on
Pete, who was not in the group. Her thoughts were on
Pete, who must have decided he would feel as out of place
amid this traditional sentimentality as Cheryl now felt.
Her thoughts—angry and longing, bitter and hopeful,
vengeful and forgiving—were on Pete.

She longed to see him up close and prayed he had decided to make his exit before the reception. She hungered

to look into his eyes. Maybe, just maybe, they would re
flect her own telltale emptiness. Maybe they would ligh
up in pleasure or darken with desire. She ached to breathe
in the essence of him, the smell of skin and soap that she
would know anywhere as Pete.

When she turned around to find herself face-to-face
with him, the closeness she had longed for so intensely was
so overwhelming she felt weak. She felt vulnerable.

In self-defense against her own instant vulnerability
Cheryl's anger flared. Anger at herself and at Pete for hi
rejection.

"Quite a display of generosity," she sniped quietly
surprising and appalling herself with the petty words.

He didn't answer, but he didn't move away, either. Hi
unruffled cool agitated her even more. How dare he stand
there, as unperturbed as if he were meeting her for th
first time, while she was a churning bundle of nerves
fighting not to relive every moment in his arms. She
wanted to lash out. To make him feel as small and a
bruised as she felt.

"Tuxedos. A fancy wedding gown. I'll bet everything
here came right out of your pocket, didn't it, Mr
Fontenot?"

She expected that cocksure ghost of a grin, the one he
always used when he wanted to rub her nose in his don't
give-a-damn attitude. But his face remained rigid. Not one
millimeter of emotion crept into his granite eyes.

"Your class is slipping, Slick. Huntley wouldn't be a
proud papa right now."

"*My* class isn't in question," she retorted haughtily.

He turned, abruptly. Fury rose in Cheryl's chest
choking the breath out of her lungs. She was so tired o
the breezy way he shut her out. She took a step in hi
direction and grabbed his sleeve.

"Don't you walk away until I've had my say," she ordered, surprised at her ability to keep her voice low in consideration of the celebration.

"I don't have to stand here and listen to you tell me I'm not good enough to tie your shoes," he spat back. For the first time, she saw hurt in his eyes. Had it been there before? Or had she just now noticed it? "That's what I've been telling you all along. Now just—"

"I know," she jumped in, uncertain she could bear hearing the words from his lips one more time. "Just get out of your life. Leave you alone. Believe me, I'll do just that. But not until you promise to stay out of my life. And that includes sneaking around behind my back to talk to my boss."

Once again, she caught a fleeting glimpse of some emotion he quickly took pains to hide. Dismay? Embarrassment at being caught? Regret?

Her own wounded emotions bulldozed over any compunction she might have at wounding Pete Fontenot.

"I don't sneak."

"Is that your best defense for having the gall to throw a monkey wrench in my career?"

"Sorry for the inconvenience. I thought it might be worth it if it saved your stubborn hide. Guess I was wrong."

He stalked off again. This time, she let him go.

PETE WANTED TO CRY. He couldn't remember the last time he'd cried. Maybe when his grandmother died, but he didn't think he'd still been indulging in such babyish behavior at fourteen. Maybe it had been his ninth Christmas, when Santa brought Tony and Kurt shiny new bicycles and left a new winter coat under the tree for him. By New Year's Day, he'd "found" a bike of his own, leaning against a tree miles from his neighborhood. He had pedaled furiously all the way home, his heart racing frantically, sweating as much from his fear that someone was chasing him as from his exertion.

No, he probably hadn't cried then, either.

But he felt like crying now. Instead, he gulped a cup of punch, realizing only after that it hadn't been spiked. He set the cup down in disgust. It wasn't the wedding making him so emotional, either, although he did feel a kind of pride in helping the young couple give their life together a more special start than five minutes in front of a justice of the peace. The innocent joy in their faces had put a little catch in his throat, just for a moment when he'd watched them turn to face each other and kiss for the first time as husband and wife.

He wasn't feeling sentimental about the new Reilly family. He was feeling forlorn. Forlorn and lonely, as if all the years he'd been striving so hard had been wasted. Because he was having to throw away the one thing he'd wanted to earn with his hard-won acceptance.

Cheryl's face haunted him. He could see the hurt in her eyes, no matter how hard she tried to hide it with indignant anger. He had lost her forever, he thought as he cheered with the rest of the small crowd while the bride and groom fed each other wedding cake. As he rightly should have lost her. It was the only way.

Wasn't it?

The square of sugary cake that was handed to him moments later stuck in his throat, a dry lump that he had to fight to swallow. He looked up in time to see Cheryl take a bite of the cake on her plate. She swallowed hard, then discreetly placed her dish on the table.

Wasn't it the only way? The only way to make sure she was safe? Didn't he owe her that much?

He wanted to call out to her, to stop her any way he could when he saw her slipping quietly out the door a few minutes later. He wanted to, but knew it wouldn't be fair.

CHERYL STUDIED HER CLOSET, trying once again to focus on what she could fold up and stuff into her canvas bag that would be the most versatile for a couple of days. But she couldn't. Logic escaped her for the moment, had abandoned her completely in the wake of her warring emotions.

"You're running away," Fay said dryly, stretching her short legs in front of her and slouching in the cushions of the rocking chair in the corner of Cheryl's bedroom.

"I am not running away," Cheryl said decisively, grabbing a royal-blue jacket that she could wear with both pairs of pants she had decided to pack. Couldn't she? Or would it clash with the cranberry sweater? "I am getting away. There's a difference."

Fay snorted, unladylike and unconvinced. "Going to the Bahamas is getting away. Making a mad dash for home at the last minute is running away."

Home. Cheryl slumped on the corner of her bed. She must be nuts. Was she really crawling back to Cleveland just to get away from her first Mardi Gras, which she had counted on spending with Pete? Did she really expect to lose the pain in her heart by putting 850 miles between her and the reason for her pain?

Never mind. The ticket was reserved. She was almost packed. The only detail that remained was to telephone her family and let them know she was coming for a visit.

A visit, less than a week after she saw her Dad, and almost a year since her last visit to Cleveland. Would it seem as odd to them as it did to her? Would she feel as out of place as she had the last time?

Her instincts told her she would feel even more out of place. In spite of what Pete said about her not belonging in his world, knowing him had changed her. The placid, pristine world of her parents' two-story Tudor would now seem as confining and as dull as a prison.

New Orleans, on the other hand, hummed with life. Cheryl had learned she, too, could hum with the vitality that came from living. But not without Pete Fontenot. Not quite yet.

"Why don't you just bring all this stuff out to my place on the lake?" Fay sat forward. "We'll come in for a few parades, drown ourselves in Cajun Bloody Marys, and—"

"No!" The word came out more harshly than she intended. She looked over at her friend apologetically. "I'm sorry. I just think I need to . . . get away."

"Let's think this through, Cheryl." Fay set her accountant's mind in motion. "He says he wants to keep you out of the way to protect you. Maybe that's what he means. Maybe, once all this is over, he'll . . ."

Cheryl turned off the rational arguments she didn't want to hear. She didn't want the encouragement. She didn't want the false hope. She had refused to let her own mind indulge in such fantasies, and she certainly didn't need Fay's encouragement to live in a dreamworld.

". . . doesn't that make sense?"

"I think I'd better call my parents now."

"You weren't even listening to me, were you?"

Cheryl managed a weak smile for her friend. "Fay, I've heard it all. Anything you can say has been playing through my mind for days now. But no matter how you add it up, the bottom line is that Pete Fontenot wants me out of his life. So I'm going to oblige him."

"You don't believe everything a man tells you, do you?"

Picking up the telephone, Cheryl dialed the familiar number. "I'm not that dumb," she replied, trying to convince Fay with another smile that she wasn't sneaking out of town to sulk.

"I'm not so sure."

After three rings, Huntley Steadman's voice came on the telephone line. Steadying herself, Cheryl wished it had been her mother. Good old unquestioning Mother, who wouldn't be nearly as likely as her father to think it odd that she was flying home unexpectedly.

"Dad, it's Cheryl."

"What a nice surprise." Still the same formal voice, but was there perhaps a hint of warmth that she'd never detected before?

"Thanks for the rose." She felt awkward mentioning the token of affection, an unexpected gift for an unexpected reason. Too unlike the Steadman family to be an easy topic for conversation. "It's on the mantel. It . . . I was happy that you think I'm turning out okay."

Huntley's gruff dismissal also sounded uncharacteristically awkward. She decided to let them both off the hook and change the subject quickly. "I'm . . . uh . . . thinking of coming home for a visit. Flying up tomorrow morning. Unless you've got something planned, that is?"

"Well, no," he said, clearly surprised at the news. "What time will you arrive?"

She gave him the details of the flight, but she could sense the wheels turning in his mind as he absently took down the information.

"What's the occasion?" This time, she was certain an uncharacteristic warmth crept into his voice. "It's not like you'd qualify as a frequent flier based on your trips home.''

She tried hard to keep the hesitation out of her voice. But the man who had taught her the trick to the social lie wasn't likely to be fooled, she knew. "I just thought it was time."

"Isn't this Mardi Gras weekend down there? I thought you and your young man had plans."

She hesitated too long. And tried to cover for it too nonchalantly. "It is. But I'm just tired of the crowds. It's such a circus here, with all the tourists."

She could picture him flicking his thumb against his wedding ring, speculating on her motives.

"That's too bad. I liked your young man. He's come a long way, it seemed to me. Has a lot to be proud of."

But was he? The look in Pete's eyes when he'd said he wasn't good enough to tie her shoes popped into her head. She had questioned his class. And instead of coming after her with a counterattack, he had folded at her words. This struggle she was having with Pete was about more than his fears for her life. It was about his own insecurities. Insecurities rooted in his childhood.

Surely, she told herself, *you can identify with that*.

"You're right, Dad. And I like him, too."

"Then shouldn't you stay there with him?"

The advice stunned her. "I don't think so, Dad."

"Cheryl," Huntley started firmly, in the same voice she remembered from her childhood, "I've never known you to run away from anything. You're not going to start now, are you?"

CHAPTER SEVENTEEN

CHERYL WRAPPED HER ARM around a street sign on a corner of Saint Charles Avenue and held on for dear life.

Men dressed in bikinis, their hairy beer bellies exposed to the world, women dressed in gorilla suits, an entire family costumed as the parts of a bacon, lettuce and tomato sandwich, college students in cheap paper masks and others in costumes that cost more than Cheryl's monthly rent streamed by. Some raised cups of beer in toasts to anything and everything. Some offered Cheryl refreshments from wineskins draped around their necks and drags on hand-rolled cigarettes whose greatest danger wasn't nicotine. They all blew on kazoos and swirled metallic-sounding noisemakers in the air, adding to the din of voices and laughter.

In all her days, Cheryl had never seen such merrymaking as had taken over the streets of New Orleans on Mardi Gras—Fat Tuesday, the climax of the Carnival season in New Orleans.

Fay wasn't missing out on one iota of the merrymaking, either.

Although it was still two hours until noon, Fay had already graduated from the orange juice and champagne that had started their morning to tall plastic glasses of almost warm, foamy beer being sold by a bar a half block away from the corner Cheryl had carefully chosen for their vantage point.

A vantage point that would let her spot Pete Fontenot instantly when he passed by in the trail of the Half-Fast Marching Parade, which he followed faithfully every year.

She was through running away. Huntley's words had jarred her into that decision. She knew Pete loved her. Even if he hadn't said the words, she had seen it in his eyes. She had felt it in his touch. He could say all day that it was for her own good that he wanted her out of his life. But Cheryl knew the truth: he was up to something that he wanted to shield her from.

He would just have to learn that it wasn't that easy to manipulate Cheryl Steadman.

So here she stood, stuck in the gauzy pants and bare midriff of this ridiculous harem girl getup Fay had conned her into buying. Fay was waving her feather boa under the nose of every respectable-looking male who passed their corner, batting the inch-long fake lashes that went with her Mae West getup and undulating the foam rubber padding that distorted her petite body. Cheryl had to admit, it was fun just watching her.

But it was the anticipation of crashing back into Pete's life this morning that had raised her spirits. She felt better than she had in a week, back in control and exhilarated to be taking a risk. A risk she hoped she could make pay off.

She squeezed the gris-gris resting against her breast. It had worked before; maybe it would work again.

The sound of music—real music, not the playful imitation of kazoos and party noisemakers—was her first signal that the Half-Fast Marching Parade was heading down the street. Tradition was that the band, made up of whatever well-known jazz musicians were in town for the revelry, started at the bar of the Commander's Palace in the Garden District by daybreak on Fat Tuesday and headed for the French Quarter on foot. Tradition also held that they seldom completed the trip because they made a stop at every bar along the way.

And here they came.

"Fay, this is it." She grabbed Fay's arm and pointed toward the white banner draped in front of the crowd of marching musicians. Fay turned instantly serious, joining Cheryl in straining her eyes for a sight of the man she'd only seen in the newspaper when she read Tony's story on the Friendly Faces project.

The marching musicians trailed by slowly, revving up the crowd with a spirited rendition of "Saints." Cheryl and Fay struggled to keep their front-row status amid the pushing, shoving, less-than-orderly crowds of rowdy, friendly partyers.

"What's his costume?" Fay leaned close to ask as they scanned the people passing by along the street.

Cheryl tried desperately to study every face in the knot of people coming up behind the band. It was harder than she'd thought. "I don't know."

Fay turned to her, a stunned expression on her heavily made-up face. "You don't know? What if he's wearing a mask?"

"A mask?"

Fay groaned. "A mask. This is Mardi Gras, remember? We're all in costume. He's not exactly going to waltz down the street in his jeans and a T-shirt."

"Then come on." Cheryl took Fay by the hand and dragged her into the middle of the crowd of informal marchers the band had collected along the way.

In seconds, they were part of that crowd, swept along the street to the cheers of the passersby, who would now hold their spots and wait for the twenty-plus floats in the Rex parade and the hundreds of floats in the truck parades scheduled before the evening's grand finale, the Comus parade.

Fay whooped and started to strut in time to the brassy music ahead of them. "Now this is what I call a party."

"Just don't forget why we're here," Cheryl reminded her, looking through the knot of people for that familiar shock of unruly, sandy hair. He was here. She knew that with a certainty. He was always here; he'd told her that more than once. And although the magnitude of the crowds had overwhelmed Cheryl at first, it hadn't dampened her determination to find him.

Then, and only then, would she really give herself over to the spirit of the day.

They marched for several blocks, weaving through the knot of marchers, searching the faces that weren't hidden by masks, appraising heads of hair, judging shoulders, hoping for some hint that would give Pete away. She thought once she saw a head of curly dark hair under a tweedy cap like the one Tony always wore, but by the time she worked her way to the edge of the crowd where she had seen it, it had disappeared.

Her hopes perked up as the band started one of its detours into a bar along Saint Charles Avenue. If everyone crowded into one place and simply stood still for a few minutes, maybe she would have an opportunity to spot him.

As she followed the flow of people, a hand closed over the filmy gauze of the upper sleeve of her costume. Instinctively, she jerked away and turned in the direction of the unyielding grip.

"What the hell are you doing here?" She looked up into a pair of steely gray eyes peeking out from behind the black mask of a South American gaucho, complete with silver belt and full, bright-colored pants tucked into boots.

"You look wonderful," she said, smiling into those eyes, which certainly weren't smiling at her. "But do you suppose you could loosen the death grip just a tad?"

He eased his hold on her arm. "Doesn't anything I say get through to you?"

"It's Mardi Gras," she said cheerfully, tweaking the hat strap that dangled in front of his neck. "You don't look like you're having much fun, Señor Fontenot."

It was true. His jaw was tense. His lips were stretched into a tight, thin line, and the lines over his forehead were deeply etched.

"I'm not," he snapped. "And the last thing I need is one more thing to worry about."

"Pete, you don't have to worry about me. I mean that. I love you and I want to be with you, and I came here to let you know that nothing you can say is going to keep me out of your life. Because I don't believe that's what you want." Looking deeply into his eyes to make sure he couldn't mistake the seriousness of what she said, she placed a hand on his chest. "But you don't have to... Say, what's that under your shirt?"

Pete grabbed her hand and gripped it tightly, unwilling to let her continue the exploration. He turned to Tony. "Can you do something with this woman, Tony? I've got to split in—" he looked down at his watch "—ten minutes. And if this bullheaded woman decides to follow me, I may kill her myself."

Tony grinned. "I don't know if I can handle her, Pete. If you can't, who can?"

"Oh, my gosh!" Awareness finally dawned as Cheryl kept her eyes glued to the spot under his shirt where she had felt a fine ridge running along the compact muscles of his chest. "You're wearing a wire! That's it, isn't it? Pete, what's going—"

"Could you keep quiet?" He looked around nervously. "And be a good girl? Just once? That's all I ask. Just once?"

"Pete, what's going on here?" she whispered, wondering who he was looking for in this crowd of strangers. "Where are you going in ten minutes?"

"If I tell you, will you keep your mouth shut and stay out of my hair?"

Anger flashed in her eyes. "I might. But if you don't tell me, I'll follow you until you do."

"See what I mean?" Tony said, laughter in his eyes. "I don't stand a chance."

Pete studied her, then looked over her shoulder at the tiny vamp who was watching everything, wide-eyed. "Who's that?"

"That's Fay. She's with me."

"I can see that much. Can you tell her to close her ears? Is that too much to ask?"

Fay leaned forward and grinned provocatively. "I'm too busy drinking to listen," she assured him. Then she whisked her boa under Tony's nose and snaked her arm through his. "At least, I would be if your friend would join me at the bar."

Tony shrugged as if to say he was helpless to resist, and the two shouldered their way through the crowd. Pete was left to contend with Cheryl, who had quickly become as tense as he had been all along.

"What kind of detective games are you playing, Pete?" she demanded, now desperately wishing she was wearing something a little more commanding of respect than the sexy harem pants and the sequined halter that left her flat midriff covered only with lavender gauze.

"This is no game, Cheryl. You ought to know that," he answered harshly.

"You're going to do something dangerous, aren't you?" Her heart thudded painfully. What if something happened to him? Just when she had found the courage to plow her way boldly into his life, what if something happened to him?

He didn't answer her question. He didn't have to. "It'll be more dangerous if I'm worrying about you instead of what I'm supposed to be doing."

The blood drained from her face. She cupped her hand to the side of his face, rough with a day's growth of stubble. "I understand. You don't have to worry about me, Pete. Just don't leave me in the dark. That's all I ask."

After a long hesitation, he told her about the plan for a meeting with Fletcher at a warehouse less than a mile away. Pete had a limo waiting on a street off the parade route just a few blocks from here, and the police knew his every move. As soon as Pete duped Fletcher into spilling his guts for the wire he was wearing, they would move in.

Cheryl closed her eyes. Her head spun crazily, weakly. "Oh, Lord, Pete. So much could go wrong."

He chuckled mirthlessly. "Thanks for the reminder."

She moved closer, putting her hands on his waist. "Do you have to do this? Isn't there some other way?"

"It's the best way," he said softly, tensing at her nearness and backing up a step. "I've got to go now. Will you stay with Tony? He knows where I'll be...after."

She hoped desperately that was true. She hoped desperately that everything would go exactly as planned and that, an hour from now, she and Pete and Tony and Fay could party like four people just plucked from the brink of disaster.

Holding her hands in his for one moment, Pete released her and turned to go.

"Pete?" She tossed something in his direction. He caught it, then opened his hand to look at the red flannel gris-gris that Marie had promised gave the wearer power over other people.

When Pete glanced back at Cheryl, she winked, as bravely as she could. Slipping the gris-gris into his pocket with a reassuring nod, he turned again and took two more steps toward the door.

"Pete?" He turned back. She searched her mind for a word that would change his mind, a word that would keep him from playing the hero. "Pete, I love you."

The steely determination that had kept him rigid softened. He took a hesitant step in her direction, stopped, then took the second step necessary to bridge the gap between them. He leaned toward her and pressed his lips to hers. The fleeting moment of yearning, of a promise not quite made but not entirely withheld, was over too quickly.

"And I love you, Cheryl. Too much to come to you under a shadow."

She nodded her understanding, answering the plea in his eyes.

He disappeared into the crowd, leaving her too shaken to move. Her lips burned with the brief fire of the kiss. Her heart ached with uncertainty and fear. He was gone.

FEAR WASN'T A COMPANION Pete had ever learned to live with. He had been afraid plenty of times—afraid of bigger, meaner kids who lived on the streets where he had grown up, kids who had carried knives and passed around dope like candy; afraid of getting caught the few times he had ventured over the line that his parents had taught him to respect in spite of everything he was exposed to on the streets every day. Even when he had left childhood behind, Pete had known other kinds of fear. Like the fear that had come with spending every bit of his savings to buy out Fletcher; the even greater fear of staying in business with a man who still flirted with the wrong side of that line his parents had drawn.

But that was two-bit fear. Small-time. And what Pete experienced as he sat in his limo in the empty, weed-littered lot of the abandoned warehouse near the waterfront, was twenty-four-carat-gold, grade A, number one, hit-the-big-time fear. Fear with a capital *F*.

He felt disembodied. It seemed as if every move, every sensation were happening to someone else, while he floated overhead, no longer in control of the situation. The body that sat behind the wheel of the limo, the body that was wired for sound, the body whose blood raced furiously was responsible for pulling this off. And Pete, watching from some far-removed part of his brain, wondered if this body could handle the job. His palms sweated so profusely he couldn't keep them dry, no matter how many times he rubbed them along his pant legs. Perspiration ran down his back; he wondered if moisture could throw his wire out of whack, leaving him cut off from Anderson's men, completely on his own against Fletcher.

It wasn't Fletcher he feared. It was the people Fletcher represented. Fletcher was a weasel, a rat-faced coward he had bulldozed too many times in his life to be concerned that he couldn't handle him now. But the people pulling Fletcher's strings were the real thing. Organized crime. Gangsters who had killed more people than he employed.

And there was one thing more he feared. Cheryl. He feared losing her. He feared leaving her behind. Never having the chance to share his life with her. Or worse, having something go wrong . . . having her end up the one who didn't make it through this mess.

He shoved the picture from his mind. Cheryl. It was Cheryl who was paralyzing him. It was Cheryl who made him care more than he had ever cared in his life whether or not he survived. It was Cheryl who made him want so desperately to put this behind him and get on with his life.

And it was Cheryl who made him fear that every move he made today would be the wrong move. His last move.

Cheryl. He willed himself to forget her. To forget the tremble of her lips beneath his when he had grabbed that last kiss. He should never have done it. He had been psyched for this moment before that. Or maybe it had simply been seeing her, seeing those fearless blue eyes and that dimpled grin that had turned him to jelly.

If he didn't get her off his mind, that last quick kiss would indeed be the last kiss, he told himself harshly. From the glove compartment of the limo, he pulled the flask of whiskey he had cached away there and took a long swallow of the warm liquid.

The whiskey burned down his throat. He let it burn away thoughts of Cheryl and pretended that it gave him the courage he needed to get through the next half hour.

"Okay, old pal," he told himself as he glanced in the rearview mirror. "Here's your chance. Can you really do Bogie, or not?"

Giving his reflection a thumbs-up fraught with false bravado, Pete opened his car door and stepped boldly out into the vacant lot. Telling himself this was a screen test he couldn't afford to muff, he forced himself to glance around the lot casually. The smell of garbage mixed with the smell of the river. Broken wine bottles, a blackened smudge where a camp fire had recently burned and one flat, battered shoe told him the lot was likely a favorite nesting spot for street people. It was enclosed on three sides, the only escape being the narrow alley he had driven down to get here. He cursed himself for not thinking to swing the limo around so it faced the exit.

He cursed himself for even being here. And congratulated himself on convincing Anderson to let him come in Sammy's place. The poor kid could never have handled it. He would've been a basket case instead of safely enjoying the Mardi Gras revelry with Marie from the balcony of their suite at one of the Quarter's best hotels—Pete's gift to the honeymooners.

Even from this distance, Pete heard the sounds of Mardi Gras, a steady but distant roar of people and music. But suddenly there was a loud creaking directly behind him.

He wheeled around, thinking that, if this was a movie, he should have a gun in his hand.

Fletcher walked out of the warehouse door and onto the loading dock, then dropped lithely to the ground ten yards from Pete. He was grinning. Smugly. And yet, a little nervously.

"Well, well, well." Fletcher rubbed his hands together. "So the big guy finally decided to show his face. What happened to your little buddy? I thought he and I were partners now."

"I don't think he's in your league, Fletcher."

Fletcher laughed. "I like your costume. Sorry to drag you away from the party."

Pete was impatient. The more quickly Fletcher got down to business, finished playing cat and mouse, the sooner this would be over. But he remembered only too well Anderson's much repeated warning not to invite Fletcher's overtures. They wanted no hint of entrapment to taint this tape. Fletcher had to take the lead.

But Fletcher seemed to be in no hurry. "Hope your little lady friend didn't get put out with you, leaving in the middle of the party."

Keeping quiet took every ounce of Pete's self-control. At the mention of Cheryl, Pete wanted to lunge at him and batter his pointy little face to a pulp.

It's not in the script, he reminded himself.

"So, you don't think your little buddy Reilly can play with the big guys? Think you can?"

"Sure I can." Pete spoke softly, hoping to encourage Fletcher to move closer. What if he wasn't close enough for the wire to pick him up? "You must think so, too, Fletcher, or you wouldn't have called me first."

"We're old buddies. Partners. I knew you'd want to make it up to me, the way you stole the business right out from under my nose like that." The smile that remained plastered on his face was ugly now, a sneer.

Pete didn't bother to dispute Fletcher's version of the story. The six-figure check he had written his old partner for his half of the business had doubtless evaporated into the hands of bartenders and bookies in record time.

"Every time I read about what a big shot you got to be, Font'not, I figured you owed me. Know what I mean?"

Pete didn't answer. Fletcher circled closer. He knew, logically, that there was no way Fletcher could detect the wire; but it was hard summoning his logic while face-to-face with a man who surely had a gun somewhere under that seedy jacket he wore.

"It just ate away at my gut. Know what I mean, Font'not? You haven't forgotten what it's like, have you? Envy? The way you hate the people who have everything you don't. You remember that, don't you?"

"I remember." The truth was, he did remember the envy. Sometimes it was still with him, no matter how far he'd come. But he didn't remember the hate Fletcher spoke of. It must be the hate that had made the difference, Pete thought.

"Well, I decided you'd want to do something about that. Set things right. You do, don't you?"

"Sure I do."

"Good. Good. Glad to hear that. We can really be a big help to each other, if you just keep remembering how much you owe me."

"I hope so, Fletcher."

"You got a lotta cars, don't you?"

Pete told him how many. Fletcher whistled softly. "That's good. That's real good. I'd be a rich man now if you hadn't stolen things right out from under me, wouldn't I? Well, listen, no hard feelings. We're gonna put all that behind us and start over. Partners again. You wanna hear about it?"

"Sure."

Fletcher gestured back to the warehouse. "See that building? There's about six million dollars' worth of snow in that building. You know about coke, don't you? You ain't that lily-pure, are you? Anyway, we got a gang of powder in there. And we need a good, safe way to get it spread out all over this city. In the hands of the people who can turn white stuff into green stuff. Got it?"

Pete was barely listening. The flow of words that would trigger the showdown had started. He was grateful and fearful. Grateful it would soon be over, one way or another. Fearful of exactly how the end of this scene would be written. He nodded when appropriate, remembering Anderson's admonition to get himself back in the car as quickly and unsuspiciously as possible after Fletcher spilled the story.

"So I tell Monteleone," Fletcher continued, "who better for the job than my old partner Font'not, who's got more cars than Detroit, right?"

Pete nodded again, wondering if now was the moment to begin backing out, to leave the scene safe for the authorities to come roaring in.

"You gotta keep in mind, pal, this ain't no one-shot deal. There's plenty of money in this for us. Monteleone gets a shipment like this, I'd say once a month, at least. Whaddaya say? You can buy every car in town with that kind of bread. And all the classy little blondes you want."

Pete saw red again at the reference to Cheryl. Struggling to master his anger, he barely heard the financial details Fletcher outlined.

"When do you want the cars, Fletcher? Now?"

Fletcher laughed. "I like that. You're eager to do business, now that you know what a sweet deal we're talkin' about. Don't you wish you'd saved yourself all that grief? Yeah, let's get this show rolling. Let's bring 'em in, about two an hour until we get this stuff cleared outta here."

Pete hated turning his back on Fletcher. This whole setup seemed so transparent to him, he couldn't believe Fletcher was falling for it. What if Fletcher decided just to blow him away and be done with it? His only salvation, he told himself as he walked back to his limo, was his speculation that Fletcher was in hock up to his eyeballs to Monteleone. Being in hock to someone like Frankie Monteleone was enough to make anyone willing to take desperate measures.

He almost—not quite, but almost—felt sorry for his old friend. He remembered one more time the days the three of them had peeked in the back door of the pool hall, yearning for the day when they would be old enough to go in without getting run out again. He remembered one more time the day Fletcher had covered for him long enough for him to swipe a girlie magazine so they could ogle the centerfold.

Regretting that it had come to this, he picked up the radio and gave Anderson the signal they had agreed on, while pretending to call his own dispatcher. "This is Pete. Send a car for a fare at the old coffee warehouse on Tchoupitoulas Street. Pronto."

Anderson's answering voice was reassuring. "We copy. We've got a car in the neighborhood, boss. Be right there."

Pete stayed in the car, calling out across the lot. "Got a car on the way."

"Good. Good." Fletcher ambled toward the limo, hands in his pockets. Closed around a gun, Pete had no doubt. "There's just one more thing, Font'not. No screwups. Any screwups, and you can wave your tail goodbye. That's first. Second, your pretty little friend won't be quite as pretty when Monteleone's guys get done with her. I'll see to that personally."

CHERYL HUNG OVER the open door of the cab parked on the back street Tony had led her to, listening to the crackling messages over the radio. Tony, in the passenger's seat, and Fay, pitched forward tensely on the back seat, were also waiting to hear Pete's voice.

The reporter, who was as eager as Cheryl for a sign that the operation was going as planned, hadn't been eager to take Cheryl and her friend to the cab. Pete had left it for him so he'd be as close as possible to the story, in case it resulted in busting one of the city's major crime lords. The cab, with cameras and reporter's pads in the back seat, was part of the plan.

Cheryl and Fay were not.

All three were tense. Fay's early morning revelry had dissolved into instantaneous sobriety as Cheryl recounted the story while they jogged the four blocks to the waiting cab. Tony was grim faced, making notes only halfheartedly, clearly more personally involved than professionally. Reporting this story, Cheryl was certain, was only a cover-up for his need to know firsthand that his friend was safe.

And Cheryl had abandoned all pretense of calm. She stood by the side of the car, unable even to quell her jitters long enough to sit. She jiggled the keys to the cab in her hand, knowing they would jiggle even if she tried to hold them steady. Nothing about her was steady.

Pete's voice exploded over the radio, startling them all, freezing their blood for one brief moment. A coffee warehouse on Tchoupitoulas. Cheryl strained to glean from his voice whether things were going right. Damn the man, he sounded as icily in control as always.

The police were going in. Cheryl slumped into the driver's seat.

"Then he's safe." She gulped fresh air.

When Tony didn't respond, she looked at him. His face was still grim.

"Well, he is, isn't he?" she asked, grabbing a fistful of his shirt.

"He is . . ." Tony hesitated. "He is right now."

"What do you mean by that?" she demanded.

He looked into her eyes, pleading with her not to ask more. Her expression left no room for him to deny her. He sighed, the pen going limp in his fingers. "This is always the trickiest part. When the police come in. That's when . . . when things go wrong."

"I can't sit here doing nothing anymore," Fay said from the back seat. "This is driving me crazy."

Tony turned to glare at her and, when he did, missed Cheryl shoving the keys into the ignition. The cab roared to life. Her door slammed shut as she wheeled out into the nearly empty street. Tony and Fay were flung against their seats as she accelerated.

"What the hell do you think you're doing?" Tony yelled. "Pete's gonna kill me."

"No, he won't," Cheryl said, heading for the street Pete had mentioned on the radio as quickly as she could without plowing into a car parked on the side of the road. "He'll kill me."

"Cheryl, you don't know what you're doing," Tony protested, all thoughts of his story forgotten. "This is dangerous. If you get in the way of the police, you'll—"

"I won't. I promise. I won't go to the warehouse. I'll just park on that block. I just want to be there when it's over. So I'll know he's okay."

"You won't even get close," Tony warned as she swerved around the corner and onto Tchoupitoulas. "They'll have the block around the warehouse cordoned off. You won't get—"

"Is that it?" Cheryl pointed to a weathered sign that featured an old-fashioned coffeepot next to a steaming cup. The huge windows of the old building were boarded up.

Tony looked around in disbelief. There were no police cars to be seen.

"Where is everybody?" he wondered out loud.

Cheryl looked around, too, and eased the car to the curb. "Do you suppose something went wrong?"

"They were meeting behind the building, right down that alley," Tony said absently, still looking around in bafflement for some sign that the authorities had shown up as promised. "I don't understand why—"

A sharp burst interrupted his speculation. The sound meant nothing to Cheryl at first, but when she heard three more bursts in quick succession, she recognized them instantly.

"Guns!" Fay squealed from the back seat. "Oh, Lord, they're shooting!"

Cheryl didn't waste a minute. Gunning the engine, she wheeled the car around the sharp corner into the alleyway, heading toward the sound of the gunshots. The rear of the car spun crazily, then straightened to follow its nose. Before she reached the end of the alley, Pete's big limo barreled into the opening at top speed and rammed into the cab.

Cheryl's last thought, before her forehead hit the steering wheel, was that her own stubbornness had blocked Pete's getaway.

CHAPTER EIGHTEEN

CHERYL FOUGHT BACK the blackness, groping toward the voice. She shook her head to clear the grogginess, but the movement plunged her deeper into the fog.

The voice was talking to her, but she couldn't quite make out what it said. But something about the voice was reassuring. Something about it made her determined to fight away this hazy feeling in her head so she could hear it better.

"Cheryl."

That was it. Pete's voice. She blinked once and saw a fuzzy face over hers. She blinked again. The face swam there, blurred into the darkness once more, then slowly came into focus.

It was dear and worried and covered with that sexy stubble she liked to brush her skin against. She wanted to reach up to touch his face but couldn't quite lift her arm. She felt, somewhere back of the fog, that she should be worried about why her arm wasn't cooperating. But with Pete right there with her, she felt a sort of hazy euphoria, instead.

"Are you mad at me?" she whispered, trying to smile. Hoping she was smiling but not quite sure. He couldn't be very angry if he saw she was smiling, could he?

"Mad as hell," he said. His voice sounded choked; she couldn't figure out why. "You don't belong here, Cheryl. This is no place for you."

She saw in his eyes that no matter how mad he said he was, he was still glad to see her. "Oh, yes, I do, Pete," she replied weakly. "I belong wherever you belong."

She snuggled into his arms and let the fog wrap itself around her. With Pete nearby, the beckon of the blackness was no longer threatening.

WHEN SHE STRUGGLED OUT of the blackness—how much later she wasn't sure—it wasn't into the warmth of Pete's arms or the reassurance of his voice or even the relief in his eyes.

It was into a glaringly white room and a starburst of pain. She groaned and closed her eyes again. "What have I done?" she mumbled.

A cool hand covered hers. It was too small to be Pete's. Maybe she had only imagined Pete before. She opened her eyes slowly at Fay's voice. "It's okay. Everything's okay."

"Everything?" she asked weakly.

"Everything. I promise."

Everything except that Pete wasn't here with her. She was lying in a hospital bed, her head throbbing so outrageously she couldn't imagine ever wanting to move it again, and Pete was not here.

Maybe she hadn't imagined him, after all. Maybe that *had* been him saying he was mad as hell. Maybe it was only the happiness in his eyes she had imagined.

"But..."

"I'm not hurt. Tony's only got a few bruises. You've got a slight concussion and a beaut of a shiner."

"Pete. Where's Pete?"

Cheryl wasn't alert enough to be sure whether Fay hesitated or whether she only imagined that, too.

"He's still with the captain. I'm sure he'll be up soon. You rest now."

Cheryl let her eyes drift shut, until another thought shot them open. A shaft of pain sprang up behind her eyes at the movement and the light.

"What about—" she struggled for the words "—Fletcher? Is he . . . ?"

"I . . . I'm not sure."

Fog began to settle over Cheryl's consciousness again.

"I ruined your Mardi Gras," she recalled groggily. "You'll never forgive me for ruining your Mardi Gras."

"Are you kidding? This is the most exciting Fat Tuesday I've ever had." Fay chuckled. "And to think, I could've spent the day with an optometrist."

Cheryl let herself drift away again, this time on a cloud of uneasiness. She had really done it this time, she told herself, trying to hold on to the details of the morning. There were things Fay hadn't explained, and she couldn't quite remember what they were.

The room was dark the next time her eyes shot open. Gunshots. There had been gunshots. Fay hadn't told her about the gunshots. Maybe Pete hadn't been with the captain at all. Maybe . . .

"Pete!" Her voice wasn't nearly strong enough to bring anyone's attention. She tried again. "Pete!"

This time, the hand closing over hers was big and warm and just the slightest bit rough.

"I'm right here."

"You are?" She tried to focus her eyes in the dark, then reached to find the light. Pete turned on one dim light for her. The halo illuminated his face. But without her glasses she still couldn't discern the details of his narrow face.

"You are here," she said happily.

"You've had enough sleep to get over three concussions," he teased, pushing a tendril of hair back from her face. Her face. She suddenly remembered her face. What had Fay said? A beaut of a shiner?

"I look terrible," she protested, reaching up to cover her face. He stopped the motion and leaned forward to cover her with downy-soft kisses.

"You look wonderful. You look so damn good I could scoop you up right now and make love to you the rest of the night."

She laughed softly. He wasn't mad. He wasn't even telling her he wanted her out of his life. "Pete, this is a hospital. Behave yourself."

He purred suggestively. "That's not easy, Slick. You know how sexy hospital gowns are. I'll bet this one's not even tied in the back."

"Don't you ever behave?"

"Never," he teased softly. "I'm a bad boy."

He nuzzled her neck and started working his way up to her lips.

"No, you're the best." She smiled, a soft, contented smile, and closed her eyes to keep the room from spinning. "Better than they make them at the best country clubs in Cleveland." She knew, for some reason, that she needed to talk to him about that later. Right now, she could only sigh at the soft warmth of his lips nibbling at the corners of hers. "But you still don't behave."

He grinned, a relieved grin, a grin free of any worries. "And you're the most mule-headed woman I've ever met."

"You've never even seen a mule," she protested. "What do you know?"

Before he could answer, she remembered what had jarred her awake. "Pete, there were gunshots. Are you sure you're okay?"

"I'm perfect. One of Anderson's men took a shot in the leg and Fletcher got one in the shoulder. But they'll both be okay. By the way, Anderson's happier with your performance than he was with mine."

She looked at him, frowning in confusion. "What do you mean?"

"He said the cab made one of the most effective roadblocks he'd ever seen."

"I don't understand."

"That was Fletcher in the limo," Pete said, still holding her hand. "There was some kind of snafu. Some of the captain's people showed up behind the warehouse on foot. But the backup cars never made it. Fletcher would have sailed down the street and out of our hands if you hadn't saved the day."

"I knew that."

Pete laughed out loud, only remembering to lower his voice when a disapproving nurse stuck her head in the door.

"And once you nailed Fletcher for us," Pete continued, "he was so eager to make a deal that he squealed real loud. The police picked up the people behind Fletcher, too. Fletcher's so scared he doesn't even *want* out of jail."

She yawned and nodded her drowsy approval. "Is it late?"

"No, it's early," he said. "About four in the morning."

"You should go home and get some sleep," she protested, reassuring herself of his presence once more by letting the light hairs along his forearm feather along her palm. "This is no place for you to be at four in the morning."

"I belong wherever you belong."

The words sounded disconcertingly familiar, but she couldn't place them. Soon, she told herself, all the pieces would fit together and the fog would lift completely. "You do?"

"I do."

Those words, too, were familiar. But easy to place. She giggled. "And do you promise to love, honor and obey?"

"They've got too many painkillers in you, woman. They must, if you think for one minute I'm going to promise to obey."

"That's fine," she said. "I don't like that part, either."

"That I already knew." But there was no anger in his words. "So that's settled. We'll leave that part out."

"We will?"

He laid a hand against her cheek, tenderly. "We will."

"When?"

"Soon."

Even with her fuzzy vision, she could tell he was dead serious. "How soon?"

"I don't suppose you'd be willing to get married with a black eye, would you?"

Cheryl tried hard not to giggle again, knowing the medication was making her silly. Either that, or she was growing giddy on happily-ever-after, knitting-baby-bootees, growing-old-together dreams. "Are you sure I'm not dreaming this?"

"Positive. I figure in a couple of weeks, that shiner'll be gone. Whaddaya say, Slick?"

"I say as long as I'm wearing a veil, who's going to know the difference?"

As her eyes drifted shut, he leaned over and kissed the eyelids. His breath was a whisper against her ear. "Sweet dreams."

From *New York Times* Bestselling author
Penny Jordan, a compelling novel of ruthless passion
that will mesmerize readers everywhere!

Penny Jordan

Silver

Real power, true power came from
Rothwell. And Charles vowed to have it,
the earldom and all that went with it.

Silver vowed to destroy Charles, just as surely and
uncaringly as he had destroyed her father; just as he had
intended to destroy her. She needed him to want her . . .
to desire her . . . until he'd do anything to have her.

But first she needed a tutor: a man who wanted no one.
He would help her bait the trap.

**Played out on a glittering international stage,
Silver's story leads her from the luxurious comfort of
British aristocracy into the depths of adventure,
passion and danger.**

AVAILABLE NOW!

 HARLEQUIN

SIL-1A

Take 4 bestselling love stories FREE

Plus get a FREE surprise gift!

Special Limited-time Offer

Harlequin Reader Service®

Mail to
In the U.S.
3010 Walden Avenue
P.O. Box 1867
Buffalo, N.Y. 14269-1867

In Canada
P.O. Box 609
Fort Erie, Ontario
L2A 5X3

YES! Please send me 4 free Harlequin Superromance® novels and my free surprise gift. Then send me 4 brand-new novels every month, which I will receive months before they appear in bookstores. Bill me at the low price of $2.74* each—a savings of 21¢ apiece off cover prices. There are no shipping, handling or other hidden costs. I understand that accepting the books and gift places me under no obligation ever to buy any books. I can always return a shipment and cancel at any time. Even if I never buy another book from Harlequin, the 4 free books and the surprise gift are mine to keep forever.

*Offer slightly different in Canada—$2.74 per book plus 49¢ per shipment for delivery. Sales tax applicable in N.Y.

134 BPA KBBA (US)   334 BPA YKMP (CAN)

Name _____ (PLEASE PRINT)

Address _____ Apt. No. _____

City _____ State/Prov. _____ Zip/Postal Code _____

This offer is limited to one order per household and not valid to present Harlequin Superromance® subscribers. Terms and prices are subject to change.

© 1990 Harlequin Enterprises Limited

PASSPORT TO ROMANCE
SWEEPSTAKES RULES

1. **HOW TO ENTER:** To enter, you must be the age of majority and complete the official entry form, or print your name, address, telephone number and age on a plain piece of paper and mail to: Passport to Romance, P.O. Box 9056, Buffalo, NY 14269-9056. No mechanically reproduced entries accepted.

2. All entries must be received by the CONTEST CLOSING DATE, DECEMBER 31, 1990 TO BE ELIGIBLE.

3. **THE PRIZES:** There will be ten (10) Grand Prizes awarded, each consisting of a choice of a trip for two people from the following list:
   i)   London, England (approximate retail value $5,050 U.S.)
   ii)   England, Wales and Scotland (approximate retail value $6,400 U.S.)
   iii) Carribean Cruise (approximate retail value $7,300 U.S.)
   iv)   Hawaii (approximate retail value $9,550 U.S.)
   v)   Greek Island Cruise in the Mediterranean (approximate retail value $12,250 U.S.)
   vi)   France (approximate retail value $7,300 U.S.)

4. Any winner may choose to receive any trip or a cash alternative prize of $5,000.00 U.S. in lieu of the trip.

5. **GENERAL RULES:** Odds of winning depend on number of entries received.

6. A random draw will be made by Nielsen Promotion Services, an independent judging organization, on January 29, 1991, in Buffalo, NY, at 11:30 a.m. from all eligible entries received on or before the Contest Closing Date.

7. Any Canadian entrants who are selected must correctly answer a time-limited, mathematical skill-testing question in order to win.

8. Full contest rules may be obtained by sending a stamped, self-addressed envelope to: "Passport to Romance Rules Request", P.O. Box 9998, Saint John, New Brunswick, Canada E2L 4N4.

9. Quebec residents may submit any litigation respecting the conduct and awarding of a prize in this contest to the Régie des loteries et courses du Québec.

10. Payment of taxes other than air and hotel taxes is the sole responsibility of the winner.

11. Void where prohibited by law.

COUPON BOOKLET OFFER TERMS

To receive your Free travel-savings coupon booklets, complete the mail-in Offer Certificate on the preceeding page, including the necessary number of proofs-of-purchase, and mail to: Passport to Romance, P.O. Box 9057, Buffalo, NY 14269-9057. The coupon booklets include savings on travel-related products such as car rentals, hotels, cruises, flowers and restaurants. Some restrictions apply. The offer is available in the United States and Canada. Requests must be postmarked by January 25, 1991. Only proofs-of-purchase from specially marked "Passport to Romance" Harlequin® or Silhouette® books will be accepted. The offer certificate must accompany your request and may not be reproduced in any manner. Offer void where prohibited or restricted by law. LIMIT FOUR COUPON BOOKLETS PER NAME, FAMILY, GROUP, ORGANIZATION OR ADDRESS. Please allow up to 8 weeks after receipt of order for shipment. Enter quickly as quantities are limited. Unfulfilled mail-in offer requests will receive free Harlequin® or Silhouette® books (not previously available in retail stores), in quantities equal to the number of proofs-of-purchase required for Levels One to Four, as applicable.

PR-SWPS

OFFICIAL SWEEPSTAKES
ENTRY FORM

Complete and return this Entry Form immediately—the more Entry Forms you submit, the better your chances of winning!
- Entry Forms must be received by **December 31, 1990**
- A random draw will take place on **January 29, 1991**
- Trip must be taken by **December 31, 1991**

3-HS-3-SW

YES, I want to win a PASSPORT TO ROMANCE vacation for two! I understand the prize includes round-trip air fare, accommodation and a daily spending allowance.

Name_____

Address_____

City_____ State_____ Zip_____

Telephone Number_____ Age_____

Return entries to: **PASSPORT TO ROMANCE**, P.O. Box 9056, Buffalo, NY 14269-9056

© 1990 Harlequin Enterprises Limited

COUPON BOOKLET/OFFER CERTIFICATE

Item	LEVEL ONE Booklet 1	LEVEL TWO Booklet 1 & 2	LEVEL THREE Booklet 1, 2 & 3	LEVEL FOUR Booklet 1, 2, 3 & 4
Booklet 1 = $100+	$100+	$100+	$100+	$100+
Booklet 2 = $200+		$200+	$200+	$200+
Booklet 3 = $300+			$300+	$300+
Booklet 4 = $400+	____	____	____	$400+
Approximate Total Value of Savings	$100+	$300+	$600+	$1,000+
# of Proofs of Purchase Required	4	6	12	18
Check One	____	____	____	____

Name_____

Address_____

City_____ State_____ Zip_____

Return Offer Certificates to: **PASSPORT TO ROMANCE**, P.O. Box 9057, Buffalo, NY 14269-9057

Requests must be postmarked by **January 25, 1991**

ONE PROOF OF PURCHASE

3-HS-3

To collect your free coupon booklet you must include the necessary number of proofs-of-purchase with a properly completed Offer Certificate

© 1990 Harlequin Enterprises Limited

See previous page for details